TRACKING THE WOLF PACK

Len Levinson

writing as

J Farragut Jones

TRACKING THE WOLF PACK

Published by Sapere Books.

20 Windermere Drive, Leeds, England, LS17 7UZ,
United Kingdom

saperebooks.com

ISBN: 978-1-80055-633-1

CHAPTER 1

It was night in the middle of the Atlantic Ocean, and Kapitänleutnant Joachim Kruger stood on the bridge of U-112, studying a British convoy through his binoculars. The U-boat was pointed in a north-westerly direction, the convoy headed east toward the British Isles. There was no moon, and Kruger had his U-boat trimmed low in the water.

On the bridge with Kruger was the executive officer of U-112, Oberleutnant Rudi Grunberger, and Ensign Karl Blohm. All had their binoculars trained on the convoy.

"I see only two escort vessels,' Kruger said. "One is at the head of the convoy, and the other to starboard of the convoy. Do you see them?"

"Yes, sir," said Grunberger and Blohm in unison.

"We are going to maneuver between them and strike the convoy at its heart." Kruger leaned toward the conning tower. "Steer three-two-oh! Both engines half ahead together!"

Like a dagger, the U-boat pierced through the waves as it made its way to the convoy. Below decks, the crew of U-112 was at battle stations. Torpedoman Wilhelm Kortmann stood at the controls in the bow torpedo compartment, waiting tensely for the order to fire. The helmsman stood at his post in the conning tower, making the adjustment in steering ordered by the captain.

Leutnant Frederick Wichmann-Holtz, the second engineer, stood with his back to the bulkhead in the diesel engine room, watching his crew and wondering how U-112 would fare in the battle that would begin shortly. He had previously served on

U-89, which had been depth-charged severely only six weeks ago. Wichmann-Holtz's nerves still hadn't calmed down. His engine room had sprung five leaks and his starboard diesel engine had been knocked off its mounting.

It was March 1941. Kapitänleutnant Kruger watched the convoy through his binoculars as his U-boat sliced closer to the prey. In the darkness he could see the ships' masts as they lumbered through the night. They reminded him of elephants at the circus, following each other dumbly in lines. The ships were three hundred yards apart and blacked out. Kruger planned to pass between the two escort vessels and sink ships at close range.

Grunberger had sighted the convoy that afternoon. Kruger had reported its position to U-boat headquarters in France, then followed at a distance, radioing additional position reports throughout the day. In the early evening U-121 and U-90 had arrived.

Now U-121 was on the other side of the convoy and U-90 was at its rear. The convoy was moving at 6 knots. U-boats were capable of speeds of up to 17 knots on the surface. At 0400 hours Admiral Dönitz had told them to attack. Now they were moving in for the kill.

Kruger's U-112 closed with the convoy at low speed so that he wouldn't leave a telltale white wake at his stern. He studied the escort destroyer on his starboard bow, assuming that lookouts were up there on its bridge, searching the seas for U-boats. Their eyes were probably tired and playing tricks on them in the blackness of the night. The escort ship was a thousand yards away. U-112 passed in front of it and bore down on the main ships of the convoy.

"Steer three-one-five!" Kruger said.

"Steer three-one-five!" repeated Leutnant Feiler, the wiry little man at the helm.

The U-boat changed course, heading for an opening between two of the freighters. Ensign Blohm examined them through his binoculars. They looked like mountains in the ocean of the night.

This was Blohm's first U-boat patrol and attack. He had graduated submarine school at the head of his class, and as a reward been assigned to U-112, whose commanding officer, Kapitänleutnant Kruger, was one of the great aces of the Atlantic war.

Kruger had been decorated with the Knight's Cross by the Führer himself, and his picture appeared regularly in newspapers throughout Germany. Kruger's binoculars had been given to him by Admiral Dönitz himself, and carried a personal inscription from Dönitz.

Blohm looked admiringly at Kruger, who wore a black stocking cap. He had a long straight nose, light hair, and sharp features that made him appear clever.

"How are we doing, Blohm?" Kruger asked, still looking ahead through his binoculars.

"Fine, sir."

"Keep your eyes peeled."

"Yes, sir."

Blohm raised his binoculars and looked at the British destroyer that was now astern. He thought he could make out figures on the bridge, and wondered who those sailors were and what they were thinking. He smiled as he contemplated their consternation when U-112's first torpedoes struck home.

U-112 glided over the waves and passed between two huge freighters. It was inside the convoy now, ready to attack.

The destroyer was the *Centurion*. On its bridge stood Commander William E Mulford, a husky, ruddy-faced man with a mustache, known as Moxie to his old navy chums. He wore a navy-blue duffel coat with a gray turtleneck sweater showing underneath it, and was scanning the seas for traces of U-boats, because he knew that they liked to attack at night.

He wished he had a full moon, but the night was blacker than Hitler's heart. He could see the freighters he was escorting, but it would be difficult to spot a U-boat trimmed low in the water. His Asdic — a sonar device that searched underwater for submarines — was on, sending sound impulses through the water, but nothing registered. Prior to 1939 the British navy had thought that the invention of Asdic had made submarines obsolete, but since then they'd found out that Asdic had severe limitations. Wily U-boat commanders could evade it by going deep or attacking on the surface.

Mulford ground his teeth together as he scanned the night for U-boats. He knew there had to be some out there, because his radio operator had picked up their transmissions earlier in the day. Mulford expected them to attack sometime before dawn and was surprised they hadn't tried anything yet. He felt helpless against them, with only his destroyer and two other escorts under his command. That wasn't enough to prevent a U-boat wolf pack attack. There were forty-three freighters in the convoy, and he felt certain that some of them would go to the bottom tonight.

It would be seven days before the convoy would reach Liverpool, which he'd left eight days ago with a westbound convoy. He'd turned that convoy over to its escorts in the middle of the Atlantic, then picked up this one. That convoy had lost eight ships in the waters off Iceland, and Mulford couldn't understand why it hadn't lost more. He figured that attacking U-boats must have run out of torpedoes or fuel.

Mulford had seen many ships torpedoed and many seamen hurled into the icy waters of the Atlantic. The *Centurion* had destroyed only two U-boats in over eight months of convoy duty. Mulford felt so frustrated that sometimes he thought his head would explode.

The admiralty had not been prepared for a U-boat war, although they'd had plenty of warning. There weren't enough ships for escort duty, and the ships themselves were a bunch of rust buckets. The *Centurion* was an old flush-deck American destroyer built during the First World War. It had been called the *Porter,* after an American naval hero of the War of 1812.

Mulford thought it ironic that he, a British officer, was commanding a ship named after an American who'd fought against Great Britain. The Americans had given forty old destroyers to the British navy, but America hadn't declared war on Germany. Mulford wondered what they were waiting for.

"Captain?" said Lieutenant Tommy Dugan, the officer of the watch.

"Yes," mumbled Mulford, scanning the night through his binoculars.

"Don't you think you should go below and get some sleep, sir?"

"No, I don't."

"I can awaken you if anything happens. You haven't slept for two nights, sir."

"Mind your business, Lieutenant Dugan, and I'll mind mine."

"Yes, sir."

Mulford thought he saw a white wake between two of the freighters ahead, but when he blinked it was gone. *I probably have been out here too long,* he told himself. *My eyes are seeing things that aren't there.*

He had briefly seen the wake of U-112, which was now between two rows of freighters, moving in the same direction as they were, and at the same speed. Kapitänleutnant Kruger stood on the bridge, looking first at the row of freighters to starboard and then the row to port. They appeared to be behaving normally; they hadn't spotted the U-boat yet.

Leutnant Grunberger looked through the night binoculars fastened upon the TBT (Target Bearing Transmitter). He zeroed in on the freighter on the starboard side of the U-boat.

"Fire two shots as quickly as you can at the freighter dead to starboard," Kruger said to Grunberger, "then fire two more at the freighter behind it. I'll swing the boat around so you can fire the stern tube at the freighter that's dead to port right now. See it?"

Grunberger looked up from the TBT. "Yes, sir."

Kruger turned to Ensign Blohm. "Keep a sharp eye out for escorts or suspicious movements that may indicate we've been spotted — understand?"

"Yes, sir."

Grunberger turned the knobs and dials on the TBT. "Tubes one to four ready for surface attack!" he said. "Open tube doors! Target angle left forty! Speed fifteen! Range one thousand! Torpedo depth seven! Stand by!"

In the bow torpedo compartment, Torpedoman Kortmann turned the handles on the cranks that prepared torpedoes for firing. He wore a short black beard, having not shaved since leaving Lorient two weeks ago, and his face was streaked with grease.

On the bridge Blohm could feel tension mounting. How strange to be in the center of a British convoy. How exciting to know that death was so close.

Kruger studied the first freighter target through his binoculars. "Commence firing!"

Grunberger steadied his aim through the TBT, then pressed the lever that would permit the release of the torpedoes. "Tube one — fire! Tube two — fire!"

U-112 bounced twice in the water as each of the two torpedoes shot out of her hull and sped through the water to the first freighter. Grunberger quickly aimed the TBT at the second vessel and pressed the lever. "Tube three — fire! Tube four — fire!"

U-112 jolted again as those two torpedoes were launched on their deadly mission. In the control room, hydroplane operators watched the chronograph and counted down as they waited for the torpedoes to explode.

"Right full rudder!" shouted Kapitänleutnant Kruger.

"Reload torpedo tubes one through four!" said Grunberger.

U-112 turned around so that its stern torpedo tube faced the other row of ships. Ensign Blohm kept his binoculars trained on the two freighters that Grunberger had fired at. It was eerie to be floating so silently in the middle of the convoy, and hard to imagine that torpedoes would start exploding in moments. Grunberger shouted new orders to the stern torpedo room, and Blohm wondered if the first two torpedoes had missed.

A yellow column of flame shot up from the first freighter, then the sound of an explosion was heard. The sea lit up, then the second torpedo struck home, blowing metal and British seamen into the air. Sirens and howlers pierced the winter night. Next, the second freighter's stern section exploded in a brilliant flash of light.

The flames reflected on Leutnant Grunberger's face as he sighted through the TBT. "Stern tube ready for surface attack! Open tube door! Target angle right thirty! Speed fifteen! Range twelve hundred! Torpedo depth seven! Stand by!"

"Stern tube ready for firing!" came the report from below.

"Stern tube *fire*!"

The stern torpedo charged out of its tube and raced toward a tanker on the horizon. Screams of dying men could be heard over the water as the first freighter sank stern first into the cold Atlantic. Other freighters in the convoy shot illuminating flares and snowflake bombs into the air so that they could spot the U-boat in their midst.

"Down to the cellar!" screamed Kapitänleutnant Kruger.

Ensign Blohm leaped toward the conning tower ladder. The stern torpedo struck the tanker. The explosion was so violent it shook the ocean. Tons of flaming oil burst into the sky. Grunberger looked at it for a split second, then clattered down the conning tower ladder. With a smile of satisfaction Kruger followed him down and closed the hatch.

"Level off at two hundred meters!" Kruger yelled.

"Level at two hundred meters!" repeated Chief Engineer Feiler.

The seamen at the hydroplane controls turned their wheels to hard dive. Throughout the boat hands spun levers that closed various valves. In the main motor room Second Engineer Wichmann-Holtz pulled the lever that shifted propulsion gear from diesel to electric drive.

In forty seconds U-112 was beneath the waves. The crew could hear ships breaking up and boilers exploding above them.

"Good work, men," Kapitänleutnant Kruger said into the microphone in the control room.

Standing next to the periscope, Ensign Blohm was tingling with excitement. It had all been so easy. How long could England hold out if U-boats could sink her shipping that simply?

Kruger looked up toward the sounds of destruction overhead. "Music to my ears," he said with a grin.

When the first torpedo hit its target Commander Mulford spun around on the bridge of the *Centurion*. He saw the huge orange burst of flame and heard a thunderous explosion. His stomach wrenched with the realization that the U-boats had struck again.

He leaned toward the voice tubes on the bridge. "Radio room — order the convoy to steer a new course — left three hundred degrees. Order the last ship in each line to pick up survivors."

"Yes, sir!"

Mulford looked in the direction of flames and saw another ship explode. "Send up the snowflakes."

"Yes, sir!" replied Lieutenant Dugan.

Mulford felt the old frustration crawl up his throat. He gripped the bridge rail tightly and wondered where the damn U-boats were.

The tanker exploded in a spectacular display of burning oil. Almost simultaneously the sky lit up with flares and snowflake bombs. Night became day as Mulford searched the sea for traces of U-boats.

"Sir," said his executive officer, Lieutenant-Commander Scott, "the *Laurel Canyon* has reported sighting a U-boat submerging off its starboard bow."

Mulford realized that a U-boat had penetrated the escort screen and was inside the convoy. "Order all ships to maintain formation."

"Yes, sir!"

"Battle stations!" Mulford shouted.

"Battle stations!" repeated First Mate Harrow.

Mulford held the bridge railing so tightly his knuckles went white. If he'd had enough destroyers in his escort, no U-boat would ever have got through. There was nothing he could do now except rove back and forth on the edge of the convoy and hope he could spot a U-boat.

"All ahead full!" he yelled.

"All ahead full!"

The old *Centurion* picked up speed and passed freighters on the edge of the convoy. All hands searched the water for signs of a U-boat.

"Lieutenant Gaw!" said Mulford into the voice tube.

"Sir!" replied Gaw.

"Any Asdic contact?"

"No, sir."

"Stay alert, Gaw!"

"Yes, sir."

The wind whistled past Mulford's ears as the *Centurion* ploughed through the waves toward the front of the convoy. Mulford lowered his binoculars and looked around his ship. In the gray turrets he saw men with binoculars searching the seas for U-boats. Foam flecked the waves; it would be difficult to spot a periscope out there. The Asdic could pick up a U-boat gliding beneath the surface at periscope depth, but couldn't detect a U-boat running deep. Before the war, the admiralty hadn't known U-boats could dive deeper than two hundred feet.

He studied the convoy and saw ships on the edge silhouetted against burning oil oozing from the tanker that had been torpedoed in its center. Somewhere in there, men were being fried alive.

"Sir," said Scott, "the *Creole Princess* reports that the last ship in the line isn't picking up survivors."

"What's the last ship in the line?"

"The *Martin Ingraham*, sir."

"Keep a sharp lookout here and call me immediately if you see anything. I'm going to have a talk with the skipper of the *Martin Ingraham*."

"Yes, sir."

Mulford stepped toward the door of the bridge house. Another explosion sounded from the far side of the convoy. Mulford turned to see sparks flying into the sky. Evidently another submarine attacking the convoy.

Grinding his teeth together, he entered the bridge house and made his way to the radio shack, where Petty Officer First Class Richard Lofthouse was putting his headset on.

"Get the skipper of the *Martin Ingraham* for me," Mulford ordered.

"Yes, sir."

Lofthouse spoke the call letters of the *Martin Ingraham* into his microphone, and Mulford took out a cigarette, lighting it with the gold lighter his wife had given him on their tenth wedding anniversary. He saw her in his mind: tall and angular, wearing one of her plaid wool skirts. He wondered what she was doing then. She was probably at a society party someplace, smiling at everybody and dancing with all the handsome young men.

"They're not answering, sir," said Lofthouse.

Mulford frowned as he puffed his cigarette. The captain of the *Martin Ingraham* probably wasn't answering because he didn't want to stop and make himself an easy target for the U-boats. Mulford wondered whether he should stop the *Centurion* and pick up survivors, but decided to continue searching for the U-boats.

Another explosion sounded in the distance, then another. Cigarette dangling from the corner of his mouth, Mulford left the radio shack and dashed to the bridge.

Aboard U-112, captain and crew listened to the convoy pass by overhead. They heard more explosions and knew that U-121 and U-90 were having a good night of hunting also.

Kapitänleutnant Kruger stood beside the periscope, pleased with the performance of U-112. The attack had been like a textbook exercise, the crew working together like components of a well-oiled machine. A huge celebration would be held for them when they returned to Lorient in a few days. Perhaps he would have time to go home to Berlin and see his parents.

He noticed Ensign Blohm standing beside the chart table. Blohm's black officer's cap was on the back of his head, his face ablaze with excitement. The young ensign had blue eyes, blond hair, and face of a cherub. Twenty-one years old, his father a high-ranking official in the party. Blohm had been in the Hitler Youth Organization, a fact which predisposed Kruger to dislike him, but Blohm didn't talk about the party much and had been enthusiastic about carrying out his orders. Kruger had come to like the young man.

"Well, Ensign Blohm," Kruger said, "what do you think of the U-boat war now?"

Blohm looked up from the chart table. "Very interesting, sir," he replied, his eyes glittering.

"Interesting? Yes, I suppose it could be called interesting."

They listened to the convoy pass by overhead. There was a tremendous churning of propellers and more explosions. Kruger's skilled ears told him that the convoy was changing course. But they'd never get away from him. Not now.

"Bring the boat to periscope depth," Kruger said.

"Periscope depth!" repeated Chief Engineer Feiler. The U-boat angled upward as sounds of the convoy grew dimmer. Kruger looked at the depth gauge and saw the needle move toward smaller numbers. He gripped the handles of the periscope and waited for the boat to level off.

"We're at periscope depth, sir," Feiler said.

Kruger raised the periscope and looked through the eyepiece. He saw the flaming convoy heading north, boats sinking everywhere.

"Steer two-five!" Kruger said.

"Steer two-five!"

"All ahead two-thirds!"

"All ahead two-thirds!"

The U-boat changed course and headed toward the rear of the convoy. It was common for some British freighters to slow down and pick up survivors. Those freighters would be like sitting ducks in the water. Moving the periscope around in a complete 360-degree circle, he saw no escorts patrolling the rear of the convoy.

The sea was nearly bright as day due to the flares the British had sent up. Kruger wanted to get closer to the convoy, but his U-boat could only do seven knots underwater, which was the approximate speed of the convoy. Underwater travel also drained the batteries; he might need them later. He decided to be bold and surface despite excellent visibility above. He thought he could attack the convoy quickly, fire his torpedoes, then go deep again before the escorts showed up.

"Surface!" he said.

"Surface!" Feiler replied.

The men at the hydroplane controls spun their wheels. Wing-like devices on the bow forced it up through the water. In the main motor room Second Engineer Wichmann-Holtz stood at the propulsion console and prepared to shift into diesel drive. Kruger watched the needle on the dial move toward zero. The bow of U-112 broke through the surface of the Atlantic Ocean.

Kruger scrambled up the ladder, climbed through the open hatch and on to the bridge, which was dripping with seawater. He felt a shudder as the boat switched over to diesels and looked around quickly for signs of danger, but there were none.

Straight ahead was the rear of the convoy. Burning, sinking ships had lagged behind. Through his binoculars he saw a freighter picking up survivors. The freighter was at least ten thousand tons. Kruger thought he'd have a go at her.

"Both engines two-thirds ahead!" Kruger shouted.

"Both engines two-thirds ahead!" repeated Feiler.

The U-boat leaped forward in the water, its bow slicing through the moderate waves. Grunberger and Blohm joined Kruger on the bridge, scanning the sea for destroyers.

"Your torpedo tubes are loaded, Leutnant Grunberger?" Kruger asked above the cry of wind in the rigging.

"Yes, sir."

"Take your position at the TBT."

"Yes, sir."

"We'll want to move in quickly, fire our shots, then get away quickly. Speed is essential — do you understand?"

"Yes, sir."

Grunberger bent toward the TBT and sighted on the big freighter. Kruger maneuvered the U-boat at an angle so that it would face the freighter broadside. Grunberger licked his lips as he turned the dials.

"Open torpedo doors," he shouted. "Target angle straight ahead and stationary. Range fifteen hundred. Torpedo depth seven. Stand by!"

"Standing by!" came the reply from below.

Like a hungry shark the U-boat cut through the water toward the freighter. Lifeboats and rafts were clustered near it, men climbing up nets that had been thrown over the freighter's side. Ensign Blohm looked at the shipwrecked sailors through his binoculars and smiled faintly as he thought of the expressions on their faces when they realized they were torpedoed again.

Turning from the freighter, he searched the starboard side of the boat for signs of British destroyers, then glanced astern, noticing a long white wake behind the quickly moving U-boat. That wake would make the U-boat more visible, but Kapitänleutnant Kruger wanted to sink this freighter quickly then get away quickly. Kruger was a courageous U-boat commander, and Blohm wanted to be just like him someday.

Under the light of flares the U-boat charged toward the freighter.

"Adjust your range,' Kruger told Grunberger.

Grunberger turned the knobs on his TBT.

"Range nine hundred," he said.

"Range nine hundred!"

Kruger held his binoculars tightly. "Commence firing."

Grunberger pressed the lever. "Tube one — fire! Tube two — fire!"

The U-boat slowed suddenly as the two torpedoes shot out of the bow of the U-boat.

The freighter was called the *Morro Castle,* its crew consisting mostly of Cuban seamen. One of them, First Mate Rodriguez, who was standing at the port-deck rail and looking out into the water through binoculars, spotted the white wake of the U-boat.

"U-boat off port bow!" he screamed to the bridge.

Captain Guzman, standing on the bridge, felt a chill when he heard the warning. He turned to the side and scanned the waves. From his high position on the ship, he could see not only the white wake but the U-boat itself.

"Tell the escort commander," he said to his executive officer, "that there's a U-boat off our port bow, bearing approximately two hundred sixty degrees, at a range of one thousand yards!"

"Yes, sir!"

The executive officer ran back to the radio shack. Captain Guzman raised his binoculars to look at the U-boat again.

Just then the first torpedo struck.

Commander Mulford heard the explosion, but there were so many explosions taking place in the convoy that he didn't know exactly where they were coming from. The *Centurion* was at the head of the convoy and turning around to make a sweep toward the rear. Neither Mulford nor the two other destroyers in his escort had spotted a U-boat yet. Their only hope was to try to force the U-boats down so that the convoy could get away from them.

Lieutenant-Commander Scott left the bridge house and ran toward Mulford. "Sir — we've just got a message from the *Morro Castle.* They've been hit, but they've spotted one of the U-boats."

Mulford snatched the slip of paper out of Scott's hand, read the location of the U-boat and shouted into the voice tube: "All engines full ahead!"

The *Centurion* raced toward the rear of the convoy. The sea was nearly as bright as day. Mulford swept over the water with his binoculars, hoping for a glimpse of the U-boat. Earlier he'd received a message that the *Crandon* had seen another U-boat on the other side of the convoy and forced it to submerge. It had dropped depth charges but not scored a hit yet. If Mulford could put this one out of the game, the convoy might be safe from attack for a while.

The *Centurion* passed flaming vessels and lifeboats in the water. Sailors in the lifeboats pleaded to be picked up, but Mulford set his jaw and passed them by.

"U-boat off the starboard bow!" shouted Seaman Second Class Drury.

Mulford trained his binoculars in that direction but couldn't see anything.

"What's the range?" he demanded.

"About twelve hundred yards, sir."

Mulford raised his binoculars and spotted the wake of the U-boat. It was moving to the starboard side of the convoy, evidently trying for some broadside shots.

"Hard left rudder!" Mulford yelled.

"Hard left rudder!"

"Submarine dead ahead! Forward battery open fire!"

The *Centurion* sped toward the U-boat, as the forward battery fired a five-inch shell which landed in the water far to the right of the U-boat. The U-boat abruptly changed course.

"He's zigzagging, sir!" cried Scott.

Mulford leaned toward the voice tube. "Forward battery — correct your aim and keep firing! We want to force her down!"

21

The forward battery fired another shell that landed closer to the U-boat. Mulford doubted whether a direct hit could be scored at such an elusive and small target, but he just wanted the damn thing to dive. However, it showed no sign of diving. The U-boat was trying to outrun the *Centurion*, and Mulford thought ruefully that it might get away with it, because the *Centurion* was old and incapable of sustained high speeds.

The U-boat zigzagged through the water, the *Centurion* following it, firing salvos from its forward battery. Mulford doubted that he could catch the U-boat, its commander evidently too smart to submerge. Mulford's only consolation was that the U-boat couldn't attack the convoy when it was being chased like this.

The U-boat changed course again, and as Mulford was about to order a corresponding change in the *Centurion*'s course, he realized that the U-boat was turning around. In disbelief Mulford watched as the bow of the U-boat slammed against the waves and pointed toward the *Centurion*.

"The crazy bastard wants to fight it out with me!" he cried. "Forward battery continue firing! Prepare to ram!"

"Prepare to ram!" repeated First Mate Harrow.

The U-boat was eight hundred yards, and the *Centurion* roared toward her through the water. Shells from the *Centurion* splashed around the U-boat, which moved ahead slowly. Now Mulford realized what the U-boat wanted to do. It was going to try to torpedo the *Centurion*, and it was too late for Mulford to do anything about it. All he could do was present the smallest possible frontal area to the U-boat and try to ram it.

Mulford gripped the bridge rail and narrowed his eyes as the *Centurion* closed distance with the U-boat.

On the bridge of U-112 Kruger pushed Grunberger out of the

way and sighted the British destroyer through the TBT. He'd lured the destroyer into this trap, and was now going to blow it out of the water. Then he'd be able to fire his remaining torpedoes at the convoy. He thought he might be able to set a record for ships sunk in one patrol.

"Rudder amidships!" he shouted.

"Rudder amidships!" replied Leutnant Feiler.

Kruger aimed the TBT at the destroyer and zeroed in. He intended to fire one torpedo at the destroyer to make it swerve. When it did, it would present a longer target to Kruger, then he'd fire the torpedo that would sink it.

"Tube three — fire!"

The torpedo streaked out of the tube and headed toward the destroyer.

"Torpedo dead ahead!" screamed Scott on the bridge of the *Centurion.*

"Hard left rudder!" yelled Mulford, watching the track of the torpedo.

First Mate Harrow swung the wheel around, and the light destroyer sloughed to the side. Mulford wiped his lips with the back of his hand. He knew he was in deep trouble now. If the first torpedo missed the *Centurion*, he knew there'd be another, probably several more. The U-boat captain had set him up, and there was nothing that the *Centurion* could do about it now. Mulford's only hope was that he could dodge the torpedoes.

"Rudder amidships!" shouted Mulford.

"Rudder amidships!"

The *Centurion* rushed full speed ahead away from the torpedo. Mulford watched the torpedo's track as it headed toward the stern of the *Centurion*. He held his breath and prayed.

"It's passed us, sir!" said an elated voice through the tubes.

Mulford didn't feel very elated. He scanned the waters on the starboard side of the *Centurion* and swallowed hard when he saw the next torpedo. He knew that the U-boat commander had aimed it as soon as he saw which direction the *Centurion* was turning. Mulford also knew that he couldn't get away this time. The *Centurion* was going to get hit, and destroyers didn't have much armor plating.

"Torpedo dead to starboard!" shouted a lookout on the starboard rail.

"Hang on!" screamed Mulford. "All batteries fire at the U-boat target!"

The gun batteries swung their weapons around, and Mulford hoped he'd be able to take the U-boat down with him. He watched helplessly, his face draining of color, as the torpedo dashed closer.

It struck the *Centurion* amidships and blew the hull plates into the air. The old ship rolled away from the explosion, then rolled back.

"All hands remain at your stations!" Mulford shouted into the voice tubes, hoping the *Centurion* might stay afloat. "Radio room — notify the *Crandon* that we've been torpedoed!"

"Yes, sir," replied Radioman Lofthouse.

"Damage report!" said Mulford.

The ship's sections reported one by one. The lower compartments of the destroyer flooded rapidly, the ship listing severely. The engine room didn't report, and Mulford surmised that he didn't have an engine room anymore.

The *Centurion* shuddered from internal explosions. Smoke filled the air, and tongues of fire licked up the side of the ship.

"All hands on deck," Mulford ordered. "Prepare to abandon ship!"

Sailors climbed ladder wells and poured on to the deck of the *Centurion*, looking around in panic, tying on their life preservers.

"Stay calm," Mulford called to them through his big bullhorn. "Make all lifeboats ready — but no one will abandon ship until I give the order."

Mulford watched detachments of sailors remove canvas covers from the lifeboats. He looked toward the U-boat and saw that it was speeding on the surface after the convoy. Mulford had expected the U-boat commander to fire another torpedo and finish the *Centurion* off, but evidently he wanted to save his torpedoes for bigger game.

The *Centurion* was sinking deeper into the water, stern first. Mulford knew that when ships were torpedoed, they either sank immediately or managed to stay afloat long enough for crews to get away safely, without panic. He'd been on convoys where crews had abandoned ships that never sank completely.

Ahead, Mulford saw explosions and flashes of light. The wolf pack was still attacking the convoy. Flares weren't going up anymore. Evidently Commander Herbert of the *Crandon* going to leave disabled freighters behind and try to elude the wolf pack through changes of course in the darkness.

Mulford realized that the *Centurion* definitely was sinking and nothing could save it. The stern deck was already awash, his crew looking expectantly to the bridge for the captain's order to abandon ship.

Mulford sighed. This was the first time he'd ever been on a ship that had been sunk. "Away all boats!" Mulford hollered. "Abandon ship!"

The officers and men boarded their lifeboats and lowered themselves into the sea. Sick at heart, Mulford made his way into the bridge house and put on his life jacket. His father and uncle had been killed in the Battle of Jutland, and his younger brother Nigel had died on the Royal Oak after being torpedoed by a U-boat in Scapa Flow. Mulford, a Scotsman, had graduated from the Royal Naval Academy and had the navy in his blood. Although he had no desire to go down with his ship, he fully intended to be the last one to abandon her.

He'd loved the *Centurion*, even though it was an old scow. It had been his first command, and he'd been proud of the way he'd welded his crew into a fighting team. He looked around at the helm and gyrocompass. Above the window at the front of the bridge house was the brass plaque that told when and where the *Centurion* had been built.

The *Centurion* lurched; Mulford thought it was time to get going. "So long, old girl," he whispered. "You've always had a lot wrong with you, but you've been kinder to me than my own wife."

He left the bridge house and climbed down the ladder to the deck. The rear quarter of the *Centurion* was underwater now, no smoke issuing from her two stacks. Mulford angled his body as he stumbled toward the rail and looked down. Three lifeboats were down there, and in one of them Lieutenant Dugan stood up and waved his hat.

"Over here, sir!" Dugan shouted.

Mulford lifted one leg over the rail. He saw boxes and lengths of wood floating in the water; he needed to miss all that debris. Lifting his other leg over, he felt cold wind buffet his face. He'd heard that some men died from the shock of landing in cold water.

Hanging on to the rail behind him, he thought, *What the hell.* Letting the rail go, he stepped into the air, covering his groin with one hand, his face with the other, and bringing his feet close together.

It was thirty feet down and seemed like an eternity of falling. He hit the water, dropping below the surface like a rock. The cold water made him black out for a few seconds, then he floated upward, numb from head to toe. His head broke through the water. Lieutenant Dugan's lifeboat was there, hands reaching out to him. They grabbed him and pulled him into the lifeboat.

Mulford lay on the bottom of the lifeboat, as his crew wrapped him in blankets. His teeth chattered and eyeballs stung from the saltwater.

"Have a nip of this, sir," said Chief Bosun's Mate Ronald Buckles.

Buckles held a canteen filled with rum to Mulford's lips. Mulford took a swig and it burned all the way down, heat radiating throughout his body.

"Anybody got a cigarette?" he asked.

"There she goes," somebody said.

Mulford raised himself and looked at the *Centurion*. Its bow was sticking straight up in the air and sinking quickly into the Atlantic. It emitted a sound like a sigh and disappeared beneath the waves.

Someone placed a cigarette between Mulford's lips, and someone else lit it with a lighter. Mulford puffed the cigarette, feeling strangely elated. His ship had been sunk, but he was glad to be alive. And most of his men had got away, too.

"You okay, sir?" asked Lieutenant Dugan.

"Yes," Mulford replied. "Anybody hurt in this boat?"

"No, sir."

"Is there a compass handy?"

"Yes, sir."

"Then steer a course toward England."

"Yes, sir."

Mulford raised himself higher and leaned his back against a gunwale. He saw the *Centurion*'s other lifeboats bobbing close by in the water. Rescue ships should arrive before long. They'd all have to sit tight until then.

"Pass me that rum again, will you, boys?" Mulford asked.

They passed him the flask; he took another drink. The blankets and rum were returning his body temperature to normal. He handed the flask back and puffed his cigarette, hoping that someday he'd be able to pay the German navy back for sinking the *Centurion*.

CHAPTER 2

U-112 glided past the ancient stone fortress of Port Louis and saw Lorient straight ahead. Most of her crew were on the bridge. Hanging from the periscope were six black pennants, each representing a ship that had been sunk. The tonnage of the ship was stenciled in white on each pennant, and the score added up to 42,000 tons, a very successful patrol.

It was a sunny winter day, with the air so crisp that a sailor could almost hear it crackle. Houses with red, gray, and blue roofs lined the river, a few puffy white clouds drifting across the sky. U-112. had been on patrol for six weeks. Its crew gazed joyfully at civilization.

Kapitänleutnant Kruger stood on the forward section of the bridge, scanning the harbor through his binoculars. He wore his white captain's hat and brown leather coat, a faint smile on his lips. Ensign Blohm stood beside him, binoculars hanging from his neck and his hands on the bridge rail. He was dressed identically to Kruger except for his navy-blue hat, because only the commanding officer of a ship was entitled to wear a white hat.

Ensign Blohm anticipated seeing Christina, one of the nurses at the hospital on the base. He'd met her before going out on the patrol; they'd had dinner together once. Christina was blond and blue-eyed like him. He was madly in love with her although she was two years older. She'd been educated in a convent school and was a nice girl, unlike many nurses on the base.

U-112 approached the inner harbor. Kruger ordered a reduction in speed. Crowds of sailors lined the quay, waving their hats and cheering. A navy band on the end of a pier struck up the Badenweiler Marsch, Hitler's favorite march. Near them a group of nurses waited with flowers. Ensign Blohm studied them through his binoculars but couldn't see Christina among them. Perhaps she was on duty at the hospital.

Kapitänleutnant Kruger deftly brought U-112 alongside the pier. Sailors threw lines to the U-boat's crew. The U-boat was tied fast to the pier, and a gangplank laid toward it.

Flotillenkapitän Werner von Weisacker, commander of the Fourth U-boat Flotilla, approached the gangplank with several members of his staff.

"Welcome home!" he shouted, mounting the gangplank and boarding U-112.

Kapitänleutnant Kruger stood on the foredeck and saluted Weisacker, who returned the salute and then warmly shook Kruger's hand.

"Good to see you," Weisacker said.

"It's good to be back, sir."

Weisacker looked up at the tonnage flags. "You've had a marvelous patrol."

"The boat suffered no malfunctions, and my crew was superb."

Weisacker smiled. "And the captain?"

"The captain merely did his duty."

A news photographer came aboard, along with the nurses. The photographer took pictures of Weisacker shaking Kruger's hand, and then Weisacker stepped to the side and shook the hand of Oberleutnant Grunberger.

"Welcome home," Weisacker said.

"Thank you, sir."

The band played on. Sailors on the pier waved their hats in the air. Weisacker continued shaking hands as nurses gave bouquets of flowers to grinning, bearded U-boat men, horny as billy goats after six weeks at sea. The U-boat men would have liked to grab the nurses and drag them below, but behaved like gentlemen, smiling shyly and contemplating with pleasure a night of debauchery in the brothels of Lorient.

Weisacker shook the hand of every officer and crew member. Every crew member received a flower from giggling nurses. Then Weisacker led the crew ashore. The officers got into Mercedes-Benz limousines; sailors boarded trucks. They were driven to the former French Naval Prefecture. In one of the huge old halls they sat for a sumptuous dinner washed down by champagne. Kruger, his face flushed with drink and food, told of the U-boat's adventures while on patrol. Weisacker and his staff applauded boisterously after each story, listening with special attention as Kruger described how he sank the British destroyer that had tried to ram the U-boat. The air was thick with cigar smoke. The bleary-eyed assembly smiled as Kruger told them how he'd maneuvered the British destroyer into his trap and torpedoed it.

"Well," said Weisacker, raising champagne glass into the air, "I suppose that's one British commander who'll think twice before he tries to ram another German U-boat. That is — if he's still alive."

"The destroyer sank slowly," Kruger told him. "I think most of the sailors got away alive."

"Then perhaps you'll meet again on the high seas," Weisacker replied, "and you'll have another chance to send him to the bottom."

"Perhaps," Kruger agreed.

Weisacker, his eyes glazed with drink, held out champagne glass. "To U-boat 112!" he said.

All the men staggered to their feet and held up their steins. "To U-boat 112!"

They drank heartily, then cheered so loudly that people outside on the street could hear them.

As dawn broke over the ocean, the first light of day fell on five lifeboats bobbing on the waves. Mulford opened his eyes and saw most of his men asleep in the lifeboat. The lookout on the bow was on his knees, peering ahead through binoculars, as the helmsman held the tiller underneath his arm, his beard encrusted with salt.

Mulford had been sleeping next to the helmsman. He raised himself up, hoping a rescue ship would find them soon, because the temperature was dangerously cold. He and his men had to huddle together for warmth. He'd discovered that one of the men had a compound fracture in his left leg.

The lifeboat had enough food for a week, but he was afraid of stormy weather. If a typical North Atlantic winter gale struck, the puny little lifeboats wouldn't last very long. Fortunately his crews had lowered the lifeboats carefully, no food or any other supplies lost. Usually when crews abandoned ships, they inadvertently wrecked most of the lifeboats in initial confusion, but his men were in the Royal Navy, not the merchant marine, and knew what to do.

Mulford wondered why a rescue ship hadn't come yet. He'd radioed his position after he was hit. What was taking the rescue effort so long?

He heard a sound like a waterfall and looked around.

"My God!" said the lookout on the bow.

A U-boat surfaced only three hundred yards away. Mulford stared at it in horror because he'd heard stories of U-boats machine-gunning survivors of torpedoed ships. Maybe it was the U-boat that had sunk him last night, coming back to finish the job.

He saw men appear on the bridge of the U-boat. Some climbed down the bridge ladder and manned the cannon on the deck, while others took their stations at the machine guns on the platform behind the bridge.

The U-boat turned its snout toward the lifeboats and motored closer. The men in Mulford's boat looked at each other, and Lieutenant Gaw went for the .45 in one of the lifeboat's lockers.

"Leave it alone!" Mulford shouted.

Gaw pulled the .45 out of the locker. He had brown hair and a freckled face. "I want to get one of them before they get me!"

"I said leave it alone!" Mulford looked at Gaw, who was in the middle of the lifeboat. "Give me that pistol!"

Gaw hesitated a moment, then made his way to Mulford, holding the pistol out. Mulford took it and jammed it in his belt underneath his jacket, where it couldn't be seen.

"We don't want to provoke them," Mulford said. "But if they show any sign of firing on us, you can be sure I'll take a couple of them with me."

The U-boat came closer and slowed down. Mulford could see its captain in his white hat on the bridge. The U-boat men at the guns gazed at the lifeboats but didn't appear as though they were going to shoot.

The U-boat captain waved toward Mulford's boat. "What ship are you?" he hollered in German-accented English.

Mulford cupped his hands around his mouth. *"Centurion!"*

"How long have you been on the ocean?"

"Since last night!"

"You have food and water?"

"Yes!"

"Good. I shall radio your position to England. The best of luck to you, Englishmen!"

The U-boat captain waved again, then issued an order to officers on his bridge. The U-boat turned and gathered speed, moving away from the lifeboats, heading in a southwesterly direction.

Mulford breathed a sigh of relief. "Let's have breakfast, boys," he said.

At twelve noon the crew of U-112 assembled in ranks in front of the Prefecture, stood at attention in the cold breeze and waited for Admiral Dönitz to arrive. Karl Dönitz commanded the U-boat fleet and liked to greet U-boat men returning from successful patrols.

Kapitänleutnant Kruger stood in front of his men, wearing his dress dark-blue greatcoat with Knight's Cross dangling from his neck, brim of his white hat low over his eyes, his head throbbing with a hangover. He and his men had drunk huge quantities of beer until late in the night.

After the admiral finished with them today, they'd start all over again. Kruger looked forward to a visit to the Crescent Palace, the fanciest brothel in Lorient. The most beautiful women in Brittany worked there, and he couldn't wait to get his hands on some of them.

The brass band began to play as Admiral Dönitz marched into the square at the head of a large contingent of officers from his staff. Dönitz, tall and lean, known as "The Lion" to his men, had been a U-boat officer in the First World War, and developed wolf-pack tactics used so successfully against British convoys in the new Atlantic war.

After executing a sharp column left, he marched several more steps, came to a halt ten yards in front of Kruger, his staff forming three ranks behind him. Dönitz waited a few seconds for dramatic impact, then delivered his speech.

"On behalf of our Führer and his navy," he said, "I want to welcome you back to port. We men of the U-boat Command have three duties: to pursue enemy ships, attack them, and destroy them. In the light of your recent successful patrol, it would appear that you understand your duties full well. My congratulations to all of you. Your exploits have added new glory to the U-boat Command. I'm very proud to be your admiral. With men like you, the enemy cannot hold out against us much longer."

Admiral Dönitz stepped forward and shook Kruger's hand. A photographer dropped to one knee and took the picture.

"My warm congratulations to you, Herr Kapitänleutnant," Dönitz said to Kruger.

Kruger looked into the admiral's eyes. "Thank you, sir."

Dönitz continued to hold his hand tightly. "It is a great honor to command men such as you."

"It is an honor to be led by men such as you, sir."

Dönitz smiled faintly. "Keep up the good work."

"Yes, sir."

Dönitz stepped around Kruger and moved toward the rank of officers. The first on the left was Oberleutnant Grunberger. Dönitz clasped his hand.

"Congratulations," Dönitz said. "It was an excellent patrol."

"Thank you, sir."

"You're the executive officer of U-112?"

"Yes, sir."

"You've got a sharp eye, Herr Leutnant."

"I wish it were sharper, sir."

Dönitz raised an eyebrow. "If it were, we'd have to designate a special ship to deliver more torpedoes to you because you use them up so quickly."

Grunberger felt at ease with his admiral and thought it would be all right to make a joke. "I wouldn't want to be selfish, sir. I only want my fair share."

Dönitz held his hand tightly. "We have U-boats on our drawing boards that can carry twice as many torpedoes as you carry now. Keep up your good work, and perhaps one day you'll command one of them."

"I'd like nothing better, sir."

Admiral Dönitz sidestepped to the next officer, Leutnant Manfred Feiler, and held out his hand. At the end of the line of officers, Ensign Blohm faced straight ahead, but out of the corner of his eye he could see Dönitz shaking hands with Feiler.

"Well," Dönitz said, "you're the man who keeps U-112 going."

"I try," Feiler said dryly.

Blohm listened to the conversation, wondering if the admiral would remember him. They'd met once at a party in the chancellery in Berlin. Blohm had been a midshipman from the naval academy at Flensburg then, and attended the party with his father, one of Joseph Goebbels's section leaders in the Propaganda Ministry. Blohm's mother and twin sister Wilhelmina also had been there.

Admiral Dönitz continued down the line, shaking hands and joking with the other officers. Finally he came to a halt in front of Blohm. He shook Blohm's hand and smiled broadly. "So we meet again," Dönitz said.

"Yes, sir," Blohm replied, his chest swelling with pride. The admiral had remembered him. Blohm hoped the others had heard.

"I saw your father in Berlin last week. He told me you had gone out on your first patrol."

Blohm smiled nervously but didn't know what to say.

"What did you think of it?" Dönitz asked.

"It was wonderful, sir," Blohm blurted out.

Dönitz smiled. "I'm sure you performed your duties well."

"I did my best, sir."

"You can learn a lot from Kapitänleutnant Kruger and the other officers of U-112. You must pay close attention to them, Ensign Blohm."

"I do, sir. I consider myself fortunate to be serving under such officers."

Dönitz nodded. "I can see that you're a fine young officer, Ensign Blohm, and your father is justified in being so proud of you. Follow your orders to the letter, be courageous, and I'm sure you'll have a brilliant future ahead of you."

"Thank you, sir."

Dönitz shook Blohm's hand again, the photographer snapping the picture. Dönitz stepped away and walked back to the first rank of enlisted men. Blohm stood stiffly, his chin tucked in. He knew that his father had enough influence to get one of those pictures in *Signal* magazine.

He wondered what Christina would think when she found out that he'd become famous.

Dusk was falling on the ocean as the men of the *Centurion* huddled together in their lifeboats. Wind was picking up, sky becoming cloudy, waves taller, spray covering the men as boats tossed up and down.

Mulford shivered among the men in his lifeboat. The rum ration was nearly gone, and he wondered where the Royal Navy was. His feet were wet, he had a headache, and he silently cursed the German U-boat that had sunk him.

Something must be done to stop the U-boats and their relentless destruction of British convoys. Britain had always been a great power, and still was. It hadn't been defeated at sea yet. If more escorts were available, they could keep the U-boats away from the convoys. Surely the admiralty could build more escort craft. If the destroyers were faster, Mulford was sure he could have blown that U-boat out of the water. Instead the U-boat had sunk his first command from underneath him.

"Ship dead ahead!" shouted Radioman Lofthouse in the bow.

Mulford bolted upright and looked straight ahead, but couldn't see anything. His hands and feet numb from the cold, spray hitting him in the face, he crawled over his men and took the binoculars from Lofthouse's hands. He peered through the lenses, his heart quickening as he saw two ships steaming toward him through the dusk.

"Lieutenant Gaw!"

"Yes, sir!"

"Send up a flare!"

"Yes, sir!"

Lieutenant Gaw opened a locker and took out a Very pistol. He loaded it, pointed it into the air, and pulled the trigger. The pistol exploded, wreathing Gaw with white smoke as the projectile shot into the sky and burst into light. Moments later a light flashed on the horizon.

"They've seen us!" Gaw yelled.

"What are they saying?" Mulford asked Lofthouse.

Lofthouse squinted at the signals. "They're saying that they're on the way, sir."

A cheer went up in the lifeboats. The men slapped each other on the shoulders and shook hands.

"I knew they'd find us!" Lieutenant-Commander Scott said happily.

"We might as well have a little celebration," Mulford replied, reaching into his duffel coat and removing the hidden flask of rum he saved for this very occasion. He unscrewed the top, tilted it into his mouth, took a gulp, then he passed it to Lofthouse. "A double ration for the man who spotted the rescue ships!"

The men hollered their approval as Lofthouse raised the flask to his lips. "To the good old *Centurion*!" he said.

"To the *Centurion*!" they replied.

Lofthouse drank his double ration. Mulford could see the rescue ships, and had to admit to himself that there had been moments when he thought they'd never be found and would die of starvation or hunger in the trackless wastes of the Atlantic. Now their ordeal was almost over. Lofthouse passed the flask to Gaw, and Mulford swore that he'd never let himself be torpedoed again. He wouldn't chase any more U-boats unless he was sure he had enough speed to overtake them quickly.

The rescue ships steamed closer. Mulford observed his men, their morale high again, and he marveled at the resiliency of the British sailor, his eyes becoming misty as he realized that he loved them all. They were his brothers. One day they'd be together again on another ship and would avenge the *Centurion* a hundred times over.

"It's empty, sir," said one of the sailors, holding the flask upside down.

"You didn't get any, Hughes?" Mulford asked.

Hughes shook his head.

Mulford proclaimed: "When we get ashore — drinks for everyone on me!"

The men raised their fists and cheered again. The boat rocked from side to side as they crowded around Mulford and slapped him on the back. Mulford looked over their heads and saw two rescue ships ploughing through the ocean toward them.

He figured his wife had been told that the *Centurion* had been sunk, and he wondered what she'd say when she saw him walking into their home.

U-boat officers were billeted in the Hotel Beau Séjour when they were in Lorient. Ensign Blohm stood in front of the mirror in his room, adjusting his black necktie, his hands trembling with excitement. He was anxious to go to the hospital to look for Christina. The ceremony with Admiral Dönitz had ended only an hour ago, and Blohm had rushed back to his room to change clothes. He hadn't called Christina because he wanted to surprise her. He couldn't wait to see the look on her lovely face when she opened her door and saw him there.

There was a knock on his door.

"Who is it?"

"Open up, you little bastard!"

Blohm recognized the voice of Oberleutnant Grunberger. Blohm walked to the door and pulled it open. Sure enough, Grunberger was there with a bottle of cognac in his hand and his cap askew on his head. Beside him, also disheveled and with bottles, were Feiler and Wichmann-Holtz.

"Let's go, you little sprout!" Grunberger shouted, and the rest of them laughed.

"Go where?" asked Blohm.

Grunberger blinked in amazement. "Do you mean to tell me that you really don't know where we're going?"

"No, sir."

"This is our first free night in port and you don't know where we're going?" Grunberger asked in disbelief.

"No, sir."

Grunberger looked at Wichmann-Holtz. "I believe this lad is beyond all hope."

Wichmann-Holtz shook his head. "No lad is beyond all hope."

Feiler poked the top of his bottle into Blohm's chest. "Haven't you ever heard of the Crescent Palace, sonny?"

"You mean the brothel, sir?"

Wichmann-Holtz jabbed his elbow into Grunberger's gut. "I told you the lad wasn't beyond hope. He's heard of the Crescent Palace. That's a start, anyway."

Feiler nodded. "The situation isn't hopeless by any means."

Grunberger looked disapprovingly at Blohm. "You exasperate me, sonny. I've tried to make a sailor out of you, but it's been an uphill fight all the way."

"I've always tried to do my best, sir."

Grunberger took a drink from his bottle of cognac and slapped the cork back in place with the palm of his hand. "There's more to being a sailor than merely carrying out orders to the letter, Blohm. You've got to have the soul of a sailor, and that you don't have yet. And you've got to have the heart of a sailor, too, and I regret to say that you don't have that yet either. You can acquire all these characteristics if you come with us to the Crescent Palace, but of course if you don't want to go out for a night of fun and frolic with your fellow officers, that's all right. We won't hold it against you — will we, gentlemen?"

"Of course not!" they all said in unison.

Blohm realized he was on the spot. They were suspicious of him already because his father was in the party and he'd been in the Hitler Youth. If he didn't go to the brothel, they'd cold-shoulder him on the boat, which would be very unpleasant. It might even be harmful to his career.

"But I had intended to see a certain girl," he protested, his face growing red. He'd never been to a brothel in his life and didn't want to go to one now. Only people of no moral background did that.

"A girl?" asked Grunberger. "What girl?"

"You wouldn't know her," Blohm said.

"No? What makes you think so? I know lots of girls — don't I, gentlemen?"

The other officers nodded and grumbled, indicating that Grunberger was popular with girls.

"You see?" Grunberger asked Blohm. "What's your little lollipop's name?"

Blohm blushed. "I'd rather not say."

"You wouldn't tell her name to your fellow officers?" Grunberger raised his eyebrows and looked at the others.

"This is worse than I thought," Feiler said.

"Obviously the lad isn't one of us," Wichmann-Holtz said sadly. "We might as well be on our way."

"No, no!" said Blohm, trying to stop them.

"Then what's the little lady's name?"

"Christina Kemp," Blohm admitted.

Grunberger placed his index finger on his chin. "Sounds familiar. Feiler, isn't that the one you used to bed down with?"

"Might have been. It's hard to keep track of them all."

"Now just a minute!" Blohm said angrily. "Christina doesn't sleep with men!"

"No?" asked Grunberger, reeling in the hotel corridor. "Then who does she sleep with — other women?"

"Perhaps Dobermann Pinschers," offered Feiler.

"Maybe French poodles," contributed Wichmann-Holtz.

Blohm stood stiffly in front of his door. "You men are sullying the honor of a very fine young German woman!"

Grunberger looked at the others. "Did we say she wasn't a fine young German woman?"

"Of course not!" Feiler replied.

"Just because she used to suck Feiler's *knockwurst*, that doesn't mean she's not a fine young German woman. Why, all the fine young German women do that whenever they can." Grunberger narrowed his eyes at Blohm. "Evidently you don't know much about young German women."

Blohm didn't know what to do. He didn't want to argue with his superior officers, but he didn't like to hear German women spoken of in that way.

"Oh shit," said Feiler, "let's just grab him."

Grunberger held out his hand. "No — we mustn't force him, gentlemen. If he doesn't want to join us, that's quite all right. We'll just have to accept the fact that he thinks he's better than us, and draw appropriate conclusions." He smiled wistfully at Blohm. "Well, we're sorry to have bothered you, sonny boy. We're only ill-mannered louts, I'm afraid, but I'm sure we'll find plenty of interesting things for you to do when we go on our next patrol, won't we, gentlemen?"

"We sure will," said Feiler, looking crossly at Blohm.

"I can think of a couple of things that need to be done in my engine room just off the top of my head right now," added Wichmann-Holtz.

They turned and walked away.

"No — wait!" shouted Blohm.

"Did you hear something?" asked Grunberger, pulling the cork out of his bottle.

"It was just wind in the rigging, Herr Oberleutnant," replied Feiler.

Blohm dashed into his room and put on his hat. He made sure he had his money and identification, then ran out of the room and locked the door. He caught up with the others halfway down the corridor. Grunberger was leaning against the wall, drinking cognac from his upended bottle.

"Who's this?" asked Feiler.

"It looks like Ensign Blohm," said Wichmann-Holtz.

"I wonder what he wants?"

"I can't imagine."

Grunberger lowered his bottle and burped. "What can we do for you, young ensign?"

Blohm shuffled his feet nervously. "I want to go with you," he said weakly.

Grunberger looked down his reddening nose at Blohm. "You do?"

"Yes."

"But we're so far beneath you, Blohm. How could you possibly want to go anywhere with men such as us who sully the honor of fine German nurses?"

"You're my fellow officers," Blohm said hopefully.

Grunberger looked at him sternly and then smiled. "How touching. The lad disapproves of us, but he's going to stick with us because we're his fellow officers. What a fine display of camaraderie. What a great soul you have, Blohm." Grunberger placed his arm around Blohm's shoulder and breathed alcohol fumes into his face. "Come along, my boy. We'll show you the meaning of life, won't we, gentlemen?"

Feiler and Wichmann-Holtz laughed and slapped Blohm on the back as they made their unsteady way down the corridor to the stairs. They descended the stairs, nearly falling down and breaking their necks, then reached the lobby, where a drunken officer was passed out in a big stuffed chair. They went outside to hail a cab.

Wichmann-Holtz held his hand up at the curb, but no cabs were in sight. Blohm looked across the square to the Lorient marketplace, feeling apprehensive about the evening that lay ahead. He felt unsure of himself, and he hated to be in situations with uncertainties. That was why he liked military life so much: everything — up until now — was so clear-cut.

An old Citroën taxi cab rounded the corner and came to a stop in front of the hotel. The four officers piled in. Feiler, who wound up in the front seat beside the mustachioed driver, told him the address of the Crescent Palace.

The sun was setting as the taxi cab drove toward the outskirts of Lorient. They passed over winding cobblestone streets lined with boxy stucco buildings, and finally stopped in front of one of them. The officers pushed their way out, and Blohm wound up paying the driver. The street lamps went on as Grunberger approached the door and knocked. On the sidewalk Blohm could hear music coming from inside the building.

There was a peephole in the door, and movement could be detected behind it. The door opened. A woman aged approximately fifty-five with dyed blonde hair appeared, wearing a white chiffon evening gown.

"Gentlemen," she said in French-accented German, "welcome to the Crescent Palace." She bowed and indicated the interior of the building with her delicate hand.

"Oh, don't be so formal with us!" Grunberger said boisterously, wrapping his arms around her waist and lifting her into the air.

"Let me down!" she laughed, squirming with delight.

Grunberger kissed her cheek noisily. "When I'm away at sea, I dream of you every night."

"Liar!" she squealed.

"I do!"

"You tell that to all the girls!"

"So what if I do? I mean it every time I say it."

"You're incorrigible," she said as he set her down. Her eyes fell on Ensign Blohm. "Well, look at the pretty lamb. What is his name?"

Blohm clicked his heels together. "Ensign Karl Blohm, madame."

She fluttered her enormous false eyelashes. "I am Madame Rupembre, but you may call me Cecille." She turned to Grunberger. "Why, he looks pure as an angel."

"That's his problem," grunted Feiler.

"Oh, you're always such a cynic, Leutnant Feiler."

"I don't think he's ever had any," Feiler added.

Cecille looked at Blohm and smiled, her lips plastered with bright red lipstick. "No?"

Blohm looked at his feet and blushed.

"I told you," Feiler said.

Wichmann-Holtz sidled up to Cecille. "Find him someone who'll break him in right, will you? Maybe if the boy gets his pipes cleaned, he'll be easier to get along with."

She winked at Blohm. "I'm sure he's fine just as he is." She linked her arm in his and led him into the corridor. "Come with me, my boy, and I'll introduce you to someone who's just dying to meet you."

She led Blohm into a corridor. At its end Blohm could see bodies twisting and dancing in tobacco smoke. The sound of the jazz band was loud, and shouts of joy punctuated the music. They came to a large dance floor with mirrored balls hanging from the ceiling and six musicians sitting on an elevated platform, blowing horns and banging drums. On the dance floor U-boat officers danced drunkenly with pretty young girls in evening gowns.

Cecille looked around the room. "I don't see her right now, so I'll go and find her for you. I hope you won't get frightened and run away in the meantime, will you?"

"No ma'am," Blohm said, aghast at the bacchanalia before him.

Cecille walked away. Feiler pointed to the right corner of the room. "Look who's here!" he said.

They all turned in the direction of his finger. Blohm's eyes goggled at the spectacle of Kapitänleutnant Kruger dancing in his shirtsleeves on top of a table. Kruger held a bottle in his hand as he kicked his feet in the air like a chorus girl, surrounded by officers and girls who clapped their hands in time to the music.

"I think we'd better report to our commanding officer," Feiler said.

"By all means," Wichmann-Holtz agreed.

Wichmann-Holtz grabbed Blohm by the sleeve and dragged him toward Kruger. Feiler and Grunberger followed, passing little round tables where U-boat officers sat drinking and fondling girls. Blohm was horrified. It was all so undignified, so un-German to him. How could the brave officers of the U-boat arm reduce themselves to the level of animals?

Kruger jumped up and down on the table, tripped and fell off it, but a forest of hands caught him and pushed him upright again. He raised his bottle to his lips, swallowed some of the champagne, and screamed with all his strength. He made himself bow-legged and staggered around on the table like a gorilla. He flapped his arms like the wings of a bird and made himself cross-eyed. Blohm couldn't believe that this was the man he'd seen in action on the bridge of U-112 only two days ago.

Kruger saw his junior officers and stopped cold, staring at them. The people clapping their hands on the periphery of the table turned and looked in the same direction.

"You're making an utter fool of yourself!" Grunberger said, puffing out his chest in mock seriousness.

"A disgrace to the U-boat arm!" Wichmann-Holtz agreed.

"If the folks in Berlin could see you," Feiler said, "the home front would collapse."

Kruger, spittle running down his chin, held out his arms to them. "My children!" he shouted. "My children have come to see me!"

Grunberger cupped his hands around his mouth. "How many girls have you slept with so far, Herr Kapitänleutnant?"

Kruger smiled crazily and held two fingers up in the air. The crowd around the table applauded him.

Feiler wasn't impressed. "That's all?" he asked.

Kruger held out his hands. "But I've only been here for two hours!"

"A very deficient performance nonetheless," Wichmann-Holtz said superciliously.

Kruger placed his hands on his hips. "How dare you criticize your commander in that insolent manner!"

"A thousand pardons, sir," said Wichmann-Holtz.

"Only a thousand?" screamed Kruger.

"Ten thousand?" Wichmann-Holtz said hopefully.

"Still doesn't sound like enough," Kruger replied, teetering drunkenly on the edge of the table.

"It seems to me, sir," Grunberger said, "that ten thousand apologies should be enough to cover anything short of murder."

"You think so?" Kruger asked.

"Yes, sir."

Kruger's bloodshot eyes came to rest on Ensign Blohm. "My God — I don't believe it!"

Blohm tried to smile.

"Is it my baby that I see there?" Kruger demanded.

Feiler slapped Blohm on the back. "It is indeed, sir."

"How'd you get him here?"

"We dragooned him, sir."

Kruger waved his arms back and forth. "Out of my way, you peasants!"

The officers and girls between Kruger and his men stepped to the side. Kruger let out a war whoop and jumped to the floor, tripping over his feet and falling to his side before rolling over a few times and winding up on his back.

"Somebody help me up," he said.

Feiler extended his hand and pulled Kruger to his feet. Kruger drank from his bottle, then staggered to Blohm. "My baby," he said, placing his hand on Blohm's head. "Have you been laid yet?"

Blohm stared at the great U-boat ace whose picture appeared regularly in *Signal* magazine and the *Völkischer Beobachter.*

Kruger knitted his eyebrows together. "I believe I asked you a question." He turned to Grunberger. "Didn't I ask him a question?"

"You certainly did, Herr Kapitänleutnant."

"That's what I thought." Kruger returned his gaze to Blohm. "Well?"

"No, I haven't, sir," Blohm muttered.

"Speak up! You sound as though you've got a mouth full of shit!"

"No, I haven't, sir!"

"Why not?"

"I … ah…"

Feiler stepped forward. "We just got here, sir."

"What took you so long?"

"We had to argue with him. He didn't want to come."

Kruger looked horrified. "You didn't want to come?" he asked Blohm.

"No, sir."

"Why not?"

"I had intended to see a young lady, sir."

"Oh? Which one?"

"I'd rather not say, sir."

"Why not?"

"I'd just rather not say, sir, if you don't mind."

"But I do mind, my boy." Kruger placed his hand on Blohm's shoulder. "You shouldn't keep secrets from your commanding officer. You know that, don't you?"

"Her name was Gretchen, I think," Wichmann-Holtz said.

"No, it was Helga," said Feiler.

"You're both wrong," Grunberger told them. "It was Christina."

Kruger clasped his hands together. "Christina — what a lovely name. I believe I read somewhere that one of the Führer's most trusted secretaries is named Christina, which means that evidently it is a hallowed name as well as a beautiful one."

"I believe," Feiler said, "that you are referring to Miss Christa Schroeder, sir."

"Yes, that's the one."

"But Blohm's young lady's name is *Christina,* sir."

"Oh — I've made a little mistake. Well, these things happen." Kruger wiped the drool from his mouth with the palm of his hand and looked at Blohm. "You're a great disappointment to me, lad."

Blohm's heart sank. "Why, sir?"

Kruger stared coldly at Blohm, who thought his commanding officer was about to describe his deficiencies as an officer in the U-boat arm. He tensed his stomach, expecting the worst.

Kruger frowned. "You disappoint me because you evidently were going to attempt the seduction of a pure-blooded German female tonight."

"Oh, no, sir. It was nothing like that."

"It wasn't?"

"No, sir."

"Well," said Kruger, with comic seriousness, "I'm so glad to hear that, because you, a son of a leading party official and yourself a former member of our illustrious Hitler Youth Organization, should not be out at night trying to deflower Aryan maidens."

"We are friends, sir. It was nothing like that, I assure you."

"No?"

"No, sir."

"Then what were you going to do with her, Ensign Blohm, if I may be so boorish as to ask?"

"Um … I thought we might take a walk, sir."

"A walk — how nice. Where?"

"Oh — perhaps the park, sir."

"You mean the park where everybody is screwing in the bushes?"

Blohm's eyes darted around nervously. If anyone else ever had dared to talk to him in that manner, he would have smashed him in the face. "I didn't know that, sir."

"Know what, Blohm?"

"What you just said about people in the park."

"Screwing?"

"Yes, sir."

Feiler guffawed. "I don't believe him, sir. He was going to try and screw a nice young German maiden in the park."

"I was not!" Blohm said angrily.

Grunberger reached out and pinched Blohm's nose. "You were going to try and stick it in her, you dog."

Blohm's face turned red. Everyone was laughing at him, and he wanted to leave immediately, but knew if he did he'd have great difficulties with his fellow officers when they went on patrol again. But he didn't care. He turned around and was about to make a dash for the door when he saw Cecille approaching with a young dark-haired woman.

"Ensign Blohm," she said enticingly, "where are you going?"

"Home."

"But you haven't met Julie yet."

"How do you do, Ensign Blohm," Julie said with a dazzling smile, holding out her hand.

Blohm took her hand but didn't know what to do with it. If she were from a decent family, he would have kissed it, but she was only a French prostitute.

Julie laughed. She was a year or two older than Blohm, with a pretty face, an upturned nose and curly black hair, and wore golden earrings. "I don't think he likes me," she said.

"Of course he does!" bellowed Kruger.

"No, he doesn't," she insisted.

Kruger pushed Blohm's shoulder. "Don't you like Julie?"

"How can I like someone I don't even know, sir?" Blohm asked nervously. He was aware that all eyes were on him, and wanted to run and hide.

"Well, if you go upstairs with her, you'll know her," Kruger said.

"Upstairs?" Blohm looked up and saw a walkway with a wrought-iron banister above the dance floor. On the other side of the walkway were doors.

"He's afraid," said Wichmann-Holtz.

"Doesn't know how to do it," added Feiler.

"Maybe he's a queer," offered Grunberger.

Cecille leaned toward Blohm and whispered into his ear: "Young man, if you don't know what's going on here, I'll explain it to you. If you don't do what your comrades want you to, they'll never accept you as one of them and will make life very difficult for you in the future. Therefore I think you should go upstairs with Julie. She's very experienced — you won't have a bad time at all. You might even like it — who knows. But I don't think you should incur the wrath of your comrades so early in your career."

Blohm looked at Julie as Cecille counseled him. She had large breasts for a slim girl, and looked clean. However, the color and texture of her hair, plus her vaguely Latin features, indicated that she had very little Aryan blood in her, if any at all. It was possible that she might even be partially Jewish. But Cecille was right. His career would be in jeopardy if he didn't go upstairs with this girl.

Blohm squared his shoulders and smiled. "I'd be very happy to go upstairs with the young lady," he said.

"Ah," said Kruger, clasping his hands together, "how gallant is my young gentleman!"

Grunberger smiled. "I knew he'd see the light sooner or later."

Kruger reached into his pocket. "I want to pay!"

"No — let me!" said Grunberger.

Cecille pushed Blohm and Julie toward the stairs. "Move along, you two. I have some business to discuss with these two gentlemen."

"But I insist on paying!" Kruger cried.

"Of course you'll pay," Cecille purred. "Stop worrying, and for goodness' sake stop braying like a donkey."

Julie took Blohm's hand and led him to the stairs. Her hand was small with long, elegant fingers. The band played a slow tune. Officers danced with their heads on women's shoulders. Cigarette smoke was thick in the air, and a group of officers at a corner table laughed uproariously.

Blohm was frightened. He'd never been to bed with a woman before, and he wasn't sure he knew what to do. If something went wrong, Julie would tell Kruger and the others, which would be catastrophic.

They approached the stairs, and a *Leutnant* was descending with a blonde who looked Swedish. Blohm stepped to the side and let Julie precede him up the stairs. He noticed that her waist was slim and her backside shapely. He arose into the scent of her perfume, which reminded him of roses.

They reached the landing, and she took his hand again, smiling confidently. "You're like a little girl," she said.

"I'm nothing like a little girl!" he retorted angrily.

He realized that he didn't feel erotic at all. He would never be able to do it to her. She wasn't his type, and there was too much pressure on him. *If only I had left the hotel before Grunberger and the others showed up.*

She stopped at one of the doors and took a key from her purse. Blohm looked over the railing and saw officers and women swirling over the dance floor. Balloons hung from the ceiling, and on the far wall was painted a mural of naked women dancing in a field of flowers. The odor of whiskey and tobacco floated up from the room below.

Julie opened the door to the room. "Are you coming in?" she asked tauntingly.

"Yes, of course."

He entered the room cautiously. She lit a low-wattage electric lamp next to the bed. The lampshade was pink, giving the room an atmosphere of warmth. There was a dresser with a large mirror, a closet door, and a window overlooking a courtyard. On a wall hung a landscape painting that Blohm thought amateurish.

Julie closed the door, latched it, sashayed to the mirror, looked at herself, raised her little finger to her face and flicked something away from the corner of her lip. "You've never done this before, have you?" she asked, looking at him in the reflection of the mirror.

"What makes you think that?" he asked indignantly.

"I can tell. This is my business, you know." She turned around and leaned against the dresser, looking him up and down. "You're awfully good-looking."

"Thank you," he said icily.

"Would you like to take off your clothes now, or would you like me to take them off for you?"

He blushed. "Do you think you could do me a favor? I don't feel right about this, and if I gave you some more money, would it be all right if we didn't — ah, go to bed together, but when we went downstairs, we could pretend that we did?"

She smiled. "I knew you didn't like me."

"No, no, it's not that at all. I'm sure you're as lovely as any other woman here, but well, I believe in love, and this isn't love."

Her smile became broader. "No, this isn't love," she agreed.

"Would you do it for me?" he asked, reaching into his pocket. "I'll pay you well!"

"Of course I'll do it for you, and it's all right — your friends downstairs will pay." She reached into her purse and took out a package of cigarettes.

"I'll pay you more. I have plenty of money."

She raised her eyebrows. "You do?"

"Yes — how much do you want?"

She lit her cigarette. "It wouldn't be proper for me to be paid twice." She closed one eye because of the smoke. "Well, we'll have to stay here for a while to make it appear that we did the deed. Why don't you have a seat, or you can lie down on the bed if you like."

There was a wooden chair against the wall; Blohm sat on it. Julie turned around, looked at her face in the mirror again, applied some lipstick and powdered her cheeks. Blohm examined at the curve of her rear end and realized that she had an extraordinary figure, was young and wouldn't look like a prostitute at all if she weren't wearing so much makeup.

"Who are you in love with?" she asked, widening her eyes and applying mascara.

"Oh, no one really."

"I thought you were in love with someone."

"Well, there's a nurse at the hospital whom I like an awful lot."

"Is she pretty?"

"Yes, very pretty."

"Do you think you'll marry her?"

"I don't know. I really don't know her that well."

Julie examined her face in the mirror, then puffed her cigarette and sat on the edge of the bed, removing her shoes. "I might as well relax while I have the chance."

"Yes — why don't you lie down?"

"I think I will." She fluffed up the pillows and lay down, reaching for an ashtray on the night table. Inhaling her cigarette, she blew a column of smoke into the air.

Blohm felt overcome by sadness. She was only a year or two older than he, yet she was a prostitute sleeping with anyone who had enough money to buy her. He decided she must be very poor, then thought of his twin sister Wilhelmina and how terrible it would be if she ever had to become a prostitute.

"You must hate us very much," he said.

"What was that?"

"I said you must hate us very much."

She adjusted the pillow so that she could look at him without raising her head. "No, I don't hate you."

"I think if I were you, I'd hate the Germans."

She shrugged. He decided that she didn't want to admit her true feelings because she feared getting into trouble with the Gestapo.

"Is Lorient your home town?" he asked.

"Yes. Where are you from?"

"Berlin."

"I went to Berlin once when I was a little girl," she said. "My mother took me to a museum full of artifacts from Egypt, I remember."

"Oh yes, the Egyptian Museum. I've been there many times. Why were you in Berlin?"

"My parents liked to travel a lot."

"What did your father do?"

"He had a small business — I don't want to talk about that, if you don't mind."

"No, that's all right."

"That chair's not very comfortable," she said. "Would you care to lie down?"

It was true — the chair was wooden and rickety. He looked at his watch. "I don't mind sitting here."

"You should stay here for a good while," she said, "so that your friends will think you're a great lover and so forth."

"I find this whole thing rather embarrassing," he said.

"As I said before, you're very much like a little girl."

"I regard that as an insult," he told her.

"You shouldn't," she said, stubbing out her cigarette in the ashtray. "I'm sure you're a very brave man with enormous reserves of willpower and physical strength, but in a certain part of your mind, you're as delicate as a little girl. You're the first man who's come up here to my room and refused to go to bed with me. True, there were some too drunk to do anything, but no one before ever told me he couldn't go to bed with me because he didn't love me. You must be a very romantic person."

"I don't think one has to be a little girl to be romantic. I believe that life can be finer than it is, and people should try to conduct their lives on as high a level as possible."

She laughed, covering her mouth with her long fingers.

He felt that she was insulting him again. "What's so funny?"

She stopped laughing and sighed. "Oh, nothing."

"You were laughing about something. Please me what it was."

"Well, it's best not to talk about certain things."

"Why not?"

"You really don't know why not?"

"You mean because you're French and I'm German?"

"Yes, that's what I mean."

"I wouldn't tell anyone. I'm not a blabbermouth."

"Well, we girls who work here are supposed to avoid certain subjects."

"Like the war?" he asked.

"Yes."

"Ah," he said, "I know what you were thinking. You thought it amusing that a person could talk about living life on the highest possible level when there's a gruesome and bloody war going on and I'm an integral part of it."

She reached for another cigarette, not replying.

"Is that it?" he asked.

"I prefer to change the subject. What does your father do?"

"He's an official in the party."

"Oh," she said. "You are ideological?"

"Very."

"Ah, I see."

She lit her second cigarette and inhaled. He looked at the way her gown outlined her body, and suddenly he was titillated by the thought that she was a beautiful young woman and he could do anything he liked with her.

"Now I know why you don't want to sleep with me," she said. "You think I'm a mongrel of some type."

Blohm didn't know what to say, because that was exactly what he thought.

"Do you really think that?" she asked.

"I do believe that the Aryan race is the highest development of human nature thus far," he replied.

"Highest in what way?"

"In every way."

"What about all the great men of history who weren't German?"

"There is Aryan blood throughout Europe, because Aryans have interbred with adjacent peoples over the millennia."

"So you believe that, for instance, if Balzac was a great writer, he must have had some Aryan blood in him."

"Yes," Blohm said. "Something like that."

She puffed her cigarette. "I see."

He shifted uncomfortably on the chair. "I suppose I've just insulted you, but I didn't mean to."

She waved her hand. "Don't worry about it."

"I don't suppose many U-boat officers have talked to you this way."

"As a matter of fact, you're the first one."

"The navy has tried to keep the party out, but the party will win in the end."

There was silence for a few moments.

"You probably think I'm a fanatic of some kind, don't you?" he asked.

"I'd rather not answer that question," she replied.

"Oh, go ahead, you can answer it."

"No, I don't think I should."

"I realize it's difficult for some people to grasp the essentials of National Socialism. We had many enemies in the early days. My father was in the party since nineteen twenty-two, and let me tell you that it wasn't easy to be a National Socialist in those days. But now we've won. The truth of our philosophy could not be stopped."

"Have you ever seen Hitler in person?"

"Oh yes, I've attended many of his speeches. I even met him once personally."

She raised her head from the pillow. "You did?"

"Yes."

"What was he like?"

Blohm's eyes took on a faraway look. "He's very intelligent, and when he looks at you, you can feel the power of his personality deep in your soul. His knowledge is vast, and you have the impression that he's not an ordinary human being at all, but an avatar of some kind — a man of the future. He talks about destiny and honor and justice — never anything mundane or trivial. When you are with him, you know that you are in the presence of one of the greatest men who ever lived."

She gazed at him as he spoke, and his face was radiant with conviction. "It must be wonderful to believe in something as strongly as you do," she said. "I imagine it gives your life a solid foundation and makes you feel secure."

He nodded and made a fist. "It makes me strong and gives me the courage to persevere in the most difficult situations."

"Like this one?"

He smiled. "This one isn't so bad."

"I don't believe in anything anymore," she said wistfully. "I believed in God when I was a little girl, but I've lost my faith."

"You'll get married someday, and then you can believe in your husband."

She shook her head. "No, I never could believe in a man. I know them too well."

"You don't like men very much, I suppose."

"It's not that. It's just that — oh, I don't know." She looked at the clock ticking on her dresser. "Maybe it's time we went downstairs."

He looked at his watch. "Yes, we have been here a while, haven't we?"

She sat on the edge of her bed and put on her high-heeled shoes. Blohm caught glimpses of her legs and thought that she really was quite a fine-looking young woman, except for her curly black hair. He wanted to ask if she was part Jewish, but realized she'd never tell him the truth if she were.

They left the room and heard raucous laughter below. The band played, and officers danced drunkenly with prostitutes. Blohm wanted to leave the Crescent Palace immediately — he couldn't stand the place.

They descended the stairs and faced each other at the bottom. "Well," she said, "good luck on your next patrol."

"Deep in your heart you probably hope I'll be sunk."

She smiled. "No, not really."

"If I were you, that's how I'd feel."

"But I'm not you. Goodbye." She waved, turned, and disappeared into the crowd.

Blohm stood at the foot of the stairs for a few moments, feeling a strange sense of loss. She evidently was an intelligent girl from a good family — how terrible that she had to sleep with drunken, loutish men in order to earn her living. Part of his mind told him that she deserved her fate, because she had inferior racial characteristics, but another part of his mind was saddened by her predicament. This clash of attitudes produced a mild headache above his left eye.

He couldn't leave without saying goodbye to his fellow officers. As he searched for them, a drunken officer with a blonde girl in tow bumped against Blohm at the bottom of the stairs. The officer didn't excuse himself, and Blohm felt like slapping his face. He thought that alcoholic beverages should be banned throughout the Reich, because alcohol corroded people's minds and ruined their character.

He made his way across the dance floor, dodging German officers slobbering over French prostitutes. His plan was to walk around the periphery of the room and look for his fellow officers, but he spotted them immediately, sitting at a corner table with a bunch of girls.

They hadn't seen him, and he knew he was in for another ordeal. Somehow he'd have to tolerate their taunts and stupidity, because it wouldn't do to become enemies with them. He was the youngest officer on the U-boat and had to expect this sort of thing, but when he became a commander he wouldn't tolerate drunkenness and whoring among his officers. They would pay dearly for what Kruger and the others were doing to him now.

Taking a deep breath and bracing his shoulders, he walked toward the table. Officers roared with laughter as they drank champagne and kissed girls, who giggled and squirmed, rubbing their breasts against the officers, touching them between their legs.

"Look who's here!" shouted Feiler when he saw Blohm approach.

"It's my baby!" yelled Kruger, standing up. "Make a place for him!"

The officers and women moved to the side and made room for him next to Kruger. The table was round, in a corner with an upholstered bench lining the walls. Kruger grabbed Blohm's hand, shook it, and dragged Blohm to the seat beside him.

"Well," said Kruger, his eyes glazed and hair mussed, "how did it go?"

"Fine, sir."

"Was it the way you supposed it would be?"

"I think so, sir."

Kruger laughed loudly and pounded Blohm on the back. Feiler pushed a glass in front of Blohm and poured cognac into it. A young woman sat on the other side of Blohm. She leaned over, poking her tongue into his ear. A shiver went up his back, and he wanted to push her away, but didn't dare.

Kruger raised his bottle in the air. "I salute you, young ensign."

Blohm decided he'd better play the game. He raised his glass and said, "I salute you, my captain."

Everyone touched glasses and drank. Blohm sipped his cognac and considered it to be of high quality. Opposite him, Wichmann-Holtz's hand was in the bodice of the young blonde he was sitting beside. Grunberger appeared to have his hand up his girl friend's dress. An officer walked by with a toreador cap on his head, and Blohm wondered where he'd got it.

Kruger put his arm around Blohm's shoulder and said in a low, slurred voice: "I'm sorry if I've caused you any great embarrassment, Ensign Blohm, but I'm only trying to make a man out of you. You can see that, don't you?"

"Yes, sir," Blohm said.

"Good. Very fine. Superior."

Kruger hugged Blohm, and Blohm realized his captain had genuine affection for him. Kruger was trying to be helpful, albeit in a clumsy, rowdy way, and Blohm felt the warm spirit of camaraderie swell in his breast. He'd intended to leave as soon as he could, but now decided to stay and get drunk with his fellow officers. Taking part in their pleasures seemed to be necessary. He didn't want to be considered stuffy and arrogant.

He raised his glass to his lips as the girl on his right massaged his thigh. Blohm thought that if he could get drunk quickly enough, he wouldn't have to go upstairs with her.

He looked toward the dance floor and saw wild, drunken dancing. A dark head and feline eyes emerged from the smoke, and he saw Julie ascending the stairs with a tall officer whose jacket was half-unbuttoned. Her arm was around his waist as she helped him up the stairs. Blohm knew what would happen. They'd go to her room and she'd take off his clothes, then hers. They'd get in bed together and the drunken oaf would clumsily invade her body. She'd wiggle her hips and try to show him a good time.

"You've become sad," said the woman on his left.

"Just tired, I guess," he said with a smile.

"So tired at your age? You should be ashamed of yourself."

"He has a right to be tired!" bellowed Grunberger. "He's just been upstairs with one of the ladies."

"Ah, I see," said the blonde. "But you'll recover quickly," she told Blohm, "and who knows, you might want to go up those stairs again, perhaps with me?"

"Perhaps," Blohm said, looking at the staircase. Julie and her officer were out of sight now. Soon they'd be in bed together, and the drunken officer would breathe his foul breath into her face.

Blohm reached for his glass and took a deep swallow, because he didn't want to think about that anymore.

CHAPTER 3

Mulford sat in the back of a taxi cab and looked at the fashionable homes of Mayfair. He was on his way to see his wife, whom he hadn't seen for three months. He wasn't particularly anxious to see her, because it probably wouldn't be very pleasant, but it was expected of him.

He'd married her out of sheer lust seven years ago, but never did learn why she married him. She was so vague and ethereal, sometimes rather silly, the type of socialite who'd go to a filthy restaurant in Soho where boorish waiters spilled soup on her, then tell her friends how quaint and charming the experience had been.

The taxi cab stopped in front of his home, which she'd painted beige shortly before the war. On that gray, cold day, the lilac bushes on either side of the stairs were bare and forlorn. He paid the cab driver, got out of the cab and looked up at his home, although really it was *her* home. She'd paid for it; her name alone was on the deed.

Mulford carried his valise up the steps of the house. He'd called his wife from Liverpool last night and told her he'd catch a flight to London today, and she said she planned to be home for most of the day, so perhaps she could see him.

In the privacy of his thoughts, Mulford referred to her as the Iceberg. She seldom showed any emotion beyond a faint smile or frown. On the rare occasions when she laughed, her voice sounded false and hollow. He considered her an extremely superficial person without a brain in her head, but the characteristic that appealed to him most was that whenever he was able to get her naked in bed, she became a wild screeching animal, scratching and bucking like a wild horse — a truly amazing and exotic sexual experience.

Then, after it was over, she'd pretend that nothing had happened, and drift away slowly on her iceberg. Mulford thought she was the strangest person he'd ever met in his life, and didn't know whether he loved her or hated her.

He rang the doorbell and waited patiently for someone to open it. Glancing behind him, he saw faces at some of the windows across the street. Some of his neighbors spent their entire lives observing comings and goings on the street. They'd been behind those very same windows when he'd left home last time, and they were still there. He'd like to become friendly with one of them so he could find out what his wife did in his absence. He often wondered if she had a lover, but couldn't imagine her loving anyone. She was too much in love with herself.

The door opened and Agnes McKinnon stood there, mouth agape. "Commander Mulford!"

Mulford realized that his wife evidently had not told Agnes he was coming. "Hello, Agnes dear," he said in his Scottish brogue. "How's every little thing?"

Agnes was sixty years old, and her gray hair was like an electrified mop on her head. She was gasping for breath, her eyes popping out of her head.

Mulford placed his hand on her shoulder. "Calm down, dear."

"We read in the paper that your ship was sunk, sir! Are you all right?"

"I'm fine," he replied. "Can't you see?" He held out his arms and smiled.

"You look as handsome as ever, sir."

"You're so kind, Agnes. Is Mrs Mulford in?"

"She's having tea with Olivia Kent-Taylor."

"Would you inquire whether I might join them?"

Mildred pursed her lips. "Stop being childish, sir. She's your wife and you know very well that you don't need permission to sit down with her."

Mulford wagged his finger at her. "I don't know that at all, Agnes. For all I know, my wife might be discussing something extremely important with Mrs Kent-Taylor, such as a trip to an antique dealer or a charity ball. Please do what I asked you, if you would be so kind."

She wrung her hands. "But I'd feel so foolish, sir."

"That's part of life, Agnes. We must grow accustomed to feeling foolish. Imagine how foolish I felt when my very ship was sinking underneath me."

"That must have been just awful, sir," Agnes said with genuine heartfelt compassion.

"It was," Mulford agreed, "but I tried to think of your fine biscuits, which gave me the will to live."

She moved her hand through the air as though she were pushing something away. "Oh, you're always making fun of me."

"You think I am, but I'm not. I mean every word I say, and I would be very grateful if you'd make my presence known to my dear wife."

Agnes gave him a cross look and left the vestibule. Mulford hung his topcoat and service cap in the closet, then took a briar out of his jacket pocket and stuffed it with tobacco from his old pigskin pouch. He was taking a book of matches from his pocket when Agnes returned.

"Mrs Mulford did not appreciate your little joke," she said.

"What did she say?"

"She told Mrs Kent-Taylor that you always did have a deplorable sense of humor."

Mulford smiled. "Well, on that note I think I'll go in to see my wife."

He strode toward the tea room, passing paintings of his wife's ancestors, and furniture that any antique dealer would sell his children into slavery to obtain. Entering the tea room, he found his wife and Mrs Kent-Taylor sitting at the table with teacups. Behind them were large windows festooned with plants.

Mulford walked to the side of his wife and kissed her cheek. "Vanessa, my dear, how good to see you."

"Welcome home, darling," she said elegantly. "You remember Olivia Kent-Taylor?"

"Of course. How do you do, Mrs Kent-Taylor?"

"So good to see you again, Commander Mulford."

Mulford sat on one of the white cane-backed chairs and proceeded to light his pipe.

"Surely you're not going to light that thing up now," Vanessa said. She had long blonde hair and small, perfectly formed lips. Mulford often thought she looked like a beautiful actress who was playing the part of an elegant woman onstage.

"You mean my pipe?" he asked.

"Were you planning to light anything else?" she replied dryly.

"No."

"Please don't light that dreadful thing now, William. You know how pipes and cigars make me cough."

"Do they?" he asked. "I hadn't noticed."

"Stop trying to be funny. I can see that you're trying to become a regular comedian, and it doesn't suit you at all."

Mrs Kent-Taylor cleared her throat. She was a sparrow of fifty with graying hair cut in a bob. "I understand your ship has been sunk," she said. "I'm so glad you're all right."

"So am I," Mulford replied, thinking of how strange it was to be sitting here in his wife's tea room, surrounded by flowers and speaking with a fashionable lady from the upper reaches of society, when only ten days ago he'd been standing on the bridge of the *Centurion* as it was sinking into the Atlantic Ocean.

"All of England owes you, and those like you, a great deal," Mrs Kent-Taylor said. "Every one of you men wearing a uniform is a hero, as far as I'm concerned."

"That's generous of you to say, ma'am."

Vanessa lifted her teacup, little finger curled daintily in the air. Mulford felt himself becoming enchanted by her again; it always happened whenever he was in her presence. She sipped some tea, then returned the cup to its saucer. "We were talking about the bombing last night," she said. "Lady Holbrook's home was utterly destroyed, but fortunately she and Lord Holbrook were at the theater."

"Utterly destroyed?" Mulford asked. "You mean it was leveled?"

"No, no," replied Mrs Kent-Taylor. "Part of the roof and a few rooms on the east wing were hit, that's all."

"At least they don't have to sleep in the street," Mulford said.

Vanessa wrinkled her brow with annoyance. "Lord and Lady Holbrook never will have to sleep in the street. They have homes all over England."

"Everywhere," Mrs Kent-Taylor added.

Agnes arrived with a fresh pot of tea and a cup for Mulford.

"Would you get me a Scotch?" Mulford asked her.

"Now really, William," Vanessa said. "It's only two o'clock in the afternoon."

"That's true," Mulford agreed, "but he who starts early, finishes early. Agnes — a Scotch, please."

"Yes, sir."

Agnes left the room. Vanessa scowled at Mulford. Mrs Kent-Taylor looked at her watch. "I have an engagement," she said.

"So soon?" asked Vanessa.

"I'm afraid so."

"I'll see you to the door."

Mrs Kent-Taylor and Vanessa rose from their chairs, then did Mulford.

"It's so good seeing you again, Commander Mulford," Mrs Kent-Taylor said.

"It was good to see you too," Mulford replied with a bow of his head.

"Do be careful in the future."

"I'll do my best."

"We'd hate to have anything happen to you."

"So would I."

Vanessa's eyes shot daggers at Mulford as she led Mrs Kent-Taylor out of the room. Mulford took out his pipe and lit it, filling the room with the fine aroma of Egyptian and Latakia tobacco. Agnes arrived with the glass of Scotch and soda.

"Where's madam?" asked Agnes.

"She's seeing Mrs Kent-Taylor to the door."

"Oh, my goodness!" Agnes exclaimed.

Agnes ran out of the room, and Mulford gulped down a quarter of his Scotch. It wasn't his first drink of the day — he'd started in Liverpool shortly after he awoke, for he always kept a bottle in his room.

Vanessa returned to the tea room, fanning the air. "My word, you've lit the damned thing up even though I asked you not to."

"You love the smell of tobacco and you know it."

"I do not. It's dreadful."

She sat and poured herself some fresh tea. Mulford liked the way she always kept her knees together so no one could look up her dress. She was dainty and absurd, and he felt the urge to make love to her.

"How have you been, my love?" he asked.

She sighed. "Oh William, I think I'll just fall down and die if this war keeps on. You can't buy anything anywhere and it's difficult to sleep at night with all the bombing. Quite often I've had to leave my bed in the middle of the night and go down to the cellar with Agnes. The Germans actually drop bombs on Mayfair — can you believe it?"

"How dare they."

She frowned. "You're making fun of me. You always do, and I find it most annoying. I didn't mean that Mayfair was supposed to be sacrosanct, but it has no military significance whatever, and there's no decent reason to bomb it."

Mulford sat in a cloud of pipe smoke. "Ah, but it does have a military significance, dear. I live here, let's not forget."

"You're joking with me again," she said wearily. "Why do you always joke with me?"

"I'm merely expressing the great joy I feel to be with you again, Vanessa. Seeing you is like walking into a garden filled with beautiful flowers."

She smiled. "That was sweet of you to say, William. Do you say things like that to your little American girl friend — what's her name?"

Mulford coughed. "I'm afraid I don't know who you're talking about."

"Oh, sure you do — the American girl who's slept with nearly every man in England. Helen, I think her name is. Yes, Helen. The one who chews gum like a cow in the pasture."

Mulford puffed his pipe. "I've told you a million times that I only know her because her brother and father are naval officers and I met them when I was an attaché in Washington."

Vanessa wrinkled her thin nose. "Oh, really, William — must you go on this way? Everyone knows that you've been carrying on a tempestuous relationship with the silly little slut, much to my social embarrassment. People feel sorry for me because of the way you're carrying on with her. 'Poor Mrs Mulford,' they all say. 'Her husband is having an affair with an empty-headed young American girl who is evidently trying to sleep with every male in England?' This is what people say, William. It's most distressing. I wish you'd leave her alone, or at least be more discreet."

"Vanessa, I'm surprised at you," Mulford said. "I don't know how you can say such terrible things about a person whom you hardly know."

"I may not know her personally, William, but I know quite a lot about her. All London is talking about her, for goodness' sake."

Mulford looked at her disapprovingly. "All London is not talking about her. Only you and your gossipy friends who don't have anything better to do than invent lurid stories about this poor unfortunate American girl. Your gossipy friends do not constitute the entire city of London, though you may find that hard to believe."

Vanessa raised her eyebrows. "Poor unfortunate girl? You make her sound like an orphan, when in point of fact she's never alone, according to my information."

"According to your gossip, you mean."

She sniffed and straightened her back. "I think we're having another quarrel."

"Appears that way."

"You're gone for three months, and then suddenly here you are back again and we're quarreling."

"It's your fault. You insulted a friend of mine."

Vanessa bared her teeth. "She's your lover — admit it!"

"She's not my lover. I haven't had time for a lover. I've been to sea for most of the past two months."

"If you hadn't been to sea, then you would have had time for a love affair — is that it?"

Mulford's pipe was out. He set it beside the ashtray and took another drink of Scotch. "I know why you're saying I have a lover. It's because you have a lover yourself, and you want to think that I have one too, so you won't have to feel guilty."

She placed the palm of her hand to her breast. "How can you accuse me of such a thing!"

"The same way that you accuse me."

"I need a cigarette," she said. "I would like to cry too, but I've cried too much for you already and I don't have any tears left."

"Is this a melodrama or a tragedy that I've suddenly fallen into?"

"Just an ordinary normal afternoon at home."

She opened the sterling silver cigarette case on the table and placed one of the cigarettes in her mouth. Mulford gave her a light with the matching lighter.

"Women like you ought to be put in prison," Mulford said. "My ship was sunk underneath me exactly ten days ago, this is my first hour at home with you, and all you can think of saying are insults and innuendoes concerning a rather mixed-up young American girl and myself. Women like you ruin the morale of men like me — you're a threat to the war effort."

"Oh, I see," she replied huffily. "You're an adulterer, but that's all right because your ship was sunk underneath you. It was probably sunk underneath you because you were preoccupied with that strange American girl."

"No, actually I was preoccupied with the fact that seven ships had been sunk in the convoy."

She took a speck of tobacco from her tongue and flicked it away. "I realize you've just been through something terrible," she said, "and I know that men on your ship were hurt, and I know that I shouldn't be selfish, because after all I'm nothing more than a foolish woman who spends too much time in society, but it is very painful for me to know that my husband is unfaithful to me, particularly so in view of the fact that everyone else seems to know about it. I'm afraid I'm a very vain person, William, because my jealousy and rage have blotted out the war and the seven ships in your convoy that were sunk, and the good men aboard your ship who were hurt." She covered her eyes. "I told you that I didn't have any more tears left for you, but evidently I was wrong."

Mulford looked at her, amazed. He hadn't seen her break down like this since the early days of their marriage. The bombing and lack of sleep must be wearing her down, he thought.

He fell to his knees before her and placed his hands on her thighs. Looking up at her, he said: "I'm sorry, Vanessa."

"No, it's all right," she blubbered. "It's not your fault."

"I'm just a weak man," he admitted.

"No, you're not."

"Yes, I am. But I do love you, Vanessa. I really do."

"If I thought you did, I wouldn't mind so much. But you know how vain I am, and I can't bear to think that you prefer a little gum-chewing American to me. I suppose I should be compassionate and understanding, and realize that the war is putting you under great pressure and warping your morals — not that you ever had any morals in the first place — but I just can't accept your infidelity, William; I'm sorry."

He laid his face on her lap. "You shouldn't have to accept my infidelities, Vanessa," he said into her dress.

"Infidelities? You mean there's more than just the American girl?"

"No."

"Are you sure?"

"Yes. And I really do love you, Vanessa. Really. But sometimes I have the feeling that you don't love me."

"What makes you think that I don't love you?" She worked her fingers into his thick hair and raised his head so that she could look into his eyes. "If I didn't love you, why would I marry you?"

"Sometimes I wonder about that, Vanessa."

"And why would I have stayed with you for all these years?"

"To tell you the truth, I have no idea. You seem so distant."

"That's because you're always away. When you come home, you're like a stranger almost. I have to get used to you all over again. Why, I see Olivia Kent-Taylor more than I see you."

"It's the war," he said.

"You were like this even before the war — always at sea on a training exercise or going to other countries."

"You could have come to America with me."

"I can't bear America. I told you that."

"Yes," he remembered, "you visited America when you were a little girl."

"Dreadful place, utterly devoid of charm or culture. An entire nation of nincompoops. They don't even have the sense to fight Hitler. They don't realize that if they don't fight the maniac over here, they'll have to fight him over there, and they won't have us to help them."

"They'll come into the war," he said soothingly. "They may be stupid, but they're not that stupid."

"Well," she said, "I imagine you know more about Americans than I."

"I did spend six months in their country," he agreed.

"Six months of bliss with your little American gum-chewer."

Mulford's hands were on her legs, and he knew how long and shapely they were. He squeezed them gently and blew warm air on them through the silky material of her dress.

"Don't do that, William."

He raised the hem of her dress and kissed her knee.

"You're taking advantage of me," she whispered.

"I want to take advantage of you."

"What if Agnes walks in?"

"I don't care."

"William!"

He pulled her to the fluffy yellow rug, rolled her on to her back, and kissed her aristocratic lips.

"Are you crazy?" she demanded, gasping for air.

"Not exactly."

"I think we should go upstairs," she moaned.

"I've always wanted to do it with you on the floor of your parlor."

"You bastard," she said through clenched teeth, digging her fingernails into his shoulder.

CHAPTER 4

A light rain fell as the crew and officers of U-112 crossed the narrow gangplank and boarded their vessel, the navy band on the pier playing the Badenweiler Marsch as usual. Deep ocean swells entered the harbor of Lorient, raising and lowering the floating U-boats.

A large crowd of sailors, nurses, and civilians were on the pier, waving goodbye. Kapitänleutnant Kruger assembled his men on the foredeck of the U-112 and saluted Flotillenkapitän Weisacker, who stood with his staff on the pier and saluted back.

"Happy hunting!" said Weisacker with a smile.

Kruger ordered his men to report to their stations and prepare the U-boat for sea. They climbed the bridge and entered the conning tower or took positions on the deck near cleats tied to the pier.

Inside the U-boat Wichmann-Holtz made his way back to the engine room, past crates of food and hammocks filled with potatoes and loaves of bread. Hanging from a pipe on the ceiling was a huge bunch of bananas. A can or box was stuffed into every nook and cranny of the boat.

He passed through the engine room, a narrow cavern filled with two huge diesel engines and supporting machinery. His mechanics followed him and began turning wheels and pressings levers. He shouted orders and soon the electric motors started up.

Ensign Blohm's duties aboard the U-boat were mostly administrative. He had nothing to do as the vessel was preparing to get under way. Standing on the bridge, he looked at the crowd of civilians, noticing a few of prostitutes from the Crescent Palace, but couldn't see Julie among them.

He'd been thinking of her since his night there, and had reached the conclusion that he should have gone to go to bed with her. He'd often found himself thinking of her intelligent face and shape of her body. Sometimes he thought that she must be more Aryan than originally estimated.

Beside him on the bridge was Kapitänleutnant Kruger, watching everything taking place on deck. Kruger wore his long brown leather jacket and white cap, looking every inch the heroic young U-boat commander: stern, sober, punctilious, quite different from the man who'd been dancing drunkenly on the table at the Crescent Palace two weeks ago.

Grunberger climbed the ladder from the conning tower to the bridge and saluted Kruger. "All hands present and accounted for, sir. The engine room is ready. All decks cleared for departure."

"Excellent." Kruger returned Grunberger's salute. "Cast off all lines!"

The men on deck cast off the hawsers. Sailors on the pier hauled them in. The crowd cheered and the band played on. Flotillenkapitän Weisacker held his hands behind his back and chatted with his staff officers on the pier.

"Rudder amidships!" shouted Kruger. "Both engines slow astern!"

U-112 backed out of its pen into the oily water pockmarked by rain. Bouquets of flowers fell on to the deck, thrown by nurses in ranks on the pier. Flotillenkapitän Weisacker and his officers waved goodbye, and the officers and men of U-112 waved back.

"Hard right rudder!" said Kruger.

"Hard right rudder!" repeated Feiler in the conning tower.

The U-boat turned around in the river and pointed toward the bay.

"All stop ... both engines half ahead!" yelled Kruger.

"Both engines half ahead!"

The U-boat moved toward the bay, its signal horn emitting two short toots. Kruger adjusted his leather collar and looked at the sky. "Filthy day."

Blohm looked back at the pier, proud to be leaving on his second patrol, anticipating that it also would be successful. It was inconceivable that anything catastrophic could happen to U-112.

"Switch to diesel drive!" said Kruger.

"Diesel drive!"

There was a coughing, rumbling sound as the diesel engines started up. In the control room Wichmann-Holtz watched Chief Mechanic Bogatz pull the levels in the propulsion control unit. U-112 trembled as the mighty diesels took over.

"Both engines three-quarters ahead!" said Kruger.

"Both engines three-quarters ahead!"

U-112 gathered speed as it headed for the bay.

"Well, here we go again," murmured Kruger.

Grunberger nodded. "Off to sea for the greater glory of the Reich," he said sarcastically, glancing at Blohm. "Right, Blohm?"

"Yes, sir."

Grunberger chuckled. Kruger raised his binoculars and looked ahead. Soon they'd be in the bay, where a British Sunderland might swoop down at them from out of the sky.

On the deck a seaman threw the flowers into the water. Blohm watched them float astern like a long broken necklace.

The headquarters of the Western Approaches Command Centre was in a heavily protected basement on a grimy waterfront block in Liverpool. In one of the conference rooms, a group of escort commanders sat on unfolded steel chairs, waiting for Admiral Sir Percy Noble to arrive and deliver a speech. Wrens in their blue uniforms fastened a map of the Atlantic Ocean to the wall, and Commander Mulford sat in the rear row, puffing his briar. He'd returned to Liverpool from his furlough only three days ago and was awaiting orders.

The door opened and Admiral Noble entered the room. All officers shot to attention.

"You may return to your seats," Admiral Noble said in his clipped, aristocratic accent. He had been appointed commander of Western Approaches Command by Winston Churchill only a month ago.

The officers sat again. Noble was accompanied by Commodore Pug Stephenson and Captain Randolph Farnsworth. Noble looked at the map and thanked the Wrens for putting it up. Stephenson and Farnsworth sat on chairs beside the lectern. Noble looked over the audience for a few seconds before beginning his lecture. He was fifty years old, with dark hair, a Roman nose, and the reputation for being the best-dressed admiral in the Royal Navy. This reputation appeared justified, for his uniform fit him perfectly.

"Good morning, gentlemen," he said, shuffling papers atop the lectern. "I thought I'd take this opportunity to speak with you so that perhaps we could get to know each other a bit better, and make an assessment of the problems that will be facing us in the months ahead." He looked up at them and smiled. "First of all, there's no denying that our situation still is quite critical. Our enemy is skillful, ruthless, and exacting a heavy toll on our shipping despite all our efforts. Most of the winning factors have been on his side, but it won't be that way for much longer." He looked at them significantly, then continued. "Our principal obstacle, as we all know, has been our inability to detect the enemy. We do not have sufficient patrol ships and aircraft, our Asdic has not performed to our expectations, and our ships have been easy targets. However, all this will be changing slowly over the next several months. New escort vessels will arrive from our shipyards, and new, sophisticated electronic gear is being developed to enable us to locate the U-boats. I can't tell you specifically what these inventions are because of security reasons, but I can promise you that they'll change the face of the Battle of the Atlantic. Therefore I must impress upon you the importance of holding fast until the new equipment becomes operational. Germany is in danger of choking us to death right now — let's make no bones about that. We must fight on as best we can and hold our losses to the minimum. I realize that it's frustrating and discouraging to see so many of our ships being sunk, but we must continue to carry out our defensive mission as best we can, firm in the knowledge that in the months to come we shall go over to the attack and drive the U-boats from the seas."

Noble gazed at his audience and saw that the escort commanders had skeptical expressions on their faces, as though they thought he was giving them a pep talk without any real substance.

"I know that many of you with great experience in this battle have come to believe that we can never defeat the U-boats. You've seen too many ships sunk around you, you've been unable to track down the U-boats that have sunk them, and some of you have even had your own ships sunk underneath you. But you must beware, gentlemen, of thinking that this situation is permanent. It is not permanent, and in fact it will be over quite soon. I am not making this up out of the whole cloth — you shall see for yourself shortly."

Noble placed a new sheet of paper on top of the ones on the lectern. "There is one more important point that I would like to make. Our Radio Intelligence Unit makes regular interceptions of German communications between their U-boats in the Atlantic Ocean and U-boat Headquarters in France. The problem is that these communications are in a highly sophisticated code that we thus far have been unable to break. The communications are sent and received through a special coding machine, and our intelligence people feel that they'll never break the code until they have one of these machines. Fortunately, we have managed to get hold of some similar machines used by the German military, and only last month we captured the German weather ship *München* in the North Atlantic. The *München* had a coding machine on board, but it was set only for relatively low-grade codes and not the complex ones used by the German U-boat arm. Therefore, I want each and every one of you to make a special effort to try to capture a German U-boat coding machine. I know this won't be easy, because Germans scuttle their U-boats whenever there is a danger of them falling into our hands. Yet a day will unquestionably come when events will move too quickly for the crew of a U-boat, and the opportunity will arise where it can be captured. I want you to know that I expect you to take advantage of that opportunity and seize one of the machines. They are located in the radio shacks of the U-boats, just forward of their control rooms. This is what they look like."

Noble turned toward two of the Wrens standing nearby. She unrolled a four-foot-square poster and held it up. Printed upon it in black and white was the picture of a device that resembled an old-fashioned typewriter. A complex system of rotors was located where the paper would normally be inserted.

"Make sure you bring us the cipher machine and not an ordinary German typewriter," Noble said. "We don't need any of those, and I hope you understand that the man who brings me a U-boat coding machine will not only make a significant contribution to the war effort but also will make a significant contribution to the advancement of his career within the Royal Navy. We also want any coding books that might be in the vicinity of the coding machine. Any questions?"

No one raised his hand.

"Good," said Noble. "Now we'll proceed with a discussion of escort strategies and certain revisions that I'd like all of you to inaugurate, beginning today."

U-112 motored on the surface of the Bay of Biscay. The rain had stopped but the sky was still thick with dark, threatening clouds. Ensign Blohm stood on the bridge with Oberleutnant Grunberger and a few members of the crew. They all held binoculars to their eyes, scanning the ocean and sky for signs of danger.

U-112 was moving along at fifteen knots, close to her top speed, on her way to a grid in the Atlantic Ocean where she was to rendezvous with three other U-boats and form a wolf pack. They would lurk in the square and wait for a convoy to appear, or move to another square if ordered to do so by Admiral Dönitz.

It was late in the afternoon of the day they'd left Lorient. Dinner would be served soon, and Blohm couldn't wait because he was hungry. The salt air always affected him that way. He wondered why, since he wasn't doing any heavy exercise or work. Watch on the bridge was tiresome only to the eyes.

"Aircraft bearing red three!" shouted one of the seamen on the bridge.

Jolted by the shout, Blohm swung his binoculars around. He saw the big plane diving toward them, extremely close because of the low cloud ceiling.

"To the cellar!" screamed Grunberger.

The sailors jumped into the hole at the top of the bridge, clattering down the metal stairs. Blohm went in next and Grunberger was last, closing the hatch. The nose of U-112 inclined into the water.

Kruger climbed into the conning tower. "What is it?"

"A Sunderland," replied Grunberger.

An explosion shook the submarine violently and Blohm was thrown to the side, hitting his head against a meter. Dazed and frightened, he dropped to one knee.

Kruger held on to a pipe. "You should have fought him with machine guns!" he shouted at Grunberger. "You didn't have time to get away from him!"

Grunberger's face was pale. He realized what Kruger said was true.

Another explosion shook the U-boat. Blohm could hear creaking in the hull.

"Take it down to two hundred meters!" Kruger shouted. "Both motors at full speed!"

Blohm pulled himself up and held on to a conduit pipe. A U-boat's hull was thin and could be holed easily. The bulkhead next to him might burst and drown him at any moment. He held the pipe tightly and focused his will on controlling himself. If the boat was sunk, it wouldn't help to lose control of himself. All he could hope to do was die like a man.

"I think that will be all for a while," Kruger said. "He's probably climbing now. There'll probably be a few more depth charges when he makes his next pass, but he doesn't know where we are. Blohm, go below and check the damage."

"Yes, sir."

Blohm climbed the ladder to the control room and saw chaos everywhere. A crate of French apples stowed between hydroplane wheels had tipped over and spilled on to the floor. Cans of food rolled about, and a jet of water squirted in through a pipe seam. Sailors frantically tried to stop it, turning little wheels to halt the flow. The stream of water slackened perceptibly.

"I think we've got it!" said one of the sailors.

Blohm bent as he passed through the forward hatch and entered the petty officers' quarters. The floor was covered with cans of food. One of the petty officers was slumped against the wall, bleeding from his head. Another petty officer dabbed the wound with a handkerchief.

"Has the pharmacist's mate been sent for yet?" Blohm asked.

"Yes, sir."

Blohm entered the galley, which smelled like beef stew. The pot on the stove had been thrown to the deck. Blohm had to walk on his tiptoes so that he wouldn't step in spilled stew completely.

"Get this cleaned up right away!" he barked at the cook.

"Yes, sir."

In the engine room mechanics worked furiously on one of the exhaust manifolds of the starboard engine.

"What happened?" Blohm asked Wichmann-Holtz.

"A broken gasket," Wichmann-Holtz replied, his face pale.

"Are you all right?"

"Of course I'm all right."

Wichmann-Holtz's hands were shaking. Blohm recalled a story he'd heard about U-89, Wichmann-Holtz's previous boat. It had been depth-charged for eight hours and nearly sunk, but had managed to limp back to Lorient afterward. Evidently the experience hadn't been the best thing in the world for Wichmann-Holtz's nerves.

Blohm entered the motor room and saw the electrician's mates inspecting their machines. "Anything wrong back here?" he asked.

"Nothing we can see yet, sir," said one of them.

"Good."

Blohm turned around and returned to the engine room, where he saw Wichmann-Holtz watching his mechanics work on the broken manifold. An explosion could be heard in the distance, and a few seconds later another. Wichmann-Holtz's head turned in the direction of the sounds, his body stiffening.

"They sound very far away," Blohm said. "He'll never find us now."

Wichmann-Holtz looked at him. "Not this time, anyway."

Blohm returned to the conning tower and made his report to Kapitänleutnant Kruger, who received it silently, his foxy face indicating he was deep in thought.

"Blohm," Kruger said, "if you're ever alone on the bridge and a plane dives on you from low cloud cover, fight back with the machine guns — is that clear?"

"Yes, sir."

"Also, you should always turn to windward if you can. That will force the plane to bank and the wind will slow him down for a few moments. Those few moments might mean the difference between a whole U-boat and a shattered one."

"Yes, sir."

Kruger took out a cigarette and lit it up. "We cannot tolerate mistakes of any kind on this boat. I realize that it's human to err, so in that case we'll have to become superhuman, because the slightest mistake can mean the end of all of us, such as what almost just happened. All right, return to your duty stations. We'll stay down for a few hours to make certain that Sunderland goes away."

Kruger descended the ladder to the control room, leaving Blohm and Grunberger in the conning tower, along with Feiler at the helm.

"Take it easy, Grunberger," Feiler said. "We got away, and you won't make the same mistake again."

Grunberger blew air out the corner of his mouth. "That one was almost too close for comfort."

"It was close but not a direct hit, and that's all that counts in the end." Feiler looked at Blohm. "What are you doing standing around? Don't you have anything better to do?"

"Yes, sir," said Blohm, descending the stairs to the control room.

Commander Mulford walked down a corridor of the Command Centre and stopped at a desk. "Admiral Noble asked to see me," he said to the pretty Wren sitting there. "I'm Commander Mulford."

She smiled — an adorable little brunette. "He's expecting you, Commander Mulford. You may go right in."

"Thank you."

Mulford opened the door and entered the office of Admiral Noble, who was standing at the window looking out the window at ships in Liverpool Harbor. He turned around as Mulford saluted, and saluted him back.

"I was just looking at Convoy L-51 forming out there and wondering which ones will make it back to America," Admiral Noble said.

"That's like betting the horses sir," Mulford replied. "You never can know for sure."

"That's true, I suppose. All we can be sure of is that approximately thirty to forty percent of them probably will be lost." Admiral Noble sighed and pointed to a chair. "Have a seat, Mulford. I've got a new job for you."

Mulford sat on one of the green leather chairs in front of the desk. Hanging on the wall on the right side of the windows was a photograph of the king next to another of Winston Churchill.

"A new assignment, sir?" Mulford asked. "I thought I was going to get one of the new destroyers."

Admiral Noble sat behind his desk and opened his cigar humidor. "Care for one of these?" he asked. "They're from Cuba."

"Don't mind if I do," Mulford replied, reaching over and picking one out of the humidor.

Both men tore the cellophane off the cigars and lit them. The air around the desk became thick with blue smoke.

"Excellent cigar," said Mulford, sniffing the fragrant smoke appreciatively.

"Yes — fortunately the boat carrying them got through."

"What's this about my new assignment?"

"You're going to America."

"America?" Mulford was aghast. "Me?"

"Yes."

"But what about my new destroyer?"

"Your exec is going to be promoted. He'll take command of it."

"Scott?"

"Yes — don't you think he's qualified?"

"Of course he's qualified — I trained him myself. But what about me?"

"You're going to America."

Mulford groaned. "But sir…

"I know you'd rather take your new destroyer out and sink U-boats with it," Admiral Noble said soothingly, "but we need you in America. It'll only be a matter of time before they're in the war all the way, and they need an anti-submarine warfare adviser. I've decided to send you because you've been to America before and know many people in the American navy, and because you've had a great deal of experience in anti-submarine warfare."

Mulford frowned. "I wish you could send somebody else, but if you think I'm the best man for the job, I'll go and do my very best, sir. You can rely on me."

"I knew I could, Mulford," Noble replied. "That's another of the reasons I selected you."

It was night on the North Atlantic. Ensign Blohm lay on his narrow cot in the officers' quarters, thinking of the events of the day. U-112 was running on the surface, heading for its designated square in the ocean, searching for convoys at the same time. An alarm might sound at any moment forcing him to dash to his battle station on the bridge. His job would be to command the gun crews should they be needed and take command of the bridge if senior officers were killed or wounded.

Blohm was now aware of how quickly someone could be killed on the boat, and how easily one could be sunk. If that Sunderland bomber had been a little quicker and more accurate, U-112 would be at the bottom of the ocean right now, an iron coffin for himself and the rest of the crew.

Never in his life had he come so close to being killed. Until today he'd had the vague notion that he might live forever, but now realized that death could strike him down at any moment, although he was only twenty-two years old. *I could die before I've hardly even lived,* he thought. *There are so many of life's pleasures that I've never tasted.*

He remembered Julie, the prostitute in the Crescent Palace. *I should have bedded her down while I had the chance.* He'd never had any sex in his life and was intensely curious about it. He'd imagined that someday he'd marry a nice German girl from a good family and find out about it then, but he had no steady girlfriend because he'd spent most of his life in uniform and in the company of other males.

He decided that he'd like to make love to a woman before he died. Often while going about his duties he had been assailed by lurid thoughts of naked, writhing women. He sometimes thought that sexual intercourse with the woman you loved would be the most intense and wonderful experience in life.

Now he was glad that he'd met Julie, because he would have found it immensely difficult to go to the Crescent Palace and just pick out any old girl. He would simply go there the next time they were in Lorient and take her up to her room, just like the other U-boat officers. He thought of her strong young body, high bosom, and shapely rear end. She had a pretty smile, and that curly hair of hers made her look wild.

He almost never thought about Christina. She was a nice German girl, and he didn't want a nice German girl. He wanted a prostitute like Julie who would be easily accommodating to his needs. Thinking of her, he felt an erection growing in his pants and couldn't wait to get back to Lorient. *I was such a fool before. I should have taken her while I had the chance.*

With a bottle of Scotch in his hand, Mulford stumbled over a carpeted corridor of the Hedgewick Hotel in Liverpool. His hat was askew on the back of his head, and his jacket was unbuttoned. It was two o'clock in the morning.

He stopped in front of a door and squinted at the number on it. "I think this is it," he said to himself, "and if it isn't I'll find out soon enough." He made a fist and pounded on the door.

"Who is it?" demanded a voice inside.

"Your commanding officer — open up!"

There were footsteps in the room and the door opened a crack. Standing behind it, his eyes narrowed to slits and his jaw hanging open, was Lieutenant-Commander Michael Scott.

"Good morning, sir," he said. "Are you drunk?"

"Of course I'm drunk!" roared Mulford.

"Then you'd better come in before you wake everybody up."

Mulford staggered into the hotel room. The shades were drawn, and a lamp illuminated a photograph of Scott's wife and two sons which was displayed prominently on the dresser. They lived in Cornwall in a charming old stone house by the sea.

Mulford collapsed in the chair near the window. "Have you heard the news, Scotty?"

"What news, sir?"

"The news about you."

Scott sat on the edge of his bed and lit a cigarette. He wore shorts and a T-shirt. "News about me?" he asked, puffing the cigarette. "No, I haven't heard any news about me. Couldn't it have waited until the morning, sir?"

"No!" said Mulford.

"What is it then?"

Mulford growled and shook his head. "You're going to get the new *Centurion* and I'm going to goddamn America!"

Scott's mouth vacillated between a smile and a frown. "Really?"

"Yes."

"You mean I'm going to be promoted?"

"Yes, and I'm going to goddamn America." Mulford raised his bottle to his lips and gulped some down. "You want some of this?"

"I think I'd better."

Mulford handed Scott the bottle. He had short light brown hair combed to the side, was six feet tall, growing just a trifle flabby.

"Where did you hear all this?" Scott asked, handing the bottle back.

"Noble told me. I don't suppose I should have told you, but what the hell."

"I have rather mixed emotions, sir," Scott said. "On one hand I'm very happy to be getting my own command, but on the other I'll be sorry to see you go."

"Horseshit," growled Mulford.

"I really will, sir. We've been together for so long."

"I hate America," Mulford said.

"It's supposed to be a very beautiful country."

"It's like a big kindergarten. Nobody has any sense over there, except maybe Roosevelt."

"Perhaps you can show them the light, sir."

"No one can show them the light — they're all blind."

"I'm sure you'll feel differently in the morning."

Mulford raised his bottle to his lips. "Don't be so sure." He burped. "Maybe it's time I went to bed."

"It is rather late, sir."

"Sorry to bother you, Scotty."

"That's all right, sir."

"You'll be a fine commander; congratulations."

"Thank you, sir."

Mulford arose unsteadily and held out his hand. "Good luck, Scotty," he slurred. "They couldn't have picked a better man."

"It's kind of you to say that, sir."

"Sorry you had to hear it from an old rum pot like me."

"There's no one I'd rather hear it from, sir."

"You're full of shit, Scotty."

"Not completely, sir."

Mulford began to cough uncontrollably. His face became red, his eyes bulged, and he nearly dropped to one knee. Scott slapped him on the back.

"Are you all right, sir?" Scott asked, alarmed.

Mulford coughed up a big gob of something, went into Scott's toilet, and spit it out. He made a nasty throaty noise, wiped his mouth with the back of his hand, and shuffled to the door.

"Maybe you'd better sit down for a moment or two, sir."

"No, it's time I got going. Pleasant dreams, old man."

"You too, sir."

Carrying his bottle in his hand, Mulford staggered out of the room. Scott watched him anxiously for a few moments, then closed the door.

In the middle of the corridor, Mulford suddenly didn't know where he was. It happened to him occasionally when he was drunk — a complete blank-out. He leaned against the wall in the corridor and had another drink. The fiery liquid cleared his head and told him he was in the Hedgewick Hotel, Liverpool.

He decided to climb the stairs instead of taking the elevator, afraid he might step on to the elevator and find himself with an admiral or some other high-ranking officer. He found the stairs, grabbed the banister, pulled himself up, snorted like a horse, made his way to the next floor, had another swig of Scotch, and continued climbing to the floor above that, where his room was.

He walked down the corridor, paused at his door, fumbled for his keys, dropped them on the floor, bent over to retrieve them, and bumped his head on the door. It opened suddenly, and he fell into his room.

"I thought it was you," said a female voice.

Mulford looked up and saw Helen McCrary, and blubbered: "What are you doing here?"

"Waiting for you," she replied coolly.

"How did you get in?"

"I'm not telling you any of my tricks."

Mulford walked on his hands and knees into the corridor, picked up his bottle and keys, stood up, and entered his room, closing the door behind him. "Privacy is terribly hard to come by these days," he said, collapsing on to a chair. "How long have you been here?"

"Not long." She wore dark blue slacks and a pale blue blouse, and had wavy blonde hair. "I heard you were back and started looking for you in your haunts, but every bartender told me you'd just left. Finally I decided to come here. How long have you been back, and why haven't you contacted me? Have you fallen in love with your wife again, you big drunken idiot?"

Mulford looked at her; she was a twenty-one-year-old beauty. "I returned from London this morning and haven't called you because I've been busy. And yes, I'm in love with my wife again."

"I knew it," Helen said. "I knew she'd wrap you around her little finger as usual."

"She's a remarkable woman," Mulford mumbled.

"She certainly is. She's slept with just about every man of rank in London."

"That's funny," Mulford said, "because she said the same thing about you, except that she left out the part about rank and didn't confine your activities solely to London."

"And you believed her?"

"I don't know what to believe anymore." He looked at Helen and tried to think.

"Why don't you lie down?" she asked.

"Is that an invitation of some kind?"

"An invitation to what?"

"You know."

"Don't be ridiculous," she said. "You're drunk and you stink. What do you think I am?"

"You're a very nice young girl, but you have wicked inclinations."

She removed a cigarette from her purse and lit it up. "I'm very annoyed that you didn't call when you returned."

"I couldn't help it — I had a very important conference and meeting today at headquarters with Admiral Noble himself."

"That was today — what about this evening?"

"I got drunk."

"That's my point," she said, an edge to her voice. "You got drunk rather than see me."

"I was troubled."

"You should have turned to me."

"You would have troubled me more."

"Why?"

"Because I'm a married man and you're almost young enough to be my daughter."

"Is that why you got drunk?"

"Not over that, no."

"Over what, then?"

"I'm going to America again."

Her eyes widened. "You are?"

"Yes."

"When?"

"Another week or two."

"For how long?"

"An indefinite period."

She puffed her cigarette. "Where in America?"

"Washington."

"I see." She paced back and forth in front of him, tossing him suspicious glances. "Did you volunteer to go to America?"

"Of course not, and I don't want to go."

"I'm going with you."

"I thought you'd want to," he groaned.

"You don't want me to?"

Mulford tried to think. "I don't know what I want anymore."

"You don't love me anymore?"

He coughed twice. "I don't think I know what love is nowadays. There's too much happening in the world. I don't think we're good for each other, Helen."

She sat on the arm of his chair and placed her arm around his shoulders. "Because of the difference in our ages?"

"Yes. I feel like an old lecher when I'm with you."

"You're not that old, Billy. A man your age is in his prime."

"When you're pushing forty we'll see how you feel about that."

She laid her cheek against his sandy hair. "I know there's a great difference in our ages, but I love you anyway despite your drunkenness and nasty ways. I even love you in spite of your mustache."

"My mustache isn't so bad."

"It is, too. It smells like tobacco, Scotch, and whatever you had for dinner. It's unsanitary."

"Did I have it when we met?"

"Yes."

"But it didn't upset you then?"

"No. It was your warmth and rugged masculinity that captivated me."

Mulford laughed.

"I know you think I'm a silly young thing," she said, "but I'm not. I'm sure your wife is much sillier than I am."

"You're both silly. All women are silly, except when they're not being silly."

"When is that?"

"The Wrens at headquarters — when they're sticking pins in the big maps and measuring distances — they're not silly at all."

She raised her cheek from his shoulder. "I'm very serious when I'm in my office, too, but you never see me there."

"That's true."

"I'm quitting my job and going to America with you."

"I may only be there for a few months."

"Then I'll come back to England with you."

He sighed. "Look at me," he said.

She moved her face opposite his. "What is it?"

"I'm too old for you, Helen. You're wasting the best years of your life with me. You should find someone your own age and settle down."

"So I can have a happy marriage like yours?"

He groaned. "You have an answer for everything."

"You're darned tootin'."

He grimaced. "What a hideous American expression."

"You know what your problem is, Billy?" she asked. "Your problem is that you think there's no reason why anybody should fall in love with you."

"That's true because I'm nothing more than a drunken dog. And my mustache stinks on top of everything else."

She smiled and ran her fingers through his hair. "Yes, you're a drunken dog, and yes, your mustache stinks, but I love you anyway. I think you're wonderful, although of course you'd be more wonderful if you didn't drink so much and if you shaved that dreadful mustache off."

"Never," he said.

"Sometimes I think you're the way you are because you don't want anybody to love you. You're afraid you'll have to give somebody something of yourself."

"Nonsense. I'm an immensely generous man. Ask anyone — they'll tell you. The real problem is that I'm married and I shouldn't be fooling around with a woman who's old enough, or rather young enough, to be my daughter."

"Your wife is making you feel guilty," she replied.

"Yes."

"That's curious, considering how promiscuous she is."

"Funny, she said the same thing about you." He yawned. "I'm so tired I don't even know who's who anymore."

She kissed his cheek and squirmed in his lap. "I'm Helen."

"I'm drunk and I'm afraid I won't be able to do anything for you tonight, my dear. Even if I wanted to."

She stood up. "All right; get your clothes off and go to bed." She began to unbutton her blouse.

"What are you doing?"

"Getting ready for bed."

He pointed his finger at her. "You're utterly depraved!"

"If I am, you made me this way."

He covered his face with his hands. "I knew you'd blame it all on me someday."

She took his wrists in both her hands and pulled him toward the bed. "Come on," she said. "Stop being so difficult."

CHAPTER 5

U-112 was making a northerly sweep of grid AK 37, southeast of Greenland. Kapitänleutnant Kruger stood on the bridge with Oberleutnant Grunberger, Ensign Blohm, and a few members of the crew. Each had an assigned segment of the ocean to cover, and peered at it through binoculars, searching for convoys.

Kruger was becoming irritable because he'd been on patrol nearly a week and hadn't seen anything yet. On Wednesday one of the seamen had reported sighting smoke on the horizon, but the visibility was poor and Kruger hadn't been able to catch up with the convoy, if it was indeed a convoy.

"Smoke dead to starboard!" shouted Blohm.

Kruger swung his binoculars in that direction but couldn't see anything. "Anybody else see anything over there?" he asked.

"I don't," replied Grunberger.

"Me neither," said one of the seamen.

Kruger lowered his binoculars and looked at Blohm. "Are you sure you see smoke dead to starboard, Ensign Blohm?"

Blohm squinted through his binoculars. "Yes, sir."

"You're quite sure?"

"Well, there's something there, sir."

"There'd better be." Kruger leaned toward the conning tower. "Rudder left forty-five! Steer two-five-oh!"

"Rudder left forty-five, steer two-five-oh!" replied Feiler at the helm.

The bow of U-112 slapped the waves as it turned in the direction of whatever Blohm had reported. Now Blohm worried that his eyes had been deceiving him and nothing was there. Kruger really would rip into him if this alteration in course was for nothing. Holding the binoculars to his eyes, he was certain there was a faint smudge on the horizon. He hoped it wasn't just a dark storm cloud of some kind.

"I see it!" said one of the seamen.

"So do I," replied Grunberger with a wide smile. "Well, what do you know about that?"

Kruger looked through his binoculars; now he saw it, too. "It looks like a big one, and it's headed right this way. All engines stop!"

"All engines stop!"

"Ensign Blohm," said Kruger. "Take down this information and send it to headquarters immediately!"

"Yes, sir."

"CONVOY SIGHTED AK THIRTY-SEVEN. AM IN FAVORABLE POSITION, REQUEST PERMISSION TO ATTACK. Got that, Blohm?"

"Yes, sir," replied Blohm, writing furiously on his note pad.

"Don't forget to include our position in the message. Get going."

"Yes, sir."

Blohm went down the ladder like a rocket. In the control room he stopped at the navigator's table, got U-112 coordinates, then he dashed to the radio shack, where Radioman Gruber was sitting with his electronic equipment and code machine. Blohm handed him the message. "Send this out right away."

"Yes, sir."

Gruber moved his chair to the code machine and tapped out the message. Blohm watched the little rotors spin, intrigued by the complexity of the machine. Gruber completed the encoding, took the message to his radio, and tapped it out in Morse code.

Blohm stood in the doorway, thinking of the convoy bearing down on U-112. Those ships were bringing supplies to England, and the more of them that could be sunk, the closer England would be to defeat.

He heard dots and dashes over the little loudspeaker. Gruber wrote down the message, ran it through the coding machine, and came out with the decoded version, which he handed to Blohm.

PERMISSION GRANTED. MAINTAIN CONSTANT CONTACT WITH CONVOY. HAPPY HUNTING.

With a triumphant smile Blohm raced through the control room and climbed the ladder to the bridge.

"What did they say?" Kruger asked, snatching the message out of Blohm's hand. He read it quickly, then said: "Take it down to periscope depth!"

"Periscope depth!" repeated Feiler.

The klaxon went off inside the U-boat. Sailors on the bridge jumped into the conning tower hatch. Blohm went next, then Grunberger, and finally Kruger who yanked the hatch shut and turned the wheel that dogged it down.

The U-boat sank beneath the waves. Kruger took his position beside the periscope, wiping his hands on his trousers as he watched the bubble move on the depth gauge. Throughout the U-boat crewmen turned valves and spun little wheels. The radio antenna retracted into its casing.

Wichmann-Holtz shifted from diesel to electric drive. Blohm stood next to the target computer, hearing waves crash against the hull of the U-boat. Then suddenly all was still. The U-boat was underwater. Kruger stared at the depth gauge as though it were something miraculous. His body was tense, lips pinched together.

"Level off!"

"Level off!"

Blohm felt the bow of the U-boat incline upward slightly. He hung on to a pipe and watched Kruger, who looked like a cobra coiled to attack.

"The boat is level, sir!" shouted a voice from the control room.

Kruger bent over, grasped the arms of the periscope, snapped them up, put his eye to the lens and looked through. "Ah," he said. "A forest of masts."

"How many?" asked Grunberger.

"Too far away to count exactly. I'd say between forty and fifty."

"Magnificent!"

Kruger peered through the periscope. "They're like pins at a bowling alley. We'll just stand here and knock them down. Prepare tubes one and two for firing a fan shot!" He turned the periscope around in a complete circle. "Nothing's sneaking up on us — marvelous. Rudder left twenty, steer ten. Steady as she goes. Care to have a look, Grunberger?"

"Yes, sir."

Kruger stepped out of the way. Grunberger laid his long arms over the handles of the periscope, gluing his eye to the lens. "A perfect approach."

Kruger laughed. "Perfect approach? They're steaming right into our laps. It comes like this once in a lifetime, gentlemen, so let's make the most of it Your turn, Blohm."

Blohm gripped the handles, peered looked through the eyepiece of the periscope, and could see the ships clearly, even their flags and the huge crates lashed to their decks. They would pass directly in front of U-112 at a range of around two thousand meters. Blohm had received training in torpedo attacks, and wished he could direct this one.

"That's enough, Blohm," Kruger said.

Blohm backed away from the periscope. Kruger took his position behind it again. "Here they come, and they look beautiful. Which one shall I select? Let me see. Ah — is that a tanker I see before me? Why, it is a tanker indeed. A big fat tanker right on the edge of the convoy. They usually don't do that, but I'm not going to complain. Steady now. Rudder port two, steer fifteen. Take it nice and easy. Just a little closer, my darling, and I'll have you where I want you. Must be ten thousand tons at least — we're going to have some fireworks, gentlemen." Kruger stiffened behind the periscope. His voice took on a new urgency. "All right now, attention computer! Target speed fourteen, angle left thirty-five, depth seven!"

Grunberger hit the computer buttons, the correct gyro angle worked out automatically, information transmitted simultaneously to the torpedoes inside their tubes.

Kruger had one leg stretched behind him as though he intended to push the periscope. "Correct distance eleven hundred, angle left thirty-two, tubes one and two ready — *fire*!"

He remained fastened to the periscope as the U-boat jerked twice, indicating that the torpedoes were off. Blohm's ears popped at the rise in air pressure; the compressed air that launched torpedoes was released directly into the boat instead of the ocean, where it would make a telltale bubble.

"Tracking nicely," Kruger said, "yes, very nicely. I think they'll both hit — yes — no — I don't know — it's getting difficult to see."

A loud booming sound was heard in the U-boat. Aa split second later there was another.

"They both hit!" yelled Kruger, still peering through the periscope. "Burning oil flying into the air — what a mess! Here — take a look, Grunberger!"

Grunberger dove at the periscope and saw flaming wreckage on the high seas. His head jerked slightly as he tried to get a better view.

"That's enough. You're next, Blohm."

Grunberger stepped away, and Blohm looked into the eyepiece. The tanker was split in half, its bow and stern in the air. The sea around it was covered with burning oil. Little black figures leaped into the flames.

Kruger slapped Blohm gently on the back. "You've got a good pair of eyes, Blohm. If it weren't for you, we might have missed the damn thing."

Blohm swallowed hard as he realized that all those people were burning to death because of him. In a corner of the screen, he saw a ship coming. "Patrol boat!" he said, backing away from the periscope.

"Let me see!" said Kruger, pushing his face against it again. "Ah, a destroyer — looks like a new one to me. I think I'll give him a couple right down his throat."

"Don't you think you should save your torpedoes for the convoy, sir?" Grunberger asked.

"It'll be easier to get the convoy with the escort out of the way, and I like to sink the ones who are trying to sink me.

Prepare tubes three and four. Attention computer: target speed eighteen, angle left five, depth six, hold on now, steady as she goes — come on, you son of a prostitute — *fire*!"

A slight shock passed through the U-boat, and Blohm's ears popped again. Kruger was rigid at the periscope, his white cap on the back of his head.

"He'll see the torpedo and turn," Kruger said in a whisper, "thus falling right into my trap — *What's that? Take her down to the cellar!*"

Kruger folded away the arms of the periscope and it whined down to its well. The bow of the U-boat dipped downward; hydroplanes moved to their most extreme angle. Kruger held on to the computer. "He fired something at us ... very strange."

An explosion shook the U-boat. Lights went out. Blohm felt his arm nearly yanked out of its shoulder socket.

"Emergency lights!" yelled Kruger.

Another explosion sounded nearby. Blohm heard a hissing sound down below. He gritted his teeth and prayed that the U-boat could dive away from the depth charges.

The lights came on, revealing Kruger still hanging on to the computer apparatus and Grunberger grasping a pipe. Kruger's hat had fallen off, his legs were splayed apart. "Hard left rudder!" he shouted. "Both motors ahead full! Take her down to two-fifty!"

Another depth charge exploded, this one not so close. The U-boat only shook slightly.

"Hard right rudder!"

The U-boat snaked its way to the depths of the ocean. From above they still could hear the tanker breaking up. Kruger wiped his forehead with the back of his sleeve. "He must have seen our periscope," he said. "Very strange. He fired the depth charges at us — never saw that before. He must have shot them out of a cannon or something. Well, it won't do him any good. This is a big ocean and we're awfully small."

There was the sound of a ping on the hull.

"Asdic," said Kruger. "Well, that won't help him, either."

The sound of the destroyer's propellers passed overhead. Kruger looked up and smiled.

"He has no idea of where we are. Hard left rudder!"

"Hard left rudder!"

Kruger looked at the depth gauge; U-112 was down to two hundred meters, its bow still dipped as it headed deeper. The sound of more propellers came from the surface.

"Another one," Kruger said. "A regular party. The convoy must be wide open up there. If some of our boys happen to show up, they'll have a field day."

The Asdic continued to hit the hull of the U-boat. Aa chill went up Blohm's spine. Uncanny how the ships up there could reach them with electronic impulses.

"Hard right rudder!" yelled Kruger.

"Hard right rudder!"

Kruger looked at the depth gauge, where the needle was nearing 250 meters.

"Level her off!

"Level off!"

"One motor ahead one-third!"

"One motor ahead one-third!"

Kruger looked around, smiling. "I don't think we have much to worry about now, gentlemen."

The Asdic pinged against the hull, then three depth charges exploded simultaneously overhead, but they were far away and only shook the U-boat slightly.

"They're just wasting their time," Kruger said. "Bunch of damn fools."

More charges exploded.

Kruger wrinkled his nose in disgust. "They haven't the slightest idea of where we are. Their Asdic is a joke. I'll have to tell headquarters about their little cannon that shoots depth charges. That's certainly a new wrinkle. Rudder left thirty!"

"Rudder left thirty!"

Grunberger shifted position and held on to a pipe with his other hand. "We may lose the convoy now."

"Probably, but headquarters wouldn't have given me permission to attack unless they had another wolf in the neighborhood. That convoy is in for some fun, let me tell you."

A depth charge exploded above and behind them. The Asdic pings sounded weak.

"A ten-thousand-ton tanker isn't bad," Kruger mused, "but of course we wasted two torpedoes. Still, our performance couldn't be faulted. We did everything by the book."

Grunberger grinned. "I think you like destroyers too much."

"I just like a good fight," Kruger replied. "Destroyers are armed but freighters aren't."

A depth charge exploded far away, echoing across the vast reaches of the ocean. Blohm felt himself relaxing; the ordeal was over.

"The fools don't know we can submerge to this depth," he said. "They set their depth charges too shallow."

CHAPTER 6

Mulford climbed the steps of his Mayfair home, puffing his briar and carrying a bouquet of flowers. Mildly inebriated, he rang the bell and whistled a tune.

Agnes opened the door. "Commander Mulford!" she exclaimed.

"'Tis I."

She pulled a strand of gray hair away from her eye. "Why do you always ring, sir? This is your home!"

"I don't like to take all of you by surprise." Mulford entered the vestibule. "Where's my lady?"

"In bed, sir."

"At one o'clock in the afternoon?"

"Um … she's sick, sir."

"What time did she get in last night?"

"I don't remember, sir."

Agnes looked guilty. Mulford knew she was lying. Vanessa must have come home very late if she was still in bed. "I think I'll go up to see her. I want to say goodbye. I'm going to America. I'll be gone for quite a while."

"Oh, sir!"

"Can't be helped." Mulford climbed the stairs. "It's for the good of England."

He tiptoed down the corridor and stopped at Vanessa's door. Pressing his ear against it, he could hear nothing inside. Turning the knob slowly, he pushed the door open. Vanessa was sprawled on her back in bed, one knee in the air and her head to the side. She'd thrown the covers off; she was wearing a diaphanous white gown. Her bed was large and covered with a white canopy. The afternoon sunlight managed to work its way through the heavy drapes and give the room a faint glow.

Mulford sat on the edge of the bed and looked at her. Her hair was mussed, face devoid of makeup. He thought she looked beautiful and bent over to kiss her cheek.

She made a faint moan. "Don't, Jeremy," she whispered, turning away from him.

Mulford sighed, recalling how much they'd loved each other when they'd married seven years ago. He'd been thirty and she was twenty-five. They'd vowed to love each other forever, and indeed did love each other for several years, but then things began to deteriorate. He couldn't remember what had happened. It was strange how you forgot important things as you grew older.

"Darling," he said softly, placing the palm of his hand against her warm cheek.

She opened her eyes and saw him. She gazed at him expressionless for a few moments, then her eyes widened. "What are you doing here?"

"This is my home. Why shouldn't I be here?"

She pulled the covers over her body and frowned. "You could have knocked first!"

He pulled the covers off her. "Don't cover yourself up."

"Don't get any ideas," she said, crossing her legs and arms.

"I wouldn't dream of it." He handed her the flowers. "For you."

Her face melted into joy and appreciation. "How sweet of you." She accepted them and brought a blossom to her lovely nose. "I love roses. The queen of flowers, they are."

"What is the king of flowers?"

"There is no king of flowers. All flowers are ladies. What are you doing here?"

"I've come to say goodbye. I'm leaving for America."

She sat bolt upright in bed. "You are?"

"Yes, my love."

"America?"

"Yes."

She propped up her pillows on the headboard, then lay back and looked at him crossly. "I suppose you're taking your little American gum-chewer with you."

"Who's Jeremy?"

Her jaw fell open, and he had his answer.

"You talk in your sleep," he told her. "It's very dangerous."

"I find it difficult to respect a man who listens to a woman who talks in her sleep."

"I merely came in here to awaken you with a kiss and present you with these flowers when you started talking about Jeremy."

She groaned. "What did I say?"

"Wild horses couldn't drag the words out of me."

"That bad."

"Yes," he lied.

"I think I'm going to cry."

He took out a clean folded handkerchief and handed it to her. She dabbed her eyes, but Mulford couldn't see any evidence of tears.

"We are not nice people, William," she said.

"No, I don't suppose we are."

"I do love you, you know."

"I love you too, Vanessa. More than anything in the world."

Her eyes went soft on him. "Do you really, William?"

"Yes, I do."

"Come here." She held out her arms.

He lay on top of her and touched his cheek to hers. Through all the clothes he could feel her supple body, and it excited him as much as when he'd first touched it so many years ago.

"Oh, William," she breathed into his ear, "if only we could go away together to a quiet little cottage in the country and live the rest of our lives there, far from the war and the false values of society."

"I thought you didn't like the country, Vanessa. You can't stand bugs, and whenever you're in the country you complain that there's nothing to do."

"That's true," she agreed. "But you know what I mean."

"I know what you mean."

"I wish we could have more of a marriage."

"So do I. I don't suppose you'd want to make love right now?"

"Why wouldn't I?"

"Well, I imagine that only a few hours ago you were like this with Jeremy. By the way, who's Jeremy?"

She touched her hand to the back of his neck. "Never mind who Jeremy is. He doesn't matter now. No one does when you're with me. Too bad that you can't be with me more."

"We've had this discussion before," he said, lifting her nightie.

"I suppose we have," she murmured, kissing his ear.

It was night on the Atlantic Ocean under a full moon. U-112 was running on the surface, looking for convoys. In the officers' mess Kapitänleutnant Kruger sat at the table alone, drinking a cup of coffee. His eyes were bloodshot because he'd just come down from the bridge after peering through his binoculars for two hours.

Wichmann-Holtz entered the tiny room, a mug of coffee in hand. His long face was sallow, a thick beard already in evidence. He sat down opposite Kruger at the table. "I thought I'd find you here."

"What's on your mind?" Kruger asked groggily.

Wichmann-Holtz ran the palm of his hand over his forehead and took a deep breath. He looked at Kruger and said: "My nerves are shot."

Kruger managed to lift one eyebrow. "You think mine aren't?"

"Everything is relative," Wichmann-Holtz replied. "I think I'm in a pretty bad way, sir. I can't stand depth-charging anymore. I know that nobody likes it, but again, it's relative. I'm afraid I'm going to lose control of myself someday and do something bizarre."

"You need a rest," Kruger said.

"I need to get out of U-boats. My personality isn't suitable for them. I've always been mildly claustrophobic. Depth-charging has a very bad effect on me. I'm afraid I'm going to lose my mind, sir."

Kruger sipped his coffee and looked at Wichmann-Holtz through hooded eyes. He'd known that Wichmann-Holtz was high-strung but hadn't realized it was a problem. "Listen Frederick — you've got to understand that it's very difficult for them to hit us. Depth charges have to land within twenty feet to do serious damage and that's not very much when you consider the ocean's immensity."

"U-boats are sunk all the time," Wichmann-Holtz replied.

"Not that many."

"It could happen to us."

"Anything could happen to anyone at any time. If you were in Berlin right now, you might get hit by a truck."

"A British bomb would be more likely."

Kruger sipped his coffee again. "Sounds as though you've got a morale problem, Frederick."

Wichmann-Holtz stared into his cup. "I'm afraid I do," he said softly. "The outlook for Germany looks very bleak to me."

"It does? How can you say that when Germany is stronger and more victorious than ever in history?"

Wichmann-Holtz's eyes glowed like hot coals. "Practically the entire world is allied against us. Strong though we are, we cannot defeat the entire world."

Kruger waved his hand contemptuously. "Our enemies don't have much fight in them. After we bloody their noses a little, they'll back off. The will to win is extremely significant, Frederick. We have it and they don't."

"I wouldn't be so sure about that, but you and I really can have very little effect on the outcome of the war, so there's no point in worrying about it." He ran his fingers through his long black hair. "My problem is that I think I'm losing my mind. I'm afraid that I'm going to do something that will let the rest of the crew down."

Kruger looked at Wichmann-Holtz for a few moments, then turned down the corner of his mouth. "You'd better not."

"I may lose control of myself."

"See the pharmacist's mate and get a sedative. If we're ever depth-charged again, swallow a couple of them right away."

"Who'll take charge of the engine room?"

"I'll send Blohm down there. Although he's young, I'm sure he's arrogant enough to keep your mechanics in line."

Wichmann-Holtz nodded. "Yes, he's certainly arrogant enough. But what about the next patrol?"

"You'll have to get out of U-boats, Frederick. I don't know how you're going to accomplish that, but you'll have to do it somehow."

"Will you help me?"

"I'll do what I can, but my influence is limited, you know. The navy needs trained U-boat personnel these days."

There was a knock on the door.

"Come in!" said Kruger.

It was Radioman Gruber with a message in his hand. "This has just come in from headquarters, sir."

Kruger took the piece of paper and held it up to the light.

CONVOY IN AK 27 COURSE 085 EIGHT KNOTS. ALL U-BOATS IN VICINITY PROCEED TO TARGET IMMEDIATELY.

"A herd of elephants," Kruger said with a grin, standing up. He looked at Wichmann-Holtz. "You'd better see the pharmacist's mate about those pills, because there'll probably be some fun pretty soon."

"Yes, sir."

Kruger left the officers' wardroom and moved aft to the control room to plot a course to intercept the convoy. He expected happy hunting very soon.

CHAPTER 7

Julie Goulard walked down the rue St Vincent in Lorient, a fresh loaf of bread under her arm. It was a sunny spring afternoon, and she wore a light sweater over a blue polka-dot dress. She was on her way to see her mother and give her some money.

She visited her mother every Thursday to give her money. Her father, a former schoolteacher, had been killed in battle against the Germans in 1940.

She entered the doorway of an apartment building and climbed the stairs. She dreaded these Thursdays with her mother, because her mother knew she'd become a prostitute at the Crescent Palace. Yet her mother accepted the money, because without it she'd starve.

Julie had wanted to become an artist, and if she failed at that she thought she might enter a nunnery, for she had been very religious when young. Now she tried not to think too much about her life, drank more than was good for her, and hoped someday soon Germans would leave France.

She climbed to the fourth floor of the building, walked down the corridor, and knocked three times on her mother's door. Then she inserted her key into the lock and opened the door. Her mother sat by the window, reading a book.

"Hello, Mother," Julie said cheerily. "How are you?"

Her mother grunted. She was wearing a soiled dress, hair unkempt, slip showing, feet in old slippers. The apartment had a bitter, stale odor.

"I brought you a fresh baguette," Julie said, placing the loaf on the table. "Care for a slice?"

"No."

"I also managed to get you a little real coffee. Shall I make you a cup?"

"I'll make one myself later."

Julie sat on a chair opposite her mother. "How've you been?"

"The same."

"Has Doctor Bercauld been here?"

"On Monday."

"What did he say?"

"He gave me more pills, but they do no good."

"Have you seen any of your friends?"

"No."

"You should get out more, Mother. You could use some fresh air. Why don't you visit some of your friends?"

"I'm ashamed to see my friends," her mother said coldly.

Julie opened her purse and took out a cigarette, lighting it with a match. Just when she thought she had toughened herself so that nothing could hurt her again, something happened to hurt her.

"You should be ashamed, too," her mother said.

"Mother," Julie replied, "half the young women in this town do what I do, and those who don't do it professionally do it as amateurs. We're all trying to get by as best we can."

Her mother snorted. "Sometimes I think it's better not to get by. Sometimes I think it's better to just lie down and die honorably."

"I don't want to die, Mother. I'm still young, and I'm certain the Germans will be out of France someday."

"They'll never be out of France. We were weak and corrupt, and we deserved what happened to us."

"I don't think we deserved what happened to us. One day the Boche will pay for everything they've done."

"Don't make me laugh," her mother said bitterly. "You take them into your bed, and then when you come here, you pretend you don't like them."

Julie puffed her cigarette and looked at her mother, wondering why she went to so much trouble to take care of her. She certainly didn't love her mother anymore, but she couldn't simply abandon her. Julie wasn't that hard yet.

"Don't look at me that way," her mother said.

"What way?"

"You know very well what way. You hate me — don't think I don't know that. You probably wish I'd die."

"I don't wish you'd die, but I do wish you'd stop being so disagreeable." Julie stood up. "I think I'd better be going." She walked to the kitchen table, removed the envelope filled with money from her purse and set it down next to the baguette. "Goodbye, Mother. I'll see you next week."

Her mother didn't answer. Julie opened the door and stepped into the hall, puffing her cigarette as she walked down the corridor to the stairs, thinking it was like this every Thursday. She wished she could find somebody to deliver the money to her mother, but didn't know anyone she could trust.

She descended the stairs, feeling despair and wondering if life would ever return to normal in France. She wondered what she'd do if it did. She wouldn't be able to work at the Crescent Palace anymore, because there wouldn't be Germans in France. Well, she'd cross that bridge when she came to it.

She heard people climbing the stairs below. Between the second and third floors she saw who they were: three

Frenchmen ascending in single file. She moved closer to the banister to let them pass as they came abreast of her.

Suddenly the man in the middle pulled out a knife and held it against her belly.

"Don't make a sound!" he hissed.

Julie nearly fainted from shock and fright. Her first thought was that they were in the *Maquis*. Sometimes they killed Frenchwomen who slept with Germans.

"Listen," she said, her tight throat distorting the word, "I can't help being what I am — I'm just trying to stay…"

"Shut up," the man said. He wore a suit with a white shirt open at the collar and a beret low over his eyes. "Come with us, and if you call for help, we'll kill you."

Julie looked at the other two men. One was the lookout higher on the stairs, and the other the lookout below. "Where do you want me to go?"

"There's a car waiting outside. You will get into it with us. Move."

"You're not going to hurt me…"

"If we wanted to hurt you, we would have done it already and been gone by now. You'll be all right as long as you do as you're told. Let's go."

Julie clutched her purse and walked down the stairs with three men following. On the sidewalk two German sailors walked by with two girls. The man in the beret veered toward an old Renault parked by the curb and opened the rear door.

"Get in."

Julie climbed into the little car. One of the men walked around to the other side and got in beside her. The man in the beret sat in the front seat beside the driver. Julie knew better than ask where she was going; they wouldn't tell her. She only hoped they wouldn't kill her as they said, but she'd been through so much already in her short life — she was ready for anything.

The driver started up the car and shifted into gear, and they all drove away.

It was afternoon in the North Atlantic. Grunberger and Blohm were on the bridge of U-112 with a few members of the crew, scanning the horizon through binoculars. Kapitänleutnant Kruger was below, asleep in his cabin.

"Plane diving out of the sun!" screamed one of the sailors.

Blohm yanked his binoculars around and saw it, a big Sunderland swooping down at them.

"Battle stations!" screamed Grunberger.

The seamen ran to the machine guns on the after section of the bridge deck, cranking wheels and slamming belts of ammunition into the chambers.

"Open fire!" yelled Blohm, squinting at the Sunderland. "Hurry up!"

First one machine gun began to stutter, then the other. The tracer bullets flew into the air like angry hornets, but still the Sunderland kept coming. Guns flashed from its turrets and bullets ricocheted off the periscope shears and bridge deck. The U-boat gunners stopped firing and ducked their heads.

"Keep firing!" shouted Blohm.

He grabbed one of the gunners by the shoulders, pulled him away from his machine gun and crouched behind it himself. Even before he took aim he pulled the trigger, hoping that bullets would distract the pilot. One of the men near him screamed and went flying off the bridge as the Sunderland's bullets ripped into him. Blohm pasted his gun sights on the plane and kept the trigger pulled back. The machine gun bucked in its mount as Blohm gritted his teeth and sent a stream of bullets zipping toward the Sunderland.

Kruger's head emerged from the conning-tower hatch. "What's going on here?"

Blohm heard bullets whizzing all around him and ricocheting off the bridge. Another seaman howled in pain and fell at the base of his machine gun. Blohm squinted in the sunlight and fired his machine gun at the Sunderland, which was now only a few hundred yards away.

"You hit him!" Grunberger shouted.

Blohm saw a thin stream of smoke trailing from the front of the plane. He kept his sights plastered on that point and continued to fire. The smoke became thicker and the plane swerved from side to side, then its nose dipped down. Blohm could see a figure in the cockpit, struggling with the controls, to no avail.

The Sunderland nose-dived toward the sea. Blohm kept firing. The front of the plane shattered, and bits of material flew in all directions. The plane crashed into the sea a hundred yards off the starboard bow of U-112, and one of the crew leaped from the cockpit into the water. The plane began to sink rapidly.

"Grunberger," said Kruger, "bring us over there."

"Yes, sir."

Blohm stopped firing and looked at the British aviator in the water, his head bloody, trying to wave to the U-boat for help.

"Rudder left twenty!" shouted Grunberger.

"Rudder left twenty!" repeated the helmsman.

Kruger climbed down to the deck as Grunberger maneuvered toward the aviator and his sinking plane. Blohm stood erect behind his machine gun. Kruger held on to the starboard rail and made his way to the bow of U-112.

Grunberger maneuvered the U-boat closer to the aviator. Only the tail of the plane still showed, and soon it would sink beneath the waves. The U-boat slowed. Kruger kneeled on the deck, drawing his navy Luger.

The aviator was bleeding profusely from a wound in his head. He coughed blood and seawater and tried to lift his hand to wave at Kruger, who could see that the man was badly wounded. If it weren't for his life preserver, he would have sunk along with his plane.

"Can you hear me, Englishman?" Kruger shouted in German-accented English.

The aviator nodded weakly.

"I don't have a doctor and there's nothing I can do for you. I can either leave you like this or give you a bullet. Which would you prefer?"

The aviator's mouth wrenched in pain. Kruger figured he was around twenty-five, and noticed the wedding band on his finger.

"Kill me," the aviator uttered.

Kruger raised his pistol, took aim, fired. The aviator's head blew apart, brains splattering into the water. Kruger stood, placed the Luger in its holster, and returned to the bridge, where everyone was staring at the man in the water.

"Let's get out of here," Kruger said. "Both engines full ahead!"

"Both engines full ahead."

Kriebl, the pharmacist's mate, was examining the wounded U-boat men. Kruger walked back to Blohm and held out his hand. "Good work. I'm very impressed. You shot down a Sunderland."

Blohm shook Kruger's proffered hand. "Thank you, sir."

"It just goes to show you — the man who keeps his nerve in the final moments always will win. You have nerves of steel, Blohm. You'll go far in this navy. I'm going to put you in for the Iron Cross."

"That would be very kind of you, sir," Blohm's chest swelled with pride.

Kruger turned to Grunberger. "If you had dived, they might have blown us right out of the water. Instead we fought back, so now they're the ones feeding the fishes. That's the way I want you to handle it from now on."

"Yes, sir."

"Carry on."

With a wink to Blohm, Kruger descended the steps to the conning tower.

The driver parked the old Renault next to the curb on the rue Fortuny. The man with the beret got out and opened the door for Julie. He helped her out of the car, held her arm and led her into an old wooden warehouse. The rue Fortuny was near the docks, and she could smell the salt of the bay.

They entered the building, passing crates stacked on the floor. At the rear was an office with a glass window. Julie could see men inside. She was no longer afraid; if they intended to kill her, they would have done so long ago.

The man with the beret opened the door to the office. Julie was surprised to see Jacques Berthier sitting behind the desk. Berthier was a schoolteacher in Lorient and had been a friend of her father's.

"M'sieur Berthier!" she exclaimed.

"Hello, Julie," he said warmly. "Sit down." He pointed to a chair in front of his desk.

Julie sat in the chair, glancing around at the men in the office, all of whom looked as though they were living on the wrong side of the law.

"We're sorry to have brought you here this way," Berthier apologized, "but we must be careful — I'm sure you understand."

Julie nodded her head. "Yes, of course."

Berthier leaned forward and folded his hands on the desk. He was bald and had a gray mustache. His suit looked new, and he wore a shirt and tie. "How have you been, dear?"

"I think you know how I've been."

He nodded sadly. "Yes, I know. Someday the Boche will pay dearly for what they've done to our women."

"May I smoke?"

"By all means."

She took a cigarette from her purse and placed it in her mouth. While searching for her book of matches, there was a scratching sound near her ear and a light appeared in front of her. She looked up and saw a young, tanned man in a pullover sweater.

"Julie," Berthier said, "we'd like you to help us. Do you think you would like to?"

She shrugged. "Depends on what you want me to do."

"We need any information on U-boats that we can get. Since you spend so much time with U-boat officers, and since they're usually drunk and at ease, I thought perhaps you could obtain information for us."

"What kind of information?"

"Anything — dates U-boats are due to sail, personnel on board, remarks about U-boat equipment, specifications, tactics. Information that might seem completely innocuous to you, but might be extremely valuable to us. Our British allies need to know everything they can about U-boats so they can fight them more effectively. U-boats are threatening to cut off England's supplies, and if England is defeated, we'll never be able to throw the Boche out of France by ourselves. That's why we must aid England as much as we can. Will you help us?"

"I'll try," Julie said, "but I don't know what I could do. The officers don't talk about U-boats very much when they're with me."

"You can ask questions."

"No," replied the young man who'd given Julie the light. "That might make the Germans suspicious. If she asks questions, she'll have to be very subtle. We don't want to expose her to danger."

Julie looked at the young man, who had thick brown hair parted on the side, and high cheekbones.

"No," said Berthier, "of course we don't want to expose her to undue danger, but danger is always inherent in this kind of work." He looked at Julie gravely. "We need information very badly."

"I'll do whatever I can. I don't mind a little danger. Life isn't very pleasant living under the Boche. It's merely the exchanging of one unpleasant way of life for another that conceivably could help end the unpleasantness once and for all."

Berthier smiled. "Good, I'm glad you see it that way. I'm sure you'll be most helpful to us. Your contact will be Armand here." Berthier indicated the young man. "You should meet with him regularly to relay any information you have."

"Thursdays are my only days off," she said. "I can meet him after I see my mother."

"You and Armand can work that part out between you," Berthier said. "Thank you for your willingness to cooperate with us. I'm sure your father would be proud."

Julie felt a twinge in her heart, because she knew how her father would feel if he knew she was a prostitute. She had always been his little baby. "There is a cafe called Lalys on the rue Crevel," she said. "I can meet Armand there on Thursday afternoons at two."

Berthier looked at Armand. "Is that convenient for you?"

"Yes."

"Good," said Berthier. "It's settled, then."

CHAPTER 8

"Convoy dead ahead!" said Kruger, binoculars against his eyes.

Ensign Blohm saw shadows on the horizon. It was one o'clock in the morning, and the moonlight was diminished by a light film of clouds.

"Steer left fifty degrees," Kruger said. "Both engines full ahead!"

Feiler repeated the orders. U-112 swung to intercept the convoy. Six other U-boats were also in the vicinity.

"Blohm," said Kruger, "send a contact report to headquarters."

"Yes, sir."

Blohm went down the ladder, leaving Kruger and Grunberger on the bridge. The convoy was moving along slowly at about eight knots. U-112 would intercept it soon.

Kruger swept his binoculars back and forth across the convoy. "Battle stations! Prepare tubes one through four for firing!"

Throughout the U-boat officers and men scrambled to their battle stations. In the bow torpedo compartment, seamen loaded the torpedoes into the tubes. U-112 sliced across the ocean toward the convoy, wind whistling around its periscopes and antennae. Blohm returned to the bridge.

"I've sent the message, sir."

A huge booming sound erupted before them, and a large orange ball of flame rose into the air.

"First blood," said Kruger, staring at the burning ship at the rear of the convoy, one of the stragglers.

Snowflake flares went up, illuminating the ocean around the convoy.

"Destroyer dead ahead!" said Grunberger.

"I think he's seen us," Kruger replied. "Hard right rudder!"

U-112 turned away from the convoy and headed toward a fog bank. The destroyer was far away and would probably not catch up.

U-112 entered the fog bank and disappeared. Blohm saw trails of mist streaking past Kruger, who issued orders that turned the U-boat to the east so that it ran parallel to the convoy. The U-boat was still moving at top speed. Kruger hoped to get in front of it and in position for a submerged attack in case he was forced down. They heard the sound of another explosion, then another.

"Someone's getting clear shots," Grunberger said.

Kruger looked at his stainless-steel Swiss watch. "Yes, and when escorts search for those U-boats, we'll have a clear field for ours. The night is young and we have plenty of time."

U-112 came out of the fog bank. The destroyer was nowhere to be seen. The convoy was about two thousand yards away.

"Take your position at the TBT," Kruger told Grunberger.

"Yes, sir."

"Blohm, keep your eye out for trouble."

"Yes, sir."

U-112 sped toward the convoy, which was still brightly lit from snowflake flares and flames of burning ships. The U-boat would become visible soon, but Kruger felt confident that he could fire torpedoes in the confusion of the overall wolf pack attack.

Another ship exploded inside the convoy. The sky filled with burning oil; the stricken ship was an oil tanker. The convoy altered course, heading directly toward U-112.

"They're running into our laps," Kruger said with satisfaction. "Get ready, Grunberger."

"Yes, sir."

"Steer right thirty degrees!"

"Right thirty degrees."

U-112 moved to the side so it could get a broadside view of the convoy. Blohm searched alongside the convoy for escort ships, but couldn't see any. He thought that if the convoy had been ringed by escort ships, no U-boat would be able to make a night surface attack like this. He considered the British stupid fools for not providing more protection for their vital convoys.

Kruger decided he was in a prime position for his attack. He scanned the convoy with his binoculars and picked out the fattest freighters for targets.

"Grunberger," he said, "I want the third freighter from the front, and the fifth from the front. Give them each two torpedoes, understand?"

"Yes, sir."

Grunberger zeroed in on the first target. "Tubes one to four ready for surface attack! Open tube doors! Target angle left thirty-five! Speed eight! Stand by!"

Kruger held his binoculars to his eyes. "Commence firing!"

Grunberger pressed the lever on the TBT. "Tube one — fire! Tube two — fire!"

The bow of the U-boat raised in the air as two torpedoes began their journeys. Grunberger moved his TBT to the next target and shouted its angle, speed, and range to the bow torpedo room.

Blohm scanned the convoy from front to back with his binoculars, seeing burning ships, sailors in lifeboats, and chaos. He spotted a destroyer coming around the rear of the convoy, headed in U-112's direction.

"Destroyer dead to starboard!" he reported.

"Never mind it," Kruger told Grunberger. "Commence firing."

Grunberger pressed the lever. "Tube three — fire! Tube four — fire!"

Kruger looked at the oncoming destroyer. "Reload torpedoes!"

Grunberger looked up from the TBT. "Sir, you're not going to attack that destroyer, are you?"

"Remain at your station, Herr Oberleutnant, and keep your mouth shut!"

"Yes, sir."

The first torpedo rammed into the side of the freighter, which exploded in a fierce red flash. The second torpedo hit it a few seconds later and blew the freighter in two. Its center sank into the water, bow and stern forming a huge V in the air. Sirens and howlers could be heard across the ocean, along with the hoarse shouts of men.

A small yellow flash appeared in front of the destroyer, followed by a shell hitting the water a hundred feet in front of U-112, sending a spume of water toward the bridge.

"Duck!" screamed Kruger.

They dropped behind the steel walls of the bridge as water cascaded over them and down the conning-tower hatch.

"Hard left rudder," Kruger said, standing up. "Both engines full ahead!"

The U-boat turned away and picked up speed as a torpedo struck the stern of the second big freighter. Drenched, Kruger took out a handkerchief and wiped off the lenses of his binoculars. After a few seconds he realized that the fourth torpedo had missed the second freighter. He glanced behind him and saw the destroyer in hot pursuit. Guns flashed on the bow of the destroyer. Moments later a shell whistled over Kruger's head, then a second one landed some fifty yards to starboard.

"Hard right rudder!" Kruger yelled.

"Hard right rudder!"

U-112 shifted course abruptly as another freighter exploded inside the convoy. Kruger looked astern at the destroyer, wondering if he should try to sink it. He decided that if it came too close he would try, but would otherwise save the torpedoes for the convoy.

There were more explosions inside the convoy. Tongues of flame licked at the sky, and the convoy formation appeared to be breaking apart. Ships were clearly outlined against the fire. Kruger wished he didn't have the destroyer to worry about. They were moving at approximately the same speed, but since U-112 was forced to zigzag, the destroyer would eventually catch up.

Kruger decided that the time had come to try to sink the destroyer before it came too close. As he was about to shout the orders that would turn the U-boat around, the destroyer suddenly veered away.

"He's given up the chase, sir!" Blohm said.

There was a huge roar as another tanker was torpedoed. Kruger raised his binoculars and saw men being hurled into the air like ants. His heart swelled with joy at the sight of the huge spectacle.

"Magnificent!" he said.

Blohm looked at the convoy in awe. Ships were burning and sinking from front to back. The English could do nothing to drive the wolf pack away. England would soon be unable to feed her population, forced to surrender to the forces of the Reich.

"Hard left rudder!" Kruger shouted. "Steer three-four-oh!"

U-112 turned around in the water and headed back toward the convoy. Kruger stood on the bridge and stared at the convoy, wind whistling through his beard.

"Grunberger, take your position at the TBT."

"Yes, sir."

"Sir!" said Blohm. "The destroyer's turning around again!"

Kruger moved his binoculars toward the destroyer and saw that it was indeed turning around. "Damn!" he said, realizing that he should have waited until the destroyer was gone before moving toward the convoy again, but had been too eager for more kills.

He banged the bottom of his fist against the bridge rail. "Hard right rudder! Steer one-six-oh!" Then a new thought occurred to him. "No — cancel that order! Prepare tubes one and two for firing! Grunberger, take aim at that destroyer and fire the usual two shots — one to make him turn broadside to us, and the other right into his guts!"

"Yes, sir!"

Grunberger focused on the destroyer and turned his dials. The bow of the destroyer flashed as it fired another shell. A water spout went up seventy yards off the U-boat's port bow.

"Hold fast!" Kruger shouted, looking at the destroyer through his binoculars. "Hurry up, Grunberger!"

Grunberger squinted through the TBT binoculars. "Tubes one and two ready for surface attack! Open tube doors! Target angle right five, speed eighteen! Stand by!"

"Commence firing!" shouted Kruger.

"Tube one — fire!"

The torpedo blew out of its tube. The U-boat jolted slightly in reaction. A fountain of water shot into the air next to the U-boat, dumping water on to the bridge.

"She's swerving, sir!" yelled Blohm.

Grunberger tensed behind the TBT. "Target angle right six-five, speed ten! Stand by — ready — fire!"

Kruger, Grunberger, and Blohm trained their binoculars on the destroyer as the second torpedo shot out of the U-boat and sped toward its target. Blohm clicked his teeth as he counted the seconds in his mind.

Suddenly there was a crash of water next to the U-boat, and a wall of the sea fell against the bridge, knocking the U-boat over at a forty-five-degree angle. Blohm hung on to the bridge rail as the water smashed him to his knees.

"Hard left rudder!" Kruger screamed. "Both engines full ahead!"

The U-boat turned in the water, and Blohm saw the source of the shell. There was a second destroyer bearing down hard on U-112. It fired another shell that landed directly on the spot where the U-boat had been seconds before.

Meanwhile, the second torpedo struck home amidships on the first destroyer. A split second after the first explosion, the destroyer's magazine detonated. The ship blew apart and disappeared beneath the waves in seconds.

"Perfect shot!" Kruger said, pounding Grunberger on the back.

Grunberger smiled limply. He was watching the second destroyer; it seemed to be gaining. There was a red flash on its bridge. Seconds later the shell landed near the stern of U-112 and blew it half out of the water. Blohm was pitched forward on to his face, his forehead slamming against the bulkhead. He saw a black night filled with stars and didn't know where he was.

"Hard right rudder!" yelled Kruger.

"Hard right rudder!"

The U-boat turned slowly to port. Blohm's instincts told him something was wrong.

Feiler's voice was tense in the conning tower. "I think the rudder is damaged, sir!"

"Are we losing speed?"

"Yes, sir!"

"Take her down to the cellar!"

The howler went off. Men on the bridge scrambled down the stairs to the conning tower. Kruger closed the hatch, aware that depth-charging would take place at any moment and that Wichmann-Holtz might have what might be his ultimate mental breakdown.

"Sir," said Feiler, "the propeller is behaving erratically. We're not getting the speed that we should be getting."

Feiler's mouth was tense, eyes darting around excitedly. Kruger looked at the depth gauge and saw the U-112 was descending too slowly. He cursed the lucky shot that had landed near the stern of the U-boat.

"Grunberger," he said, "take command here while I go back to the engine room."

"Yes, sir."

Kruger descended the ladder to the control room, hearing the destroyer speed closer. It would be thirsty for vengeance because of the sinking of its sister ship. U-112, with its damaged rear end, would be in for a bad time.

He made his way aft and found Wichmann-Holtz in the electric motor room, lying on his stomach on the deck, pointing a flashlight at the spot where one of the armatures had passed through the rear of the hull.

"What's the problem?" Kruger asked.

Wichmann-Holtz looked up. "A leak."

"Bad?"

"Not that bad, yet."

The first ping of the Asdic rattled against the hull of the U-boat. All the men in the electric motor room grabbed on to something and braced themselves.

"Listen," Kruger said to Wichmann-Holtz, whose face was white as snow, "we're in a bit of trouble because there's something wrong with our propellers. I think you'd better take a couple of your pills and maybe lie down."

Wichmann-Holtz bit his lip. "I couldn't go to bed. Everyone will know that I've lost my nerve."

Kruger shrugged. "If you want to get out of the U-boat service, Frederick, this is the way to do it. I'll say you had a breakdown of some kind and had to be confined to bed. They'll never let you go out on a U-boat again."

"They may throw me out of the navy," Wichmann-Holtz said.

"Extremely unlikely."

The first depth charge exploded atop the U-boat, driving it down. Lights went out, Kruger heard a hiss of water, the U-boat's nose dipped and spun out of control. "Emergency lights!" screamed Kruger.

He waited a few seconds, no lights went on. Kruger rolled against the bulkhead, then on to the overhead. The boat continued to spiral downward. Kruger slid down the other bulkhead on to the floor again, hearing screams and howls of pain all around him. *I've got to get back to the control room,* he told himself.

He tried to climb forward, but the boat continued to spin. His head hit a little wheel and he nearly lost consciousness. He heard a whimpering sound like a dog being whipped and knew it was Wichmann-Holtz. Water hit him in the face. He tried to move aft to the control room again. It appeared that U-112

137

was out of control, going all the way to the bottom where intense pressures would cave in its hull.

He thought that death was imminent, and was surprised at how calm he was.

In the conning tower Grunberger realized that the U-boat was in danger and he had to take action in the absence of the captain. His first thought was that the U-boat must be stabilized. He'd have to bring the bow up somehow.

The U-boat continued to sink as Grunberger crawled toward the intercom system. A depth charge exploded nearby, and the crackling of the hull could be heard. He wished Kruger were there; he always felt safe with Kruger. Finally he reached the intercom microphone.

"All hands aft to the engine compartments!" he screamed. "Repeat — all hands aft to the engine compartments!"

A depth charge exploded underneath the U-boat, and the emergency lights suddenly came on. The conning tower was in a shambles, the U-boat drifting on her starboard side, stern up.

"All hands aft to the engine compartment!" Grunberger shouted.

"Me too?" asked Blohm, hanging on to the depth gauge.

"You stay right where you are."

The crew of the U-boat crawled aft, and as they did so their weight gradually brought the stern of the U-boat down. Feiler descended the ladder to the control room to issue direct orders to the hydroplane operators. They struggled with their wheels, trying to stop the U-boat's spin. Slowly they brought the stricken boat under control.

Kruger crawled through the hatch into the control room and saw Feiler standing behind the hydroplane operators.

"Good work," Kruger said, climbing the ladder to the conning tower. Grunberger and Blohm watched Kruger's head emerge. "How're we doing up here?" he asked.

"Everything's under control, more or less," Grunberger said.

Kruger looked at the depth gauge; the U-boat was now at two hundred meters. In only another fifty meters it would be beyond the range of the depth charges.

"Blohm," Kruger said. "Go back to the engine room and take charge. There's a leak where the starboard propeller shaft goes through the hull — see what you can do about it."

"What happened to Leutnant Wichmann-Holtz?" Blohm asked.

"He's injured. Hurry up — you're needed in the engine room."

"Yes, sir."

Blohm descended the ladder to the control room. At the bottom was Feiler, waiting to go up. Two depth charges exploded above the U-boat, knocking Blohm off the ladder. He fell to the deck, landing on his knees. The lights went out and then came on again.

Feiler helped him off the floor. Blohm felt sharp pain in both his kneecaps. He limped a few feet, then another depth charge exploded beside the U-boat, knocking him down again. He fell against one of the seamen at the ballast-control panel, knocking the man against the gauges.

Feiler climbed the ladder as Blohm made his way aft to the engine rooms. He passed the petty officers' quarters and heard a sob from one of the bunks. Blohm walked to the bunk and pulled back the curtain. He saw Wichmann-Holtz strapped to the bunk, eyes bulging and tears dripping down his cheeks.

Blohm was astonished. He didn't know what to say.

Wichmann-Holtz looked at Blohm and growled like a madman. Blohm touched the palm of his hand to Wichmann-Holtz's hot forehead. "Take it easy," he said, soothingly. "You'll be all right."

"I can't take this anymore," Wichmann-Holtz replied through clenched teeth.

"It won't keep up much more. We're almost beneath their range."

Two depth charges exploded behind the U-boat. The lights went out again, and Wichmann-Holtz screamed in horror. Blohm closed the curtain, then felt his way toward the hatch, his ears echoing with the sound of Wichmann-Holtz's screams. The lights came on again as he passed through the hatch and continued back to the electric motor room, where Hube, the second engineer, was supervising his crew of mechanics. They were jamming slivers of wood into the cracks through which water was leaking.

"Hube, what progress are you making?"

"We'll stop it soon, sir."

"Any other leaks in here?"

"A small one in the engine room, sir."

"Can you fix the propeller?"

"We'll have to surface for that, sir."

A depth charge exploded high above, and Blume realized that U-112 had finally dropped below the 250-meter mark. He took off his hat and wiped the perspiration from his forehead with his sleeve. The worst of the ordeal was over.

CHAPTER 9

Mulford and Vanessa were having dinner at Surrey's, a fashionable restaurant in Mayfair. It would be their last dinner together for a long while, because he had to return to Liverpool next morning and depart for America the morning after that.

"I'll miss you so much," Vanessa said, slicing into her filet of broiled haddock. She wore a white satin dinner dress and pearl necklace. "I really don't know what I'll do with you so far away."

"I'll miss you, too," he said, sipping his glass of Scotch. "I hope I don't have to stay over there too long." He raised his hand; the tuxedoed waiter came scurrying over.

"Yes, sir."

Vanessa frowned as she raised her forkful of fish. "Are you going to drink your dinner, or do you think you might want to taste a bit of your roast beef?"

"I'm not very hungry," Mulford said.

She placed her food in her mouth and chewed daintily. Mulford knew he'd have to wait until she swallowed, because she'd never say a word with her mouth full. She wore pearl earrings, and her golden hair was combed back into a bun. Mulford thought her the most beautiful woman in England, and wished she weren't so unfaithful, although he was unwilling to abandon his own philandering ways.

She swallowed her food, then said reproachfully, "You're not hungry because you drink too much. Alcohol causes one to lose one's appetite."

"I can't help it. I feel sad to be leaving you."

She scooped up a forkful of peas. "Well, you'll have your strange little American girl with you, won't you?"

"Yes," he admitted.

"I'm sure she'll soothe you."

"No one soothes me like you, Vanessa dear."

"Liar."

She placed the forkful of peas into her mouth. He marveled at how she could transform the basic animal act of chewing into something lovely. Whenever he was with her, he loved her, and when he was away from her, he considered her a cruel, selfish, faithless bitch.

"What's going to become of us, Vanessa?" he asked.

"You must be getting drunk, because whenever you're drunk, you always ask what will become of us. We will go on just the way we've always gone on, William my dear. I think we both can look forward to long lives, because only the good die young."

The waiter returned with a new glass of Scotch and removed the one that Mulford had just finished. "Will there be anything else, sir?"

Mulford looked at Vanessa. "Anything else for you, dear?"

"Not right now."

"That will be all for the moment," Mulford told the waiter.

"Very good, sir."

The waiter withdrew. Mulford stared at the candle burning on the table, remembering that Shakespeare had said life was nothing more than a "brief candle".

Vanessa glanced at him disapprovingly. "Your eyes are starting to glaze over, William. I really don't think you should drink anymore."

"I'm not drunk yet," he said. "I was only thinking a philosophical thought."

"Don't make me laugh."

"I was, Vanessa!"

"What was it?"

He wrinkled his brow, trying to crystallize the thought into a coherent sentence, but found that he couldn't. "It had something to do with the impermanence of life," he explained.

"Sounds very profound," she said dryly.

Mulford reached for his glass of Scotch. "You know, Vanessa, someday I think I'm going to strike you."

"If you do you'd better kill me, because you'll never get another chance to touch me again. Care for some of this asparagus?"

"No, thank you."

"I don't think much of men who strike women," she said.

A strange voice cried out: "Vanessa!"

Mulford looked up and saw two young RAF officers approaching their table. The one who had spoken was blond and nice-looking, Mulford thought. The other was a string bean with slicked-down black hair. Vanessa turned to them and smiled as though she was delighted to see them.

She never smiles for me that way, Mulford thought ruefully.

"Vanessa," said the blond man, taking her hand, "how good to see you!"

"Nice to see you, too," she replied.

The string bean then took her hand and exchanged pleasantries with her. Then both the young men looked quizzically at Mulford.

"May I present my husband, Commander William Mulford," Vanessa said. "William, this is Captain Jeremy Thorndike and Captain Richard Tuthill."

Mulford arose and shook their hands. "How do you do," he said, scrutinizing Jeremy Thorndike and watching his complexion become tinged with pink.

"I've heard so much about you, Commander Mulford," Jeremy said. "I understand you're stationed in Liverpool."

"Yes — I'm leaving for America next week."

"Be there long?"

"Don't know yet."

"Ah." Jeremy looked at Tuthill. "Well, I guess we'd better be moving along." He turned to Vanessa again. "Very nice seeing you again, Vanessa." He looked at Mulford. "Very nice meeting you, sir."

"Very nice meeting you."

Jeremy and Richard Tuthill turned and walked away, two dashing young RAF officers with chests covered by service ribbons. Mulford returned to his seat and reached for his drink. "So that's Jeremy."

"Isn't he handsome?" Vanessa asked with a wicked little smile.

"Quite."

"He comes from a very nice family."

"Naturally."

"He's one of the heroes of the Battle of Britain, you know. Shot down fourteen German planes."

"Very impressive."

"Do I detect a note of sarcasm in your voice, my dear?"

"It's really quite amazing," he said.

"What is?"

"When I was his age, I never would have approached a woman with whom I was having an affair if she was in the company of her husband. What a brazen little bastard he is."

She made her mouth into an amused little O. "He's not little at all, William. In fact, he's as tall as you."

"He's still a brazen little bastard."

She sighed. "It's the war, William. Men like him, and you too, I suppose, face danger so often that you become somewhat inured to it. You just don't give a damn anymore."

"I'm so glad that you're doing your little bit for the war effort, Vanessa."

She sliced into her fish again. "We all must do whatever we can, William."

He sipped his Scotch, feeling angry. "You know, it's an insult when he walks up to you like that in my presence. It's as though he's rubbing my nose in it."

"Nonsense," she replied. "He doesn't even know that you know."

"I think I'm going to have a little talk with him." Mulford placed his glass on the table.

"What?"

"Calm down."

She wrinkled her eyebrows and leaned toward him. "Now William, don't do anything foolish that you'll regret afterward."

He smiled. "Why, I do believe that you're upset, Vanessa. How strange to see you upset this way."

"William," she said through clenched teeth, "if you make a scene, I'll never speak to you again in my life, and I mean it."

"I have no intention of making a scene, my dear, and furthermore, if you don't want situations like this to develop in the future, keep your ridiculous little boyfriends away from me."

Her graceful white hands became fists. "William, don't you dare get up from your chair."

"I'll be right back," he said, getting up from his chair.

He walked across the dining room, making his way between candlelit tables where well-dressed people sat and ate. He entered the bar, finding Jeremy and Richard Tuthill sitting on stools, waiting for their drinks to arrive. Mulford approached Jeremy from behind, placing his hands on Jeremy's shoulder.

Jeremy spun around, the right corner of his mouth twitching when he saw Mulford, who said, "May I have a private word with you?"

"Um … why, certainly, sir … yes, of course."

Jeremy stood and followed Mulford to a corner at the end of the bar. They stopped and faced each other. Mulford could see that Jeremy was pale but not cringing, and imagined this was the way the young man looked in the cockpit of his plane when he flew into battle.

"I hate it when someone thinks he's fooling me," Mulford said, "so I just thought I'd tell you that I know what's been transpiring between you and my wife. Is that clear?"

Jeremy was standing nearly at complete military attention, stiff and erect, with his chin high. "Yes, sir," he replied.

"And moreover, if you ever take advantage of her in any ungentlemanly way, or even besmirch her reputation, I'll kill you. Is that clear too?"

"Yes, sir."

Mulford turned around and walked back to his table, where Vanessa was nervously smoking a cigarette. He sat down, looking at her plate. "You haven't finished your fish, my dear. Is there anything wrong with it?"

"What did you say to him?" she asked coldly.

"Not very much. There was no embarrassing scene. Calm down." Mulford raised his hand for the waiter, who sped to the table.

"Sir?"

"Another of these."

"Yes, sir."

The waiter dashed away. Vanessa leaned toward Mulford. "I wish you hadn't spoken with Jeremy. I hope you didn't scare him away from me. I love him, you know."

"You do?"

She nodded. "Yes, I do."

"I didn't know that," Mulford said, frowning. "Are you sure you're in love with him?"

"I think I am, and I'm so much older than he. I'd hate to lose him. I know he'll leave me someday, but I'd like to have him for as long as I can. He's so young ... so vital. I need him, William, and I think he needs me, because he's just a boy really, and he faces death every few days up there in the sky. We make each other happy, and I hope you haven't spoiled it all."

She opened her purse, took out a handkerchief, and dabbed her eyes. Mulford stared at her in disbelief.

"You're crying!" he said.

She nodded. "Yes."

"You're crying for him!"

"Yes."

"But you never cried for me!"

"I have, but you never saw me, just as he doesn't see me now — unless he happens to look over here, of course. But he may think that you said something cruel to me and made me cry, because most men never believe that women cry over them, although we do all the time."

He placed his hand over hers. "I'm sorry, darling."

"Is everyone looking at me?"

"No, you look like a woman who's got something in her eye, that's all. I'm sure no one would guess that you're crying over your lover."

"I'm sure he'll never speak to me again," she said softly.

"Of course he will. Just call him and say hello. I didn't tell him to stay away from you. I wouldn't do that."

She looked at him. "Then what did you say?'

"I just told him that if he ever hurt you in any way, I'd kill him."

"That's all you said to him?"

"Basically."

"How very gallant!"

She smiled, and he could see that she was happy again, at the center of a big romantic melodrama, just what she loved most.

"You know, William," she said wistfully, "sometimes I think that you really love me."

"I do, my dear. I really do."

She stubbed out her cigarette in the ashtray. "You know, I think I'll finish my fish."

"It's probably cold now," he said.

"We shouldn't waste food these days," she replied. "There's a war on, you know."

CHAPTER 10

U-112 limped into port at Lorient, victory flags flying. The band played loudly if not always in unison, and Flotillenkapitän Weisacker and his staff were waiting on the pier along with a cheering crowd of sailors and civilians.

For Blohm, this welcome wasn't as exciting as his first. Now he felt like an old battle-hardened veteran, watching calmly as sailors on the pier threw hawsers to the crew members of U-112, who caught them and fastened them to cleats. Nurses from the hospital threw flowers on the deck as sailors laid down the gangplank.

The officers and crew of U-112 formed ranks on the deck. Flotillenkapitän Weisacker came aboard to congratulate everybody, then they all went to the Prefecture for the traditional drunken dinner. It lasted until midnight, then everyone returned to quarters.

Blohm was the officer of the watch that night, and had to return to the boat. He walked down the pier with four sailors who were to serve as guards with him, and saw the boat floating in the moonlit water, reminding Blohm of a dog tied to a post.

Two of the guards remained on the deck, and the other two went below to get some sleep. Blohm went below, too, intending to write a letter to his parents, but decided he was a little too drunk and the letter might not sound right.

He wasn't tired, and thought he'd take a walk through the boat. Starting in the control room, he walked aft to the engine rooms, thinking of how quiet and empty the U-boat was. Only a few days ago it had been fighting for its life in the depths of the Atlantic Ocean, and was now just a mass of dials and machinery, an engineer's paradise.

In the electric motor room he examined the packing around the propeller shafts that had given so much trouble and caused so much worry during the depth-charging a few days ago. They'd surfaced after the destroyer went away and repaired the damage, but the leaks throughout the hull couldn't be repaired permanently, and Kruger had decided that the boat might not survive another depth-charging unless it was repaired with something more than slivers of wood, so he called headquarters and requested permission to return.

Blohm thought of Wichmann-Holtz, wondering what would become of him and who would replace him. Climbing steps to the conning tower, Blohm sat in front of the periscope and recalled how Kruger had directed his submerged attacks from here.

In the stillness and safety of Lorient, the U-boat's battles seemed like a dream. Blohm thought it strange that grown men were trying to sink each other's ships and kill each other on the high seas. He remembered how Kruger had shot the British airman and blown off the top of his skull. How gruesome it seemed now, whereas Blohm had thought it routine when it had happened.

He folded his hands between his legs and looked down at the wood-slatted deck. He knew that U-112 almost had been sunk during the patrol. It had been touch and go for quite a while there. Now he was safe in Lorient, but in a week or two he'd go on patrol again. Who could say whether or not he'd return from that one?

He thought of Julie, the beautiful French prostitute. She'd been on his mind throughout the patrol, and now she was almost his. Tomorrow, after their review with Admiral Dönitz, he'd be free to go and see her. In his imagination she had taken on the aura of an exotic sexual creature, her skin smooth and without blemishes. Tomorrow night at this time he'd hold her in his arms and taste for the first time in his life the ecstasy of sexual love. He looked at his watch, wishing the hands would move more quickly.

He wondered how she'd react when she saw him come for her. She'd probably say that she knew he'd be back. That's the way women were: always pretending to be mysterious and in possession of magical powers. Tomorrow night he'd learn a few of their secrets.

Workmen came aboard U-112 at daybreak and began examining her prior to putting her into dry dock for repairs. Blohm was relieved of his watch duty and driven to the Hotel Beau Séjour, where he found his room on the fourth floor. His luggage had been delivered from the quartermaster shack. He took a hot bath, then went to bed.

Grunberger awakened him at noon. Blohm shaved carefully, put on his dress uniform, went down to the dining room, and found Grunberger and Feiler already sitting at a table. A French waitress took Blohm's order. He asked for broiled swordfish steak, French-fried potatoes and a salad. The waitress wrote down the order and walked to the kitchen. Blohm listened politely to the conversation his fellow officers were having about Wichmann-Holtz.

"I think they'll kick him out of the navy," said Feiler, slicing into a slab of roast beef.

"Naw," said Grunberger, "they'll just assign him to a surface ship."

"I don't think so. They think that if he's emotionally unstable for U-boats, he's emotionally unstable for surface ships, too."

"But it's different on a surface ship. There isn't the claustrophobia. If you're hit by a shell, you have a chance. Every sailor knows that. You can jump off the goddamned ship but if a U-boat is hit, that's the end of the story. You're crushed and smothered by a million tons of water."

"I agree with you," Feiler said, munching a boiled carrot. "But headquarters won't agree with you. Poor Wichmann-Holtz's navy career is over, I'm afraid."

"Well, I didn't think he was that interested in a career. Isn't his family rich?"

"Very rich. They own half of Stuttgart, I'm told."

"No kidding?"

"I have it on the most reliable authority."

"Why didn't you tell me before? I would have borrowed some money from him."

"I thought you knew."

"I knew he was well off, but not *that* well off." Grunberger looked at Blohm. "Are *you* well off?"

"Not really."

"Does your father make a lot of money in his party job?"

"Not that much."

"What do you think is going to happen to Wichmann-Holtz?"

"I have no idea."

Feiler snorted. "He doesn't want to commit himself."

"He's playing it smart," Grunberger agreed. "That way no one ever can tell him he's wrong."

"I don't mind being wrong," Blohm said. "Nothing wrong with making an incorrect guess. I simply don't know what's going to happen to Wichmann-Holtz, although I hope he'll be all right. I considered him a very decent person."

Grunberger nodded. "That he was. I'll miss him."

"Me too," said Feiler.

"Hey," Grunberger said, punching Blohm in the arm. "I hear you're going to get an Iron Cross."

"Really?" Blohm asked. "Where did you hear that?"

"I heard somebody from headquarters say that Kruger put you in for it."

"That doesn't mean I'll get it."

Feiler snorted. "Of course you'll get it. You shot down a plane all by yourself, for goodness' sake. There are many pilots in the Luftwaffe who've never even done that. If they don't give you an Iron Cross, there's something wrong someplace."

Blohm smiled, thinking of how nice he'd look with an Iron Cross pinned to the left pocket of his tunic.

"Are you coming to the brothel with us after the review?" Feiler asked Blohm.

"Of course," Blohm replied.

Admiral Dönitz marched into the square, leading a dozen of his staff officers, as the band played the Badenweiler Marsch yet again. The crew of U-112 stood in ranks beneath the budding branches of an oak tree. Dönitz stopped a few paces in front of Kruger, returned Kruger's salute, then advanced to shake hands and offer congratulations.

Blohm had been thrilled by this ceremony when he'd participated in it at the end of his first patrol, but now realized ceremonies were routine occasions that took place whenever a U-boat returned from patrol. Admiral Dönitz would interrupt whatever he was doing and lead his staff out for a little march.

The entire ceremony took no more than an hour. Dönitz probably could do it in his sleep.

Dönitz stepped around Kruger and marched back to shake Grunberger's hand. Blohm wondered what would have happened if U-112 hadn't returned from patrol. Standard letters would probably be sent to parents and wives, expressing regrets and continued faith in the Fatherland. A memorial service would be held somewhere. There would be speeches. That would be it.

Dönitz shook hands with Feiler, chatting amiably with him about engines and mechanical gear. Blohm figured that Dönitz probably said the same things to the chief engineer of whatever U-boat had returned from patrol.

Dönitz moved in front of Blohm and held out his hand. "Ah, Ensign Blohm," he said. "Kapitänleutnant Kruger's report said many good things about your performance in this patrol."

Blohm didn't know how to reply to that, so he smiled dumbly.

"We're putting you in for the Iron Cross," Dönitz said.

"Thank you very much, sir," Blohm said.

"I'm sure your father is very proud of you."

"I hope so, sir."

Dönitz stepped around Blohm and marched back to the first row of petty officers to continue shaking hands and making small talk. Blohm stood at attention, his eyes narrowing to slits. He could see himself being awarded the Iron Cross by Admiral Dönitz. Blohm's father would see to it that a photograph was taken. It would be printed in *Signal* magazine. All his old school chums would find out that he had proven himself a man in battle.

But thinking back, he realized that he hadn't felt much like a man when he was firing the machine gun at the Sunderland. He'd been scared to death, and so numb that if a bullet had hit him he probably wouldn't have felt it. He'd followed orders and done his duty because there were no alternatives at that moment.

But if they wanted to give him an Iron Cross for simply following orders, it was fine with him.

Admiral Dönitz marched away with his staff officers and the band, leaving the officers and crew of U-112 underneath the oak tree. Kapitänleutnant Kruger executed a sharp about-face and said: "Dismissed!"

Men cheered and threw their hats into the air, then raced off to the brothel or café of their choice. Kruger walked alone across the plaza, holding his sword steady in his right hand. Grunberger, Feiler, and Blohm stood beneath the oak tree and looked at each other.

"Let's have a drink first," said Feiler.

"Where's the nearest good café?" asked Grunberger.

"Can't we get our drinks at the Crescent Palace?" asked Blohm.

Feiler and Grunberger looked at him and burst into laughter.

"Look how eager he is!" Feiler said.

"Last time we practically had to drag him there by his hair, but now he can't get there fast enough," Grunberger scoffed.

"Let them taste it once, and they'll slobber after it for the rest of their lives."

Grunberger slapped Blohm on the arm. "How depraved you've become, my lad."

Blohm grinned. "I was a decent person before I met you two."

"You never were a decent person!"

"I need a drink!" shouted Feiler.

"Why can't you drink in the Crescent Palace?" Blohm asked.

Feiler poked his finger into Blohm's chest. "Because no self-respecting U-boat officer would ever show up at a brothel sober, that's why. Now let's go get something to drink."

"I have two bottles of cognac in my room," said Grunberger.

"Why didn't you say so before?" Feiler asked.

"Because you were talking. You're *always* talking."

"I am not always talking. Sometimes I'm drinking and sometimes I'm fucking."

"I see a cab," Blohm said.

"Get it!" screamed Feiler.

Blohm ran into the street and held his hand up. The cab stopped and the three officers piled in, telling the driver to take them to the Hotel Beau Séjour. As the cab drove away, Feiler jabbed Blohm in the ribs.

"I told you you'd get an Iron Cross," he said.

"I don't have it yet," Blohm replied.

"You will. Anybody got a cigarette?"

"I don't smoke," said Blohm.

"I know you don't, but why don't you?"

"Because it's bad for the health."

Feiler held his fist in front of Blohm's face. "You think you're healthier than me?"

"Yes."

"Horseshit!"

Grunberger gave Feiler a cigarette and lit it with his lighter. The inside of the cab filled with tobacco smoke. The cab stopped in front of the Hotel Beau Séjour. The three officers went upstairs to Grunberger's room, where Grunberger retrieved his bottle of cognac from his suitcase. He broke the seal, pulled the cork, brought the mouth of the bottle to his lips, and threw his head back. His Adam's apple bobbed up and down.

"Save some for me!" Feiler said.

Grunberger passed the bottle to Feiler, who proceeded to guzzle cognac. Finally Feiler pulled the bottle away from his lips, burped, and handed it to Blohm.

Blohm took it and drank as deeply as the others. He wanted to get drunk and crazy, so he could release himself from the tension of the patrol.

"Look at him drink!" said Grunberger, pointing at Blohm.

"Like a baby at his mother's tit!"

Blohm handed the bottle back to Grunberger. His throat and chest burned; alcohol fumes rose to his brain. "Water!" he cried. Grunberger and Feiler laughed as he ran to the sink, turned the faucet, caught water in his cupped hands, and sucked the water out of them.

"Let's get out of here," Grunberger said.

They left the room and descended stairs to the lobby, where drunken U-boat officers were sleeping on chairs or playing cards. In front of the hotel they hailed a cab and told the driver to take them to the Crescent Palace. They didn't have to give him the address; he knew exactly where it was.

The cab rumbled over the cobblestone streets. In the backseat, the three officers passed the bottle back and forth among themselves. Blohm, his head spinning, felt happy. The U-boat patrol was in the past, and he was on his way to the arms of that beautiful slant-eyed Julie.

The cab stopped in front of the Crescent Palace and they all got out. Blohm paid the driver, giving him a fat tip. Grunberger rang the bell, the door opened, and a tall

Frenchman with a bald head and a mustache was there, cigar sticking out of the corner of his mouth.

"Welcome to the Crescent Palace, gentlemen!" he roared.

"Where's Cecille?" asked Feiler.

"Inside."

"Is Julie here?" Blohm asked.

"Who?"

"Julie."

The man wrinkled his nose and shrugged. "I don't know. There are so many of them, you know, and they're all crazy."

The three officers walked through the corridor and came to the dance floor. A band was playing a fast American jazz song. Many officers were dancing with the prostitutes. The air was thick with the smell of tobacco smoke and liquor. Blohm looked around the room, trying to find Julie.

"Come on, let's sit down!" Grunberger said.

Cecille materialized from the crowd and promenaded toward them, wearing a black satin dress. "Gentlemen!" she cried. "So good to see you again!"

"Where's Julie?" Blohm asked.

"Aha! So you liked her, eh?"

"Where is she now?"

"Somewhere around here — how should I know? You'll find her, don't worry!"

Feiler pointed to the dance floor. "Isn't that her out there?"

Blohm looked at the dancers and, sure enough, saw her in the middle of the floor, dancing with a tall officer whose short blond hair stood straight up like straw. Emboldened by the cognac, Blohm strode on to the dance floor.

"Where's he going?" asked Feiler.

"He's going to cut in on that officer," Grunberger replied. "Oh-oh."

Cecille raised her hand in the air. "Don't worry about it — let Cecille take care of everything."

Blohm made his way through the dancers and tapped the officer on the shoulder, but the officer was so drunk he didn't feel anything. Julie looked at Blohm and remembered instantly who he was. Blohm tapped the officer harder, and the officer looked at him, surprised.

"May I cut in?" Blohm asked.

The officer had big ears and small upturned nose. "Cut in?" he asked. "Are you crazy?" The insignia on his shoulder boards indicated he was an Oberleutnant, like Grunberger.

"No, I just want to dance with her."

"But I'm dancing with her!"

"And I'm cutting in!"

"Oh no you're not!"

"Oh yes I am."

Cecille appeared between them and pushed them apart. "Now, boys," she said.

"I want to dance with her!" Blohm said, pointing to Julie, who appeared amused by the dispute.

"But *I'm* dancing with her!" the Oberleutnant insisted.

Cecille wagged her finger in front of Blohm's face. "The gentleman is right — he's dancing with her, and you'll have to wait your turn or leave."

Cecille placed her arm around Blohm's shoulders and led him off the dance floor.

"Wait a minute!" said the Oberleutnant.

"What's the matter?" asked Cecille.

The Oberleutnant leaned toward one side, like a tree about to fall down. "Let the kid dance with her if he wants to. It's silly, arguing over a woman."

The Oberleutnant staggered away, and Blohm walked toward Julie.

"I knew you'd be back," she said, eyes twinkling.

"I knew you'd say that," he replied.

Cecille smiled as she watched them dance. Although a madam, she was also a sentimental old lady. It looked almost like true love to her. Then somebody called her name and she had to scurry away to supervise some other brothel business.

Blohm danced with Julie on the crowded dance floor, holding her slim, shapely body close to him. "I thought of you quite often while I was at sea," he said.

"Oh?" she asked with a coquettish smile. "And what did you think about when you thought of me?"

"I thought of making love to you," he whispered into her ear, "and I regretted not having made love to you when I had the chance. I thought it would be tragic if I died on patrol without ever having tasted love."

"Love?" she asked. "Is that what we're going to have — love?"

"A form of it, yes."

She smiled and looked at him in a manner that he considered condescending. "How you've changed," she said.

"He who is not subject to change is most probably dead." As he spoke the last word, he flashed on Kruger shooting the British airman.

"What's wrong?" Julie asked.

"Nothing."

"Your expression changed so suddenly," she said. "You looked as though you just saw the devil."

He winked. "I am the devil."

"No, you're not. You just wish you were."

"Let's go upstairs."

She laughed. "You're like a wild horse tonight, aren't you?"

"Yes."

He took her arm and led her through the swirling, bumping dancers to the staircase. His hips and shoulders touching hers, he realized that soon he would know everything about women. He'd often wondered what sexual love would be like, and now at last he would find out. He expected it to be different from anything else he'd ever experienced.

They climbed the stairs, Blohm smelling the fragrance of her perfume. She'd probably slept with ten other men that evening, but he didn't care. In fact that made her more appealing to him, because it took her out of the realm of ordinary women and transformed her into a goddess of love, a Venus de Milo.

They walked on the balcony toward her room. He looked over the rail at the revelry below. It reminded him of Sodom and Gomorrah as described in the Bible. Officers danced with women, kissed them, and howled like wild animals. Some were passed out on benches, heads hanging askew, their mouths agape.

She unlocked the door to her room, and they entered. Walking toward the bed, she turned on the lamp. He looked at the bed, the dresser, and the chair where he'd sat when he'd been here last. The cognac he'd drunk distorted his flow of thought. He wondered if he'd ever left this room and whether this was still his first meeting with Julie.

She turned and looked at him, hands on her hips. "Well, what do you want?"

"Everything."

"Everything?" she laughed. "You men are like little children in a candy store. You want everything, but can only manage very little."

"You're so damned condescending. You think you know everything. I'm going to show you a thing or two."

"We'll see about that." She looked at herself in the mirror and flicked something off an eyelash. "When I asked what you wanted, I was trying to determine how much you wanted to spend."

"I want to buy an hour with you," he said.

"An hour? That's a long time."

"Perhaps for you, but I doubt whether it will be for me. How much?"

She told him the amount, nearly a month's pay for an ensign. But he'd known it would be a lot, and he'd just been paid for his last patrol. He took the money out of his wallet and threw it on the bed.

She picked it up, counted, then glanced at him slyly. "I'll be right back."

"Where are you going?"

"I have to turn in this money. It'll only take a few moments."

"Hurry up," he told her.

"Don't be impatient. I'll be back soon. You can start taking your clothes off if you like."

She left the room, leaving the fragrance of her perfume behind. Blohm took off his uniform jacket and lay it on the chair, noticing that his hands were trembling. He felt desire and fear at the same time, and worried that something might be wrong with him, preventing him from performing the sex act properly.

He was unbuttoning his shirt when she returned to the room.

"Well, here I am," she said lightly. She pulled a zipper at her side, and her red silk dress dropped to her feet. She wore nothing underneath. He stared at her in astonishment as she picked up her dress and hung it over the bedpost. He couldn't stop looking at the fuzzy dark hair at the juncture of her legs.

"Haven't you ever seen a naked woman before?" she asked.

"No."

She wore only her necklace and earrings and looked like an exotic Arabian dancing girl. Blohm felt himself getting an erection and realized he'd have no trouble performing the sex act. He felt elated to know that he wasn't impotent.

She walked toward him, pressed her body against his and kissed his lips, touching her hands to his waist. He thrilled at the sight of her nipples against his clothes. He placed his palms on the roundness of her buttocks, which were soft and smooth as silk.

She stepped back. "Take off your clothes."

He fumbled with the buttons of his shirt. She unbuckled his belt, unbuttoned his pants, and kneeling, pulled them down. Then she arose and placed her hand on his genitals.

"You're all ready to go, aren't you?" she purred.

"Yes." He threw his shirt on to the chair and stepped out of his pants.

She walked to the sink and turned on the water. "Come over here," she said.

He walked to her and she grabbed his penis, dripped water on to it and washed it with soap, all the while giving him alluring glances and mysterious smiles.

"I believe you told me last time that you were a virgin," she said.

"Yes," he replied. "I haven't had much to do with women in my life." The touch of her hands were causing chills to race up and down his spine.

She squeezed his penis. "What did you think of when you thought of me on your U-boat?"

"I thought of making love to you in bed."

She dried him with a towel. "In what way?"

"All the ways."

"Are you sure you know all the ways?"

"No."

She laughed and took his hand, leading him toward the bed. "You're built awfully well," she said.

"So are you."

"Lie down on your back."

He turned her hand loose and crawled on to the bed, rolling over on to his back. His penis stood straight up in the air. She got on the bed and walked on her knees to him, and he watched her breasts bob up and down. He reached out and cupped one of them in his hand, and thought it was the nicest thing he'd ever touched in his life. He pressed his finger against her brown nipple and stroked it gently.

"If you keep doing that, you're going to make me hot," she said, kneeling beside him.

"I'd like to make you hot."

She grabbed his penis in her fist. "You know, I really kind of like you."

He smiled wryly. "Do you say that to all the men?"

"No, but I don't suppose you believe me."

"No, I don't believe you. But that's all right."

She cocked her head to the side. "You're a strange mixture of naivety and cynicism."

"You're a strange mixture yourself, of a charming young woman and a prostitute."

"I don't think that's such a strange mixture," she said, fondling his penis. "Do you like what I'm doing now?"

"Yes."

"Are you afraid of me?"

"Not at all."

"I guess it's different for men," she said. "I was terrified when I was a virgin."

"Well, I understand a woman feels a certain pain that men don't. How did you lose your virginity?"

She smiled. "Do you want me to tell you lewd stories?"

"No, I was just wondering how you lost your virginity."

She looked at the ceiling. "Oh, it was in some woods a few years ago. I went for a walk with a certain young man whom I liked very much, and one thing sort of led to another — you know how it is."

"I'm afraid I don't," he admitted. "Were you in love with him?"

She shrugged. "Who knows what love is? Do you?"

"I think so."

"Good for you. I don't. But there are a few things I know. They say you never forget your first lover, so I guess you'll never forget this."

"But I suppose you will."

"Maybe not. You're very good-looking and you really do excite me, although I'm sure you think I'm lying."

His heart was thundering in his chest. He grabbed her waist, pulling her down on to him. "It doesn't matter to me whether you're lying or not."

She kissed his ear. "You're a real little tiger, aren't you?"

"I love you," he replied, not sure he was telling the truth but feeling compelled to say it anyway.

He pressed his lips against hers. She opened her mouth. His tongue slid inside and entwined with hers. Then he rolled her on to her back. Their humping and bumping commenced in earnest.

After a few minutes, Julie realized that she had spent two years doing these things, but somehow it had never been quite like this. No other officer had been this passionate and wild. Most had been so drunk they'd hardly been able to do anything at all, but this athletic young man was so enthusiastic, so uninhibited, that it was a revelation to her, and an extremely erotic one.

How can I feel this way? she wondered, because he was one of the hated *Boche,* defiler of her nation, murderer of her father. Yet her body was aflame with madness, and she scratched her fingernails across his back as she sucked his tongue and met him thrust for thrust.

Blohm felt himself going out of control, but his hips kept working and waves of ecstasy crashed over him. He choked and gasped, clawing at her, trying somehow to push himself completely inside her, then his groin burst, spewing sweet fire, and he cried out, raising his head high in the air.

Afterwards they lay side by side on the pillow, chests heaving. Summoning up all her energy, she leaned over and took her package of cigarettes from the dresser.

"Want one?" she asked in a voice barely above a whisper.

He was in a daze, staring at the ceiling. "I don't smoke."

"Have one anyway."

"All right."

He took one out of the pack; so did she. She lit them with her lighter. He puffed awkwardly, wondering what was the pleasure that people found in tobacco smoke.

"You have to inhale it," she said. "It's mild. You'll be all right. Watch."

He turned his head to the side and watched her place the cigarette in her mouth and inhale. He thought she was beautiful and felt a great love for her, although he knew that was ridiculous.

He put the cigarette into his mouth and repeated what she'd done, feeling the smoke scratch his throat. It felt unpleasant; he coughed, becoming a little woozy, but he was already semi-drunk and exhausted. He couldn't understand why people were always reaching for cigarettes.

"Are you sure you've never done it before?" she asked.

"You mean smoke?"

"No, I mean screw."

"I've never done it before."

She turned to the side and looked at his profile. "You were awfully good, you know."

"I know."

"How do you know?"

"Because it felt right. I've never been so strong or happy in my life."

"Well," she said, "I do this a lot — you know that — and sometimes I think of other things while I'm doing it, but you made me realize that something special was happening. You are capable of deep passion, Karl, and not many men are."

He turned toward her, their noses only an inch apart. "That's because you inspired me."

"Me?" she asked. "But how can that be, since I'm not a pure-blooded Aryan?"

"I don't know," he replied. "I'll have to think about that."

They walked down the stairs together, arm in arm. Blohm recalled seeing weddings where the bride and groom walked down stairs as he and Julie were, and thought it strange and troubling to have such strong feelings of love and passion for a prostitute who in several minutes would probably be screwing another man.

"Well," she said at the bottom of the stairs, "so long for now."

"I'll be back to see you again," he said.

"I'm here every day except Thursdays."

"Where do you go on Thursdays?"

"It's my day off."

"Do you think we could get together?"

She wagged her finger in front of his face. "You just want it for nothing. Naughty boy."

Suddenly he felt miserable. "No, it's not like that."

"I'll see you later?" she asked.

"Yes, I'll be here for a while."

She waved to him. "Ta-ta."

She walked off into the music and smoke. Blohm stood for a few moments at the foot of the stairs, looking at the rear of her body encased so neatly in her red silk dress, and recalling what she had looked liked naked.

Blohm felt desolate. He wished he could have stayed with her in that room for the rest of his life, but he was in a brothel, and the girl who had moved him so deeply was just another of the prostitutes.

I've got to get out of here, he thought unhappily. He walked across the dance floor, the orchestra blaring on the bandstand, and threaded his way among the tables. A hand grasped the bottom of his jacket.

"Where are you going?" asked Grunberger.

Blohm turned around and saw Grunberger sitting in a booth with a brunette wearing a low-cut dress, her hair in a bob.

"I was going home," Blohm said.

"So soon?"

"Yes."

"Have a seat."

Grunberger patted the chair beside him; Blohm sat down.

"This is Lisette," said Grunberger, indicating the brunette.

"How do you do?" Blohm said.

"Hi," she replied.

"How was Julie?" Grunberger asked with a wink.

Blohm shrugged, not wanting to let on how he really felt. "All right."

"Just all right?" Grunberger asked skeptically. "I heard she was a real ball of fire."

"Yes, I suppose she is," Blohm said, trying to sound worldly, "but you know, a woman is only a woman." He spotted the package of cigarettes on the table. "Mind if I take one of these?"

"Since when have you smoked?"

"Since today."

"Help yourself."

Blohm took a cigarette and lit it, recalling how he'd smoked his first in Julie's room. He felt miserable and wanted to be alone. A half-bottle of cognac was on the table, with several soiled glasses. Blohm took a glass that didn't have a cigarette butt in it and poured himself some cognac.

Grunberger laughed. "You're turning into a real old salt," he said.

Blohm forced a smile and raised his glass in the air. "To happy times," he said.

CHAPTER 11

In Washington
DC, Commander William Mulford walked down a long corridor in naval headquarters, carrying his briefcase. American naval officers approached from the other direction, looking curiously at his British uniform. He'd arrived in Washington only two days ago and was living in a room in the British embassy. Helen was staying with her family in Georgetown.

At the end of the corridor, Mulford came to a small waiting room with a secretary behind a desk. Mulford looked at his watch. "I have a three o'clock appointment with Admiral Dexter. I'm

fifteen minutes early."

"Your name, please?"

"Commander William Mulford, Royal Navy."

She looked at a piece of paper and checked off his name. "Have a seat please, Commander Mulford."

Mulford sat on one of the comfortable leather chairs and took out his cigarettes. He would have preferred his pipe, but by the time he had it packed and lit, it would probably be time to see Admiral Dexter.

He lit the cigarette and took a deep drag. On the wall behind the secretary was a poster of a ship sinking and a sailor drowning in the foreground. In large letters at the bottom of the poster were the words SOMEBODY TALKED.

Mulford opened his briefcase and went through his papers. He had statistics on the war against U-boats, diagrams of convoy tactics, discussions of Anti Submarine Warfare (ASW) strategies, and proposals for American-British cooperation in the battle against the U-boats. Admiral Dexter was chief of operations for the United States Navy, and he'd indicated that he'd wanted to meet a British expert in anti-submarine warfare, because Roosevelt and Churchill recently had signed the Atlantic Charter, and both nations would soon begin extensive operations together in the North Atlantic.

Mulford had been chosen as liaison officer, a job he didn't relish. He would have preferred to command a hunter-killer group in the North Atlantic, but was one of England's leading experts on anti-submarine warfare. He'd served on British submarines and fought against German U-boats, having developed along the way many of the tactics of anti-submarine warfare now being utilized by England. England had sent America the best man they had in this field.

Mulford wished he had a drink. Liaison work was nerve-racking because you always had to be concerned with ramifications of every word you spoke. Moreover, Admiral Dexter was no ordinary naval officer — he was the chief naval officer in the American navy.

The phone rang on the secretary's desk. She spoke into it for a few moments, hung up and looked at Mulford. "You may go in now, sir."

Mulford crushed out his cigarette and arose, smoothing the front of his jacket. His blue cap under his arm, he strode to the door, opened it, and found another secretary sitting at a desk.

"You may go right in," she said with a smile.

Mulford opened the door and entered the spacious office of Admiral Rufus Dexter, a broad-shouldered man of fifty-eight with a bald pate, his fringe of brown hair close-cropped above his ears. Mulford thought that his head looked like a cannonball with ears.

Mulford saluted. "Commander William Mulford reporting, sir."

Dexter returned the salute. "Have a seat."

Mulford sat and placed his hat on the chair beside him.

Dexter leaned forward and folded his hands. "So you're the man who's going to teach us how to fight U-boats, eh?"

Mulford smiled, trying to be diplomatic although he didn't like the taunt. "Well, I do have some experience in that area, sir."

Dexter shrugged. "Doesn't appear as though your experience is doing much good. U-boats are being extremely successful, as I'm sure you know."

"I know that full well, sir. A U-boat sank my ship underneath me a little less than two months ago."

Dexter raised his eyebrows. "And you're going to teach us how to fight U-boats? It would appear that you need someone to teach *you*."

"We know what to do, sir, but don't have what we need to implement our strategy."

Dexter scowled as if he didn't believe Mulford. "Can you tell me in general terms your overall approach to fighting U-boats?"

"Basically, sir, we believe in convoys defended by hunter-killer groups of destroyers or corvettes, supported by anti-submarine aircraft and the latest detection instruments. That is the key to winning the war against the U-boats."

"I'm not so sure."

"How do you think they should be fought, sir?"

"The convoy system that you recommend only produces large, slow-moving targets that can be spotted more easily than ships sailing singly."

"I have statistics here," said Mulford, opening his briefcase, "indicating that we lost many more ships before we started using the convoy system."

Dexter waved him off. "I'll look at them later."

Mulford slid the papers back into his briefcase.

"As I see it," Dexter said in a booming voice, "the main focus of our effort should be U-boats themselves, not convoys. I believe U-boats should be aggressively hunted and driven from the ocean!"

"In what manner, sir?"

"In the manner of sending out destroyers that otherwise would have been shackled to convoy duty, and having the destroyers hunt down the damned U-boats."

"We've tried that, too, sir, and it hasn't worked. The ocean is very large, as I'm sure you're aware. It is extremely difficult to find U-boats in it. Our strategy has been devised as the result of our knowledge that convoys attract U-boats, therefore the best place to hunt them is in the vicinity of convoys."

Dexter turned down a corner of his mouth. "But your strategy doesn't seem to be successful. U-boats have been sinking ships almost at will. They even sank yours!"

"As I just explained, that's because we don't have enough ships and aircraft. We're spread too thin."

"You might be more effective if you concentrated on ports from which U-boats sail. Get 'em before they go to sea."

"Those ports and seas around them are too heavily defended. We believe that our efforts must be concentrated on protecting convoys."

"You've just admitted that your strategy isn't working." Admiral Dexter smiled. "It appears that we have quite different views on how to combat the U-boat threat."

"Yes, sir," Mulford replied, "but I would like to point out that my views are based on actual experience fighting U-boats, and yours are not. It appears as though you're going to make the same mistakes we made before we learned the best way to deal with U-boats."

Dexter shrugged. "I'm not convinced that you've learned the best way, in view of current U-boat successes. I don't mean to be insulting, but in my experience I've noticed that the most inept commanders always say they could do a particular job better if they had more men and material, while capable commanders do the job with what they have."

Mulford realized that Dexter had made up his mind and nothing could dissuade him. "Yes, sir."

"However, I'm grateful to your country for sending you here to talk with me."

"We're happy to have been of help, sir. May I return to England now?"

"No," Dexter replied emphatically. "We've arranged with your government to have you teach a course at our anti-submarine school in Florida. I'm sure your experience will be invaluable to our young naval officers."

"I see," said Mulford, dismayed that he could not return to England right away.

"You'll like Florida," Dexter told him. "The weather is very nice there."

At dawn, sixty-five ships rode high in the water of Liverpool Bay. One was the new destroyer escort *Corinthia*. Standing on its bridge was Commander Michael Scott, its captain.

The *Corinthia* was one of four escort ships commanded by Captain Johnny Forester, whose mission was to protect the convoy of empty ships on its voyage across the Atlantic Ocean to Halifax, Nova Scotia. The escort group would remain in Halifax for a few days, and then accompany a convoy of laden ships back to London.

Scott watched the *Malay Princess* through his binoculars. It was lead ship in the convoy, steaming out into Liverpool Bay. Other ships in the convoy took their positions behind it. The *Corinthia*, last ship out, guarded the rear of the convoy.

"Lovely day, isn't it, sir?" asked Lieutenant-Commander Allan Rutherford, Scott's executive officer.

"Yes, it is," Scott agreed, still watching the *Malay Princess* through his binoculars.

Scott was pleased to have command of his first ship at last, and a modern new one like the *Corinthia* was more than he'd ever hoped for, but he felt alone and isolated on the bridge because he didn't have Commander Mulford to guide him anymore. He'd heard of many officers who'd had excellent records in lower ranks but were relieved of their first command for incompetence. He had a terrible fear that he'd do something wrong, although he had no justifiable reason for thinking that. He had been trained by Mulford himself, one of the stars of the escort service.

The ships got into position and sailed out of Liverpool harbor. High on the hills surrounding the harbor were people watching the immense spectacle. Some of them were the families of men on the ships, among them Ruthie Scott, a slim brunette, who was gazing at the *Corinthia* through her binoculars. She could see her husband clearly on the bridge of the *Corinthia*. He was gesticulating as if issuing orders. She watched as the *Corinthia* following the other ships out of the harbor, and then it was gone.

Ruthie Scott set down the binoculars and closed her eyes. "Dear God," she whispered, "in your infinite mercy, please have my husband return to me alive."

On the bridge of the *Corinthia*, Scott was glad to be under way. The tension and weeks of waiting were over at last, and now the real work would begin. He looked up to the mast of the *Corinthia* and saw the new radar gear, which would help him detect U-boats invisible to the naked eye. The *Corinthia* could achieve thirty knots, much faster than U-boats.

Scott knew that U-boat wolf packs waited for this convoy, and although one part of him was apprehensive, another was eager to do battle with the enemy. He wanted to pay the Germans back for what they'd done to so many of his friends, and he wanted to avenge the sinking of the *Centurion*.

He also knew that if he did well, there would be glory and honor waiting for him in England, and that maybe he would receive medals that would advance his career. Perhaps he'd become an admiral someday.

The convoy sailed ever farther into the North Atlantic, where the U-boats were waiting.

Ensign Blohm stood at attention in a large reception room inside the chancellery in Berlin. To his left and right were other men ready to receive the Iron Cross in the ceremony with him. One was another U-boat officer, the others from the Wehrmacht and Luftwaffe.

A door to the right opened, then Adolf Hitler walked into the room, followed by military aides, party officials, and photographers. Blohm stood rigidly with his face to the front, the corner of his eye perceiving Hitler gazing at the row of eight men. Hitler wore his tan party tunic with his swastika armband and Iron Cross pinned to his pocket. Hitler had won his Iron Cross for conspicuous gallantry against the British during World War One.

Hitler walked to a position in front of the rank that Blohm was in and studied the young men about to be decorated.

"You may stand at ease," Hitler said in his deep voice.

Blohm and the others shot out their left feet and placed their hands behind their backs.

"It is a great joy for me to meet you brave men today," Hitler said. "If the Fatherland had more like you, the war would have been won long ago, because victory always goes to that side that has the greatest courage and determination, regardless of the odds." Hitler looked into the faces of each of them, one by one. "You men know what I mean. You have stood fast and fought hard in the face of certain death, yet fate has ordained that you survive. Why? Could it be that fate always will lend a hand to the valiant and always will crush the cowardly? I believe this is so. More than twenty years ago I stood with a small band of followers, prepared to do battle against an army of lies, stupidity, and cowardice, but my small band of followers increased despite difficult circumstances, until we won. And so it will be in this war. We are ringed by enemies, but we are men of honor and courage, and shall prevail in the end. Men like you strengthen my will and steel the hearts of your countrymen. Men like you are the reason our race is the most advanced in the world. Men like you will bring your countrymen the garlands of victory, and we shall never forget you."

Hitler walked to the left side of the line, where an aide was waiting with a polished wooden box filled with medals. Hitler took out one of the medals and pinned it to the chest of a Luftwaffe pilot who had destroyed twelve Russian tanks in one day.

Camera bulbs flashed on the ceremony. On the far left side of the room, behind a velvet rope, were family and friends, among them Blohm's parents and twin sister Wilhelmina.

Hitler moved down the line, pinning Iron Crosses on tunics, chatting amiably with recipients. Blohm stiffened his spine, trying to stand even more erect, and could feel emanations of radiance coming from the Führer. This indeed was Germany's savior — who could doubt it? Hitler was unquestionably a genius, a man of great spirituality. Blohm was grateful that God had sent such a man to save Germany, and was proud to have the good fortune to live in the same era as he.

Hitler stepped in front of Blohm. Their eyes met. Blohm felt Hitler's energy pierce through to the center of his brain. Blohm saw Hitler's eyes scrutinize the features of his face and saw a corner of Hitler's mouth twitch. Then Hitler turned and took one of the Iron Crosses from the case held by the SS aide. Hitler reached toward Blohm, who felt electricity shoot through him when Hitler's fingers touched his jacket. Hitler pinned on the Iron Cross, patted it, and smiled.

"Congratulations," Hitler said, holding out his hand.

"Thank you, *mein Führer*," Blohm replied in a firm voice, shaking Hitler's hand.

Hitler's grip was strong. Blohm felt power surge from Hitler into his own body.

"I know your father well," Hitler said softly. "He is one of the old fighters from the earliest days of the National Socialist movement. I am not surprised that he would produce a hero of the German Reich. All Germany smiles upon you today, Ensign Blohm."

"Thank you, *mein Führer*."

Hitler squeezed his hand more tightly and gazed into his eyes. "It is an honor to lead men such as you, Ensign Blohm."

Hitler turned and sidestepped to the next man, a parachute officer who had distinguished himself in the battle for Crete.

Blohm remained at attention, tingling with excitement. The Iron Cross pinned to his jacket seemed to be burning into his flesh. In front of him stood the SS aide with the case of medals. Blohm remembered that day on U-112 when he had shot down the big Sunderland. It had never occurred to him that that day would lead to this one.

But now in retrospect he realized that he truly had been courageous, and that his future in the navy looked very bright indeed.

CHAPTER 12

Julie entered Café Lalys and spotted Armand sitting at a table in the corner. He wore a blue suit jacket too small for him, not matching his baggy brown trousers. She thought he looked like a student of philosophy instead of a fighter in the *Maquis*.

She walked to his table and sat down, crossing her legs and smoothing her hair. She wore a white blouse and tan skirt and carried a leather shoulder bag.

I'm sorry," she said, defeat in her voice, "but I've been unable to find out anything."

Armand looked at her sternly. "You mean after two weeks you haven't been able to find out *anything?*"

"I'm afraid that's so. The men with whom I spend time don't like to discuss U-boats. Their minds are on other things, I'm afraid."

He looked at her coldly. She realized that he didn't like her very much. She was only a French prostitute, after all, a contemptible creature to a person like him, who so obviously came from a decent family, but she had come from a decent family also. She opened her bag, took out her pack of cigarettes, and offered him one. He shook his head, so she took one for herself and lit it with a match.

"I know you're annoyed," she said, "but I'm sorry — I don't seem to be very good at this."

A waiter came to the table. She ordered a cup of coffee and a croissant. Armand also asked for another cup of coffee. The waiter returned to the kitchen, passing groups of French men and women at the tables. The cafe was in a part of Lorient where Germans rarely visited.

"If you're not good at it," Armand said, "you'll have to do something to make yourself good at it."

"What do you suggest?"

"I don't know. Can't you ask them point blank about what it's like to serve on a U-boat?"

"I do ask, but they all tell me they don't want to talk about it."

"Flatter them," Armand suggested. "Tell them you want to hear all about their heroic exploits."

"Armand — you simply don't understand. The Germans are not in my room to talk with me."

"Surely you must have conversations."

"We do, but generally about other subjects, if you know what I mean."

He shrugged. "I suppose so."

"Haven't you ever been in an *établissement*?"

He appeared embarrassed. "No."

"I didn't think so. No wonder you don't understand."

The waiter returned with the coffee and croissant. Julie buttered part of it and bit a piece off the end. She chewed and sipped some coffee.

"I don't think you really care about helping us," Armand said. "You're much too frivolous about the whole thing. You're not really trying."

"You're free to think whatever you like," she told him, "but I am trying. It's easy for you to criticize because you're not the one in contact with German officers. If I push too hard, I'm the one who'll wind up in the hands of the Gestapo, not you."

He sneered. "You think you're in danger? You don't know what danger is!"

It occurred to her that perhaps he had been in dangerous situations himself, fighting German soldiers hand to hand, stabbing them with knives. "Perhaps not," she admitted, puffing her cigarette. She placed it on the ashtray and took another bite of her croissant.

The harsh lines of his face softened. "We shouldn't argue," he said wearily. "It doesn't lead anywhere."

"You're the one who started it."

"I know, I know." He ran his fingers through his hair. "Listen, there must be a way. Have you made friends with any of the Germans?"

"Friends? Are you kidding?"

"Don't some of them see you more than one time, so that you know each other in a way?"

"Yes."

"Then why can't you work on them? Let yourself become more friendly. Get into ordinary conversations with them."

She shook her head. "There isn't time for that. It's a business, Armand. They pay, do what they want, and leave."

"Don't they ever fall in love with you?"

She snorted. "Don't be silly."

"I wouldn't be surprised if one did," he said. "You're very beautiful."

His remark shocked her because she'd thought he considered her repulsive. "Thank you." And then she remembered Blohm. "As a matter of fact, there is one who likes me very much."

Armand's eyes widened. "Who is he?"

"Only an ensign, but he's a U-boat officer and goes out on patrols."

"Then he must know quite a lot about U-boats and their tactics."

"Yes, I suppose he does." Julie regretted mentioning Blohm because she had mixed feelings about him. On one hand he was the enemy, and on the other he was a decent young man whose youthful passion actually had excited her, a prostitute, and brought her to an unfaked orgasm. "But he's only an ensign. Do you really think he knows much?"

"Of course! He has access to the most important kinds of information!"

"I *have* tried to elicit information from him," Julie said, "but he didn't want to talk about it either."

"You're sure he likes you?" Armand asked.

"Yes."

"Why don't you see him outside the *établissement?*"

"That's against the rules! I'll lose my job!"

Armand smiled. "We'll talk with the people who operate the *établissement.* They'll understand."

"They might go directly to the Gestapo!"

"I don't think so."

"Why not?"

"Because I think they might be more afraid of us than the Gestapo. They'll keep their mouths shut, but anyway, they might never find out. You will be discreet, won't you?"

"I'll need somewhere to take him."

"We'll have a flat for you."

"I'll have to see him on a Thursday. That is my only day off."

"Fine," he said. "We can postpone these meetings until midnight."

She stubbed out her cigarette and pinched her lips together. "I don't know if this is a good idea."

"You are afraid?" he asked.

"I don't know."

He placed his hand over hers and squeezed it while gazing into her eyes. "We must be brave for France."

She nodded. "Yes, you're right."

"Is this ensign in Lorient now?"

"I think he's in Berlin with his family."

"When you see him again, lure him into a date. If you're not here next Thursday, I'll assume you're with him and I'll return at midnight. Is that understood?"

"Yes."

He squeezed her hand again. "Good luck."

After the meeting, Julie walked back to the Crescent Palace, troubled by the thought of wheedling information out of Blohm. She hadn't mentioned it to Armand, but she loved Blohm in a certain strange way. It had been thrilling and a revelation to go to bed with him, and she thought he was nice underneath his reprehensible Nazi ideology. She didn't want to trick and lie to him, but now she'd put herself into a position where she had to.

She shouldn't have mentioned him in the first place, but her love of France had compelled her. She felt herself being pulled into a whirlpool from which she could not escape.

Blohm was surprised that none of his fellow officers met him at the train station at Lorient. He hailed a taxi cab and rode it to the Hotel Beau Séjour, going upstairs to his room and looking at himself in the mirror with his new Iron Cross pinned to his jacket.

It was three o'clock in the afternoon. He didn't know what to do with himself. He took out a cigarette, lit it, and sat on the edge of his bed. He'd been looking forward to seeing his fellow officers and telling them about meeting Hitler, but they weren't around. He wondered where they could be. At the U-boat pens? In a cafe? The Crescent Palace?

The Crescent Palace! He thought of Julie and the hour he'd spent with her. She had provided one of the two high points of his life, the other being the moment Adolf Hitler had pinned the Iron Cross on him. He recalled thrashing about with her on the bed and drowning in exquisite ecstasy. Incredibly, Julie, and that pleasure, were there at the Crescent Palace right then. It was no elusive thing — he could go there and get it whenever he wanted. He had enough money in his pocket. Perhaps the other officers from U-112 were there.

He placed his hat squarely on his head, left his room and walked swiftly to the stairs. He passed two young ensigns and noticed them staring at his Iron Cross. Down the stairs he went, and across the lobby. A cab was disgorging drunken officers in front of the hotel. Blohm waited until they climbed out of the cab, then dropped into the back seat and told the driver to take him to the Crescent Palace.

The cab sped over the streets of Lorient as Blohm thought of Julie's supple body and the way she caressed his penis with her tongue. His breathing became deeper, and he got an erection while imagining what he'd do to her when he saw her in just a few minutes. He wondered how she'd react when she saw him. Sometimes he thought that she'd really cared for him, although she was only a prostitute and probably acted like that with all her customers.

The cab stopped in front of the Crescent Palace. Blohm got out, straightened his jacket, adjusted his hat, walked to the door and knocked. The little window slid to the side and two little eyes examined him, then the door opened.

"Welcome, welcome!" said the man with the mustache and cigar.

Blohm entered the corridor that led to the dance floor. He could hear music and laughter, and rushed toward it like a starving man to food. Emerging from the corridor, he saw officers dancing with prostitutes and thought that it was always the same in the Crescent Palace. No matter the time of day, the Crescent Palace was a continuous Sodom and Gomorrah. The band was even playing one of the same tunes that it always played.

Blohm looked around for Julie but couldn't find her. He looked for Grunberger, Feiler, and Kruger, but they weren't there, either. He thought that perhaps Julie was in her room with a customer. Glancing toward the stairs he saw Cecille, the madam descending them.

"Cecille!" he said happily, walking toward her.

She turned to him, immediately spotting the Iron Cross. "My goodness!" She raised her hand to her mouth. "Where did you get that?"

He shrugged modestly. "It's nothing, really."

She looked at him with new interest. "You're so young…"

"Where's Julie?" he asked.

She smiled broadly and wagged her finger at him. "Naughty boy."

"Is she in her room?"

"No, this is her day off."

Blohm's heart sank. "Her day off?"

"Yes, she's entitled to a day off, don't you think? She visits her sick mother."

Blohm grinned. "Oh, come on."

"She does!"

Blohm wrinkled his nose. "Shit!"

"I have other girls here," Cecille said. "Would you like to meet Lisette?"

"Are Grunberger and Feiler here?"

"No, but they were last night."

"Shit!"

"Stop swearing — a nice boy like you." She grabbed his arm. "Come, let me introduce you to somebody else."

"I don't want anybody else."

She took his chin in her bony fingers and made him look at her. "You're not in love, are you?" she asked with a mischievous grin.

"No!" he replied, blushing.

"I think you are."

"No, I'm not."

She looked at him thoughtfully. "Do you know what you remind me of, Ensign Blohm? You remind me of the cherubs in those religious paintings in churches. There's something innocent and fine in you that is somehow unsullied by all that goes on around you."

Blohm felt embarrassed by what she said. He preferred to think of himself as a National Socialist hero rather than a cherub.

"You're blushing," she said. "I've embarrassed you. I'm sorry."

Blohm shrugged, feigning indifference. "I'm not embarrassed."

"No? You're too guileless to lie well, Ensign Blohm." She looked over his head at the dance floor. Something caught her attention. "Excuse me — I need to take care of a little problem. I hope you won't leave yet. We have other lovely girls here."

"What time will Julie be back tomorrow?"

"She'll be here when we open at noon."

Cecille walked away and was soon swallowed up by the dancers. Blohm lit a cigarette and walked to the front door of the Crescent Palace. He felt depressed and tired, and thought he might lie down for a while.

He returned to the hotel and went to bed. In his darkened room he drifted off into a twilight world somewhere between sleep and full consciousness. He imagined himself swimming underwater, miraculously able to breathe in the depths. Julie floated by, reclining on her steel-posted bed, then came U-112, its periscope retracted into its shears. He could see, through the steel hull of the boat, Kruger sleeping in his cot and Grunberger sitting at the periscope in the conning tower. Feiler stood at the helm, drinking from a bottle of cognac, and Wichmann-Holtz was strapped to his cot, a gag holding back his hysterical screams.

U-112 floated past, then Blohm saw Adolf Hitler standing on a rock formation, delivering a speech and gesticulating wildly. "I am the resurrection and the life! He who gives up everything and follows me shall rule the world!" Blohm swam past his Führer and next saw a huge air bubble floating in the water. He wondered why it didn't rise like all other air bubbles, then the bubble transformed into the face of a man with a mustache, wearing a cap of the British navy. The man opened his mouth, and a pounding sound came out instead of words.

"Open up — I know you're in there!"

Blohm stirred and rolled over. It was Feiler's voice and he was knocking on the door. Blohm got out of bed, dressed only in his white shorts, and opened the door.

"You're sleeping at this time of day?" Feiler asked reproachfully, entering the room.

"Yes," Blohm replied, rubbing his eyes.

"Let me see it."

"See what?"

"You know."

"Oh," Blohm said. He opened his closet door and took out his jacket on its hanger. The Iron Cross gleamed on the breast pocket.

"Very nice," said Feiler, reaching out and touching it. "The Führer pinned it on you himself, I heard."

"Yes."

"It must have been truly inspiring," Feiler said, a touch of sarcasm in his voice.

"As a matter of fact, it *was* inspiring," Blohm replied, his voice suggesting that he disapproved of Feiler's attitude toward the Führer.

"I don't suppose you've heard the news," Feiler said, sitting down and taking out his package of cigarettes.

"What news?"

"About Grunberger?"

"What about him?"

Feiler lit his cigarette. "Well, you might have got the Iron Cross and the audience with the Führer, but Grunberger has just made Kapitänleutnant and is getting his own boat."

"Really?"

"Yes."

Blohm sat on the edge of his bed. "My goodness." He'd always thought that U-112 and its crew were an inviolable entity. "Who's going to be the new exec?"

"I don't know yet. Maybe me."

Blohm scratched his head and yawned. "Grunberger seems so young."

"Look who's talking."

"But I'm not taking command of a U-boat."

"New U-boat commanders have to come from someplace. Even you might command a U-boat someday."

Blohm saw himself on the bridge of a U-boat, directing a surface attack at night. "I'd love to."

"Anyway," Feiler told him, "we're all supposed to report to Flotillenkapitän Weisacker's office in the morning to get the official word."

"Oh, shit," said Blohm, who'd intended to see Julie in the Crescent Palace.

"What did you think — that you could stay on furlough forever just because you won the Iron Cross?"

"Of course not."

Feiler looked at the smoke curling up from his cigarette. "I imagine we should have a party tomorrow night to celebrate your Iron Cross and Grunberger's promotion. Don't you think so?"

"Sure, why not?"

"We can hold it at the officers' club, and then all of us can go to the Crescent Palace. Why don't you get dressed and come to the officers' club with me, so that we can make the arrangements."

The next morning the officers of U-112 reported to the office of Flotillenkapitän Weisacker and received the official news. Grunberger was told of his promotion to Kapitänleutnant. He would depart for Kiel the next morning to accept delivery of his new boat and meet the crew. He would conduct training exercises with them for three weeks and then report for duty in Lorient.

New officers would be assigned to U-112 to replace Grunberger and Wichmann-Holtz, the latter transferred to a desk job in Berlin. Weisacker congratulated Blohm on the receipt of his Iron Cross. Toasts were drunk to Grunberger and Blohm. Weisacker dismissed them and the young officers departed immediately for the officers' club.

At eight o'clock in the evening, burping from a huge meal of roast chicken they'd managed to consume along with the booze, Kruger, Grunberger, Feiler, and Blohm crowded into a taxi cab and were driven to the Crescent Palace. They were welcomed by Cecille, who led them to a table on the edge of the dance floor and presented them with a free bottle of champagne.

Officers who knew Grunberger staggered over and shook his hand. Girls kissed him and told him how brave and wonderful he was. Officers whom Blohm didn't know congratulated him for receiving the Iron Cross; a picture of him shaking hands with the Führer had appeared in the local newspaper.

Girls came to the table and sat on the laps of the officers. One of them, a Swedish-looking blonde Blohm had seen there before, wiggled on to his lap and wrapped her long white arms around his neck.

"You're so brave," she sighed, and nibbled his ear. "Why don't you come upstairs with me and show me what you're really like?"

"Maybe later," Blohm said.

"You don't like me?" she asked, pouting.

"Of course I like you. How could I not like you?"

She took his hand and pressed it against her breast. "Does that feel nice?"

"Very nice."

"Wouldn't you like to kiss it?"

"A little later."

"You don't like me," she said unhappily.

Feiler, his hat crooked on his head and his eyes glazed over, elbowed Blohm in the stomach. "Take her upstairs, for crying out loud. Give the poor girl a thrill."

Blohm was drunk and had left his self-control in his hotel room. He laughed boisterously and pinched the blonde's behind.

"Feel good?" she asked.

"Yep."

"Why don't you put your hand up my dress and see if I have underwear on?"

He remembered Julie whom he wanted desperately to see.

"Where's Julie?" he asked.

"Julie doesn't have anything that I don't have."

Blohm nodded because he realized that was true. But if it were true, why did he want Julie? He looked out on to the dance floor but couldn't see her. Wasn't she supposed to be here today?

The blonde unbuttoned his shirt and placed the palm of her hand against his chest. "Mmmm," she said. "I like it."

Feiler elbowed him again. "Take her upstairs, you asshole."

"Why don't *you*?"

"Because I've got this one here." He squeezed the big breast of the stout prostitute sitting on his lap.

She turned around. "Oh, hello there," she said to Blohm.

"Hello."

"You're the one who just got a medal, aren't you?"

"Yes."

She leaned toward him and pursed her lips. "Let me give you a kiss, baby."

The blonde pushed her away. "He's mine! I saw him first."

"You're so selfish, Renée!"

Feiler buried his face in the stout prostitute's bosom. "Let's go upstairs!"

"I thought you'd never ask."

Feiler pushed the table back. The stout prostitute stood up and Feiler followed her across the dance floor to the stairs. Blohm reached over and punched Grunberger lightly on the arm. "You lucky son of a bitch."

"Lucky?" asked Grunberger drunkenly. "It wasn't luck. It was devotion to duty and heroism in the face of the enemy."

Kruger, sitting on the other side of Grunberger, raised his glass of champagne in the air. "To my ex-exec!" he bellowed. "May he sink them all!"

"Sink them all!" echoed Blohm, touching the rim of his glass to Kruger's and Grunberger's.

The girl sitting next to Grunberger was groping between his legs. Kruger burped loudly and filled his glass with more champagne while his prostitute ran her fingers through his hair.

"Hello," said a female voice.

Blohm looked up and saw Julie standing there in a clinging white knee-length dress with a low bodice.

"Hello," Blohm said, looking up at her.

"I heard you were here yesterday asking for me."

Blohm moved the blonde off his lap and stood up. "Yes."

"Hey!" said the blonde, smoothing her dress.

Julie smiled confidently at Blohm. "I've been waiting for you all day."

"I've been busy."

"Want to come upstairs?"

Blohm walked toward her and stopped a few inches away, looking at her face. He wanted to tell her how much he missed her, but his friends would laugh at him.

"Your new medal looks very nice," she said.

"Thank you. You look very nice, too."

Kruger pounded on the table. "I think I'm going to throw up!"

Grunberger laughed. "I think he's in love with the whore!"

"Blohm!" shouted Kruger. "Wait till I tell the Führer that you're in love with a whore!"

"And a French whore at that!" added Grunberger.

Blohm was hurt by their remarks, and knew the only way to fend them off was to be as coarse as they. He turned to the table, drained his glass of champagne, and said, "I'll see the both of you later. I'm going upstairs for a good fuck."

"Give her a push for me!" said Kruger.

"When you come, think of the Führer!" howled Grunberger.

Blohm placed his hand around Julie's waist and they walked to the stairs.

"You're drunk," she said.

"Partially on the liquor and partially on your beauty," he replied.

"You're sweet sometimes."

"And sometimes I must behave like a swine in order to get along with all the other swine."

They ascended the stairs and walked to her room. She unlocked the door and they went inside. Before she could turn on the lamp, he kissed her hungrily, mashing his lips against hers, trying to devour her tongue.

They tumbled together to the bed and fell on top of it. He found the zipper of her dress and pulled it down. The dress fell away. He buried his face in her breasts.

"I love you," he mumbled, feeling wild and crazy.

In the morning Blohm felt nauseous. Gagging, he staggered to the sink in his hotel room and drank some water. Then he lit a cigarette and stood at the window, looking out at the square. He thought he must be mad to be in love with a French prostitute. But he knew that he *was* in love with her, and the fact that she was a French prostitute only made it more intense.

After they had finished, she had promised to meet him on her day off next Thursday. He'd smiled when she told him that, because it meant that she truly cared for him. Now, looking out the window at dawn breaking on the square, he realized that it didn't matter how many men went to bed with her, because nothing could defile her. She was a magnificent woman and his first real love.

He dressed quickly, because Kruger had told him that he wanted to see him at the U-boat pens to inspect the work being done on U-112. He went down to the dining room, had a cup of coffee and a croissant, then walked to the U-boat base nearby. The sun rose in the west behind him, giving a pink tinge to the trails of puffy clouds in the sky. He wore his tan duty uniform and dark-blue cap.

U-112 was in a pen underneath a bomb-proof concrete bunker. Workers were swarming over her and the U-boat in the next pen when he arrived, but Kruger wasn't there yet. Blohm stood on the walkway next to U-112, lit a cigarette, puffed it, continued toward the rear of the U-boat, kneeled down on the walkway, and examined the U-boat's after section, the metal smooth and covered with primer paint. Evidently they'd repaired the entire section, and the rudder and propeller mechanism underneath. U-112 would be ready for sea pretty soon.

He heard footsteps and stood up. Kruger walked toward him, also attired in tan duty uniform, but with his white captain's hat. Kruger looked at his watch, and Blohm realized this wasn't the Kruger of the night in the brothel. This was Kapitänleutnant Kruger, and the party was over.

Blohm saluted. "Good morning, sir."

Kruger's eyes were bloodshot and his face puffy as he returned the salute. "Good morning. Did you bring a pen with you?"

Blohm took his pen out of his shirt pocket. "Yes, sir."

"Let's go aboard."

They crossed the catwalk to U-112, and Kruger stopped beside the 8.8 gun. "It's good to be back again," he said wearily. "If I don't get to sea again pretty soon, I'm afraid I'll die."

They climbed the ladder to the bridge, then descended into the conning tower. It smelled of oil and fresh paint and looked brand new. "Very nice," Kruger said, looking around. He smiled, tapped the periscope, continued to the computer, and pressed some of the buttons. "Lovely."

They lowered themselves into the control room, where workmen were fiddling with the innards of the hydroplane mechanism. The floor plates had been removed, exposing the ballast and fuel tanks underneath.

They moved aft and saw that floor plates had been removed in the petty officers' quarters and the galley too, revealing batteries below. Some had been taken away, and the bilges painted. In the engine room they were surprised to find the starboard engine missing. A crew of mechanics worked on the port engine, its pistons lying on the deck.

"Where's my starboard engine?" Kruger asked.

One of the mechanics stood up and wiped his filthy hands on a rag. "You're getting a new one, sir."

"Why not two new ones?"

"This one's in serviceable condition, sir."

In the electric motor room Kruger and Blohm saw new steel plates on the bulkhead around the new, gleaming propeller shaft. Mechanics were tightening bolts and conducting tests of motors.

Kruger said, "Looks like a good job."

Mechanics smiled in appreciation of the remark. Kruger led Blohm forward, passing compartments they'd seen already, then inspecting the forward compartment. The floor plates had been removed there, too, and the bulkheads freshly painted.

They returned to the wardroom and sat at the table. Kruger dictated some letters to Blohm and told him to type them up. One letter was to Flotillenkapitän Weisacker with copies to the chief of mechanics, and the other was to the chief of mechanics with copies to Weisacker.

"All right," said Kruger, "I'll leave you here to finish typing. Since Grunberger no longer is with us, you'll have to assume his duties until a new exec arrives. I want you to see the quartermaster and submit a list of our various requirements no later than seventeen hundred hours tomorrow. And I want you to check on our men and make sure we have a full complement when we go to sea. Then report to me and bring me up to date. Any questions?"

"When do you think we'll go out on patrol, sir?"

"I'd say within two weeks. That will be all, Blohm. Carry on."

"Yes, sir."

Kruger turned and left the wardroom. Blohm made his way to the typewriter in the radio shack, where he typed the letters Kruger had ordered, a cigarette dangling from the corner of his mouth and his hat low over his eyes. He hoped U-112 wouldn't go to sea before his Thursday date with Julie.

Days passed, agonizingly slowly. Blohm shuttled back and forth between the U-boat and the quartermaster's office. On some days he had to go to the repair office to discuss work being done on U-112, or to transmit instructions from Kruger.

On Thursday he hurried back to his hotel room, took a bath, and shaved the blond stubble on his upper lip and chin. He put on a dress uniform with his Iron Cross on the pocket, his visored blue hat worn at a jaunty angle. He left the hotel and walked across the square to the park across the street.

Julie sat on one of the benches, smoking a cigarette and smiling as he approached. She stood, he kissed her cheek, then looked at her, dumbfounded to see her without makeup and in ordinary clothes in the light of day. He thought she looked even more beautiful than when she was prettied up in the Crescent Palace.

"What would you like to do?" he asked nervously.

"Let's have a picnic. Would you like that?"

"Sounds marvelous."

They walked to a market nearby and bought bread, cheese, fruit, and wine. Blohm carried the bag as they set out for a park, passing other sailors and girls in the streets. Some Frenchmen were unable to hide their dismay at seeing French girls with Germans, but that didn't bother Blohm. If a people permitted themselves to be defeated in war, they deserved whatever indignities befell them.

The park overlooked the waterfront. Some young men were swimming at the beach, although it was early June and the water still quite cool. Blohm and Julie dined and drank wine, telling each other of their lives. Julie explained that she'd wanted to become an artist before the war broke out. Blohm told her of his days in the Hitler Youth Organization and the Naval Academy.

They finished the food and passed the bottle of wine back and forth as the flaming ball of sun sank slowly into the Bay of Biscay. Julie reached over and touched Blohm's Iron Cross, holding it in her fingers and gazing at it.

"You must be very brave to have received one of these."

"Oh, I don't know," he said shyly.

"What did you do?"

He shrugged. "Something foolish, I guess."

"What was it?"

"I shot down a British plane."

"All by yourself?"

"Yes."

She let the medal go, leaning back and looking at him. "You shot down a plane all by yourself?"

He nodded. "Yes."

"Was it shooting at you?"

"Yes."

She turned down the corners of her mouth. "That *was* very brave."

"I didn't realize it at the time, but I suppose it was. I was only following orders, and that's not hard for me because I've been following orders all my life."

"That's strange. You don't look like a military man."

"No? What do I look like?"

"A student of some kind. Of engineering, maybe. Or a chemist."

"I *was* a student until I arrived here a few months ago," he explained. "U-boat officers actually study a lot of engineering subjects. A U-boat is nothing more than a big complex machine, you know. Or perhaps it would be more accurate to say that it is a conglomeration of machines. The functions that cannot be performed by machines are done by men, but who knows, maybe machines will replace men in U-boats someday and there'll only be a handful of officers and men instead of the fifty-odd we have on our boats now."

"I hear that U-boat duty is very dangerous," she said, beginning her fishing expedition for information.

"No, it's not really that dangerous most of the time."

"But I often hear about U-boats that don't come back."

Blohm smiled superciliously. "I'd say that's usually because the commanders are incompetent. My commander, Kapitänleutnant Kruger, is excellent. He has nerves of steel. I've seen him in very tight situations, and he is always able to make calm and rational decisions."

"He's very famous, isn't he?"

"He's a hero throughout Germany. It's a great honor to be serving with him. He's sunk forty-two British ships."

"That many?"

"Yes, and he'll sink many more before this war is over."

She took a cigarette from her purse, and he lit it for her with a match. "Would you like to lie down and put your head on my lap?" she asked.

"Do I look tired?"

"A little."

He lay on the grass and rested his head on the sweetest, softest part of her body. The sun was half sunk in the water now, a cool breeze blowing in from the bay.

"What makes him so successful?" she asked. "Do you mind me asking?"

"No, I don't mind," he replied lazily. "But you wouldn't understand. It's very technical in part, and the other part is simply nerve and courage. Kruger isn't afraid of danger if it will bring him closer to a target."

"You know, I've always wondered why the British haven't figured a way to explode your torpedoes before they hit their ships. Surely there must be a way, don't you think?"

"Not that I know of," Blohm said. "Once a torpedo is on its way, it really can't be stopped. They move very fast, around forty kilometers an hour. You can't shoot one of them, particularly on the high seas."

Julie felt exasperated; she couldn't seem to elicit any useful information. "When are you going to sea again?"

"In about a week." He looked up at her. "You know, you ask a lot of questions."

"I'm very curious about your life in the U-boats," she explained. "Have you ever been depth-charged?"

"Oh yes," he said proudly. "Many times."

"What was it like?"

"Scary. Once we were depth-charged for five hours straight."

"You're very lucky to have returned to Lorient."

"Not really," he said.

"No? It seems that after five hours at least one of those depth charges might have hit you."

Blohm was relaxed, tipsy from wine, immature, and wanted to impress his girlfriend, blind to the abyss yawning before him. "They couldn't hit us," he admitted.

"Why not?"

He sneered. "Because the fools don't set their depth charges to go off as deeply as we go. We simply submerge to our maximum depth of 250 meters, and their depth charges explode high over our heads. You'd think they would know better by now, but the British are such fools."

"They must be," she said, puffing her cigarette and realizing this time she had picked up some information that might be important.

CHAPTER 13

U-435 backed out of its pen, Kapitänleutnant Grunberger standing on the bridge in his new white cap, binoculars hanging from his neck, anxious to sink British ships on his first patrol. The band played and the nurses threw flowers. Flotillenkapitän Weisacker saluted, Grunberger saluted back, and when the U-boat was clear of the pier, Grunberger gave the orders that turned the boat around and sent it humming toward the Bay of Biscay.

Grunberger had been yearning for this day ever since he was a little boy playing with toy boats in a lake near his home in Bavaria. He had been an Oberleutnant when Britain declared war on Germany in 1939, and now at last had his own command. He felt nearly drunk with authority, undisputed king of U-435, and men would jump every time he opened his mouth.

The U-boat made its way to the bay. Grunberger thought of when he'd stood on the bridge of U-112 with Kapitänleutnant Kruger, obeying Kruger's every command. Now that was all over. Now he was a U-boat commander, and hoped to become an ace like Kruger someday.

He had observed Kruger carefully during his two years of duty with him, and knew how Kruger had become a U-boat ace. Grunberger was certain he could do as well himself, and perhaps one day he too might win the Knight's Cross. Then Kruger would treat him as an equal instead of a subordinate.

Oberleutnant Marcks, his new second-in-command, went below to gather the detail that would clear the deck of flowers.

Grunberger looked ahead to the bay. Once he got out there he might be spotted by a British plane or boat. Marcks returned to the bridge with men who climbed down the ladder of the conning tower and began throwing the flowers into the water.

"Steer right forty degrees!" shouted Grunberger.

"Right forty degrees!" replied Leutnant Dolsch at the helm.

"Both engines ahead two-thirds!"

"Both engines ahead two-thirds!"

U-435 picked up speed. Grunberger breathed deeply, hoping the salt air would clean the tobacco smoke out of his lungs and give him energy. He always felt weak after leaving Lorient. Continual debauchery was bad for him, but he couldn't stop indulging. None of them could. They were all like madmen in Lorient.

Grunberger thought of his shipmates aboard U-112 and felt melancholy. He'd become close friends with Kruger, Feiler, and the rest. Now he was with a crew whom he hardly knew, and since he was their captain, wouldn't be able to relax with them. Common danger and accomplishment would eventually weld them together into a fighting team, but until then relations would be strained on U-435.

The crew cleared the deck of flowers and returned to their stations below. Grunberger, Marcks, and Ensign Hagen stood on the bridge, scanning the sea and air through their binoculars.

Marcks cleared his throat. "Lovely day, sir," he said, trying to make conversation.

"Good visibility gives an advantage to the enemy," Grunberger replied. "Keep your eyes peeled."

"Yes, sir."

"How're you doing, Hagen?" Marcks said to the young ensign.

"Fine, sir." It was Hagen's first patrol.

"Good."

Grunberger looked straight ahead. He was headed toward square AK 42, where he would take his position in a wolf pack that was forming. Naval intelligence had learned that a big convoy with ten oil tankers was headed toward England from Halifax. Admiral Dönitz had ordered that every one of those tankers be sunk.

As U-435 motored toward its position, Kapitänleutnant Grunberger wondered how many of them he'd send to the bottom.

U-435 arrived on station two days later and began cruising back and forth in its square, looking for the big convoy. After three days Grunberger began to think that the convoy had taken a different route, bypassing the wolf pack that was strung out like a necklace of teeth in its path.

On the fourth day, while Grunberger was on the bridge early in the morning, Ensign Hagen climbed the ladder from the conning tower, a piece of paper in his hand.

"A message just has come in, sir!" he said excitedly.

Grunberger snatched the paper out of his hand, thinking that the convoy had at last been spotted. Elated, he held the paper before his eyes. His smile wilted on his face as he read:

ATTENTION ALL U-BOATS. THE WEHRMACHT HAS ATTACKED RUSSIA AND IS OVERWHELMING ALL RESISTANCE. THE FÜHRER PREDICTS VICTORY IN SIX WEEKS. WE MUST DO AT SEA WHAT OUR WEHRMACHT IS DOING ON LAND. HAPPY HUNTING. ADMIRAL DÖNITZ.

Grunberger blinked and handed the message to Oberleutnant Marcks. Marcks read it and blanched. "A two-front war," he said unhappily.

"Take the bridge," Grunberger told him. "I'm going below."

Grunberger descended the ladder to the control room, went to his cabin, and closed the door. He took off his white hat, hung it on the peg, and sat on his bunk. Resting his chin on his fist, he closed his eyes and sighed. Marcks had said it correctly: Germany was now in a two-front war. She had lost the last war because she couldn't fight on two fronts, and now she was fighting on two fronts again.

What stupidity, Grunberger thought. *What's wrong with them? How can we fight the entire world?* He'd thought Hitler had been clever when he'd signed the peace pact with Stalin in 1939, but why was he going to war against him now? Did the Führer know something that Grunberger didn't? *Yes, that must be it,* Grunberger thought. *Perhaps there are new weapons or a special, unbeatable strategy.* A chill passed over him when he thought that England might attack on the other front, then what would Germany do?

Grunberger wanted to believe Admiral Dönitz. He wanted to have confidence that the Wehrmacht could defeat Russia in six weeks, but Grunberger had been an avid student of history when at the academy and knew what had happened to Napoleon in Russia. He also knew that Hitler was no Napoleon.

Grunberger felt depressed, but dared not convey that to his crew. He'd have to make a little speech to pass the information officially to them, although they'd probably found out already from gossip originated by the radioman. What could he say to them? He wished Kruger were there to handle the task. Kruger could deliver a rousing speech whether he felt it or not.

Grunberger did not think he could do that. Then he decided how to proceed: he'd merely read the telegram from Admiral Dönitz. That ought to take care of everything. Problem solved.

In the middle of the night, while U-435 was cruising on the surface, another message came through from U-boat headquarters.

CONVOY AJ 33 COURSE 85° TEN KNOTS INTERCEPT AND REPORT CONTACT.

Grunberger and Marcks were asleep when the message arrived. The third watch officer, Leutnant Holmann, received it on the bridge. It was a clear, starry night with a half-moon hanging in the sky, the sea relatively calm. Holmann read the message and wondered whether to awaken Grunberger or set a course for the convoy himself. He decided to be on the safe side and awaken Grunberger.

"Take the bridge," Holmann said to Chief Petty Officer Prager.

"Yes, sir."

Holmann descended the ladder into the U-boat and made his way forward to Grunberger's cabin, knocking on the door.

"What is it?" said Grunberger.

"Message from headquarters."

"Come in!"

Holmann opened the door as Grunberger sat up in his narrow cot and placed his feet on the deck. Holmann noticed Grunberger's hairy, muscular legs and gnarled toes. On the little stand beside the bed was a portrait of Grunberger's wife and four-year-old son. Holmann handed Grunberger the message.

"So they've found the damned thing," Grunberger said sleepily. "It's about time. Return to the bridge."

"Yes, sir."

Holmann left Grunberger's cabin. Grunberger dressed quickly, shambled forward to the officers' quarters and opened the door. The officers were asleep in their tiers of cots, some snoring, some curled up like babies not making a sound. Grunberger walked toward Marcks and shook his shoulder. Marcks opened his eyes.

"Meet me in the control room right away," Grunberger said.

"Yes, sir," Marcks croaked.

Grunberger left the officers' quarters and walked aft to the control room, where he saw the night watch at their stations, taking it easy because U-435 was moving in a straight line on the surface. He stopped at the chart table and looked down at their course. Grunberger placed his forefinger on square AJ 33; he figured it was about three hours away. However, the convoy was in motion, heading east, so it should take no more than two hours for U-435 to reach it provided the convoy stayed on a generally easterly course.

Marcks, his hat on the back of his head, buttoned his shirt as he joined Grunberger at the chart table. Grunberger handed him the message. "Plot a course that will intercept the convoy, then bring it to me on the bridge."

"Yes, sir."

Grunberger climbed the stairs to the bridge, smelling the cool, salty night air. He looked up at the blazing heavens and the half-moon in the sky.

"Lovely night, sir," Hagen said.

"Yes."

Grunberger raised his binoculars and scanned the horizon to the east, but there was nothing except darkness and mystery.

"Look, sir!"

One of the seamen was pointing at the sky. Grunberger looked up and saw a comet hurtling toward earth, a trail of fire behind it. It was high in the sky, just to the right of the moon, then suddenly its flames were extinguished and it disappeared from the sky.

Just like a human life, Grunberger thought, as he gazed into the dark part of the sky where the comet had come from.

The convoy was HX 167, bound from Halifax to Liverpool, and on its right flank was the escort destroyer *Corinthia*. Commander Michael Scott was sleeping in his cabin when there was a knock on his door. Scott awakened immediately, because the convoy was in the danger zone of the Atlantic.

"Come in!"

The executive officer, Lieutenant Commander Allan Rutherford, opened the door and stood silhouetted against the light in the corridor. "We're picking up heavy U-boat radio traffic, sir."

"Close?"

"We think so, sir."

"Double the watch. I'll be up on the bridge directly."

"Yes, sir."

Rutherford closed the door, plunging Scott's cabin into darkness. Scott turned on the light atop his bunk. His eyes fell on the photograph of Ruthie, who was back in Cornwall now, a schoolteacher and member of the local church council. He missed her, but didn't have time for melancholy longing.

He put on his white turtleneck sweater and blue uniform, left his cabin, and made his way to the compartment occupied by the radar operator Harold Darby.

"Keep a sharp eye out," Scott told Darby. "There are U-boats in the vicinity."

"Yes, sir."

Scott looked over Darby's shoulder at the radar screen. A bar of light moved slowly around the screen from its center. Scott could see blips of light that indicated other ships in the convoy, but nothing else on the screen. Scott knew how wolf packs operated: As soon as one of them spotted a convoy, it notified the others. Then they all moved in for the kill. According to the radar screen, the wolf pack had still not arrived, but one U-boat must be maintaining contact someplace, probably at the rear of the convoy. Scott thought it might be a good idea to go to there and try to find the trailing U-boat. If he could locate it and drive it down, the convoy could change course and perhaps elude the wolf pack for a while.

Scott picked up the radio telephone and spoke the call letters of Captain Forester, the escort commander in the destroyer *Barrow*.

"What is it, Scotty?" Forester asked.

"Request permission to scout the rear of the convoy for a trailing U-boat, sir."

"I've already sent the *Tudor* back there."

"We're picking up a lot of U-boat traffic, sir."

"So are we. When they come, we'll be ready for them. Anything else?"

"No, sir."

"Over and out."

Scott hung up the radio telephone and walked out onto the bridge. He saw officers and men facing in all directions, peering at the field of view before them through binoculars. Scott gripped the bridge rail and peered ahead into the night. Liverpool was five days away, and he knew he wouldn't get much rest until the convoy reached port. He raised his binoculars and swept the horizon, wondering when the wolf pack would attack.

Ten minutes later a seaman rushed to the bridge and handed Scott a message. It was from the *Tudor* and was addressed to Captain Forester.

HAVE SIGHTED U-BOAT BEARING 240 AND FORCED HER DOWN.

Scott knew what was coming now: a radical change in course. He handed the message back to the seaman. As the seaman was returning to the radio shack, another seaman with a message passed him in the doorway.

"This just came in, sir."

Scott looked at the message. As he'd anticipated, it was a change in course to the south.

"Steer right to one hundred forty-five degrees!" Scott shouted.

"Steer right to one hundred forty-five degrees!" repeated the helmsman.

The *Corinthia* swerved to starboard along with the rest of the convoy. Scott raised his binoculars and scanned the horizon once more, hoping the maneuver would carry them far away from the wolf pack.

At U-boat headquarters in Kerneval near Lorient, Admiral Dönitz folded his arms and studied his chart of the Atlantic Ocean. A light on the ceiling illuminated the chart table, but the rest of the room was in semi-darkness. A group of staff officers stood around the table with Dönitz.

In square AK 27 was a formation of wooden models representing convoy HX 167. In the convoy's path was a row of eight wooden U-boat shapes, and behind the convoy was one U-boat.

Dönitz raised his hand and stroked his chin thoughtfully. If the convoy proceeded on course, it would reach the line of U-boats in about two hours. He had ordered the U-boats to attack the flanks of the convoy upon contact and was confident of reasonable success.

They probably wouldn't sink all of the tankers, but at least half would be sent to the bottom. His intelligence sources indicated that there were more than fifty ships in the convoy. Dönitz was anticipating a victorious night for his wolf pack.

A young ensign rushed toward him with a message. "Sir, this just came in."

Dönitz looked at the message and frowned.

FORCED DOWN BY ESCORT. LOST CONTACT WITH CONVOY. U-380.

Dönitz passed the message to one of his aides, rested his hands on the map table, and leaned closer to the configuration of convoy ships and U-boats. The convoy would change course now, either north or south. He would need to split up his wolf pack to cover both possibilities. That meant four would move north and four south, which decreased the likelihood that his U-boats would intercept the convoy again on the tractless wastes of the ocean. He'd send the trailing U-boat due east so it would pick up the convoy again if it ever returned to its original course.

It was a cat-and-mouse game, one Dönitz was certain he could win if he had more U-boats, but at the start of the war

Hitler was more impressed by battleships like the *Bismarck* and the *Graf Spee*. Now the Führer was coming around to his position, for the *Bismarck* and the *Graf Spee* had been sunk, revealing big battleships as liabilities.

Despite the difficulties of this present chase, Dönitz was optimistic that his wolf pack could locate convoy HX 167 again. He raised his finger in the air, and an aide came running over. Dönitz dictated orders that would split the wolf pack and send the U-boats searching once more for the convoy.

Grunberger was on the bridge of U-435 when the message from U-380 came in. When he read it, he realized that the convoy would change course and new orders could be expected from U-Boat headquarters. Sure enough, new orders came within minutes. U-435 would become part of the southern wolf pack patrol.

He told his helmsman to steer a southerly course, then went to the navigation table with Marcks and plotted a more accurate course to the new square where Admiral Dönitz had told him to go. Returning to the bridge, he told the helmsman the new course, then raised his binoculars and scanned the ocean for the dark, hulking shapes of ships in a convoy.

He stood on the bridge for a half-hour, receiving reports from other U-boats about their positions and lack of luck in spotting the convoy. Finally he decided to go below and get some rest so that he could direct an attack with a clear, rested mind if the convoy were encountered.

"Take the bridge, Leutnant Marcks," he said. "Awaken me immediately if the convoy is found."

"Yes, sir."

Grunberger descended into the bowels of the U-boat and returned to his cabin. After removing shoes, hat, and jacket, he lay on his bunk with the rest of his clothes on. He lit a cigarette and smoked it, listening to waves crashing against the hull of the U-boat as it made its way through the ocean.

On the bridge of the *Corinthia,* Commander Michael Scott stood with his watch officers, looking through binoculars for the outline of a U-boat or its white wake. The breeze had increased in the last hour, dotting the tops of the waves with froth, and a half moon was sinking low on the horizon. It was three o'clock in the morning; dawn would break in another few hours. If they could elude the U-boats until then, they would have some hours of peace until the next night.

His radioman had reported messages transmitted between the wolf pack and its headquarters in France. Scott wished they had a way of knowing the German code, because those messages contained information that might save British lives.

At any rate, Scott knew that the wolf pack was out there, searching for the convoy. He peered through his binoculars, hoping he could sight the U-boats before they attacked.

All was silent in the headquarters room except for the sound of Morse code on the radio. Officers gathered around in the darkness, hoping that the wolf pack would establish contact with the convoy again.

Admiral Dönitz stood with his arms folded beside the map table, his brow furrowed in thought as he gazed at the models of ships and U-boats. His wolf pack was in position now, ready to intercept the convoy over a huge range of ocean, but there were many open areas where the convoy could go. Dönitz pinched his lips together as he realized that with only a dozen more U-boats, the convoy could not possibly get away from him. He glanced at his watch; morning would come soon.

The events of the next hour would decide whether the convoy would get away.

An ensign rushed to Commander Scott on the bridge of the *Corinthia*. "Another change in course, sir."

Scott looked at the message and saw that the convoy would swing east again. He concurred with the move because he thought it best for the convoy to continue zigzagging.

"Bring her one hundred ten degrees to port!" he shouted into the voice tube.

"One hundred ten degrees to port," replied the helmsman.

The *Corinthia* and the rest of the convoy made wide white arcs in the water as it steered toward the British Isles.

Torpedoman Kable, on watch duty on the bridge of U-435, thought he saw dark lumps on the horizon. He blinked, because he'd been on watch for ninety minutes, then peered through his binoculars again. The lumps were still there.

"I think I see something dead to starboard, sir," he said to Oberleutnant Marcks.

Marcks swung his binoculars in that direction and became electrified by what he perceived in the darkness. He'd been on U-boat patrols since the beginning of the war, and had seen convoys on nights like this before. It was the one they had been searching for. Evidently U-435 had spotted it first.

"Take the bridge!" he said to the third watch officer, Leutnant Schreiber.

"Yes, sir."

Marcks dropped down the ladder into the U-boat and dashed to Kapitänleutnant Grunberger's cabin, pounding on the bulkhead.

"Come in!" said Grunberger.

Marcks peered inside. "We've sighted the convoy, sir!"

"Have you reported to headquarters yet?"

"No, sir."

"Do so now. Then report to me on the bridge."

"Yes, sir."

Marcks ran off. Grunberger jammed his feet into his boots, put on his hat and jacket, grabbed his package of cigarettes, and left the cabin. Making his way to the control room, he saw Marcks conferring with the radioman. Grunberger climbed to the bridge and saw all the men there looking to starboard. He pushed a seaman out of his way, raised his binoculars, and looked at the convoy. U-435 was pointed in a westerly direction, and the convoy appeared to be heading to the northeast.

"Steer eighty degrees to starboard!" said Grunberger.

"Starboard eighty degrees!"

"Both engines ahead full!"

"Both engines ahead full!"

U-435 responded instantly, swinging around in the water, then roaring toward the convoy on the horizon.

"They've found the convoy, sir!" said the ensign to Admiral Dönitz.

Dönitz took the piece of paper from the ensign's hand, read the position and bearing of the convoy, then looked at his map table to relate it to the positions of the U-boats in his wolf pack. Bending over the table, he moved the U-boats into the positions where he wanted them to go.

"Plot courses for these U-boats," he said to his navigation officer, "and have them transmitted to the commanders immediately."

"Yes, sir."

Dönitz watched as the officer laid his parallel rulers on the map table and began plotting courses. He turned to the ensign who'd handed him the message. "Which U-boat was it?"

"U-435, sir."

"U-435?" Dönitz asked. "Is that Schuster?"

"No, sir. Grunberger."

"Ah, Grunberger," Dönitz said with a smile. "He used to be Kruger's exec. No wonder he found the convoy first."

Lieutenant-Commander Rutherford approached Scott on the bridge of the *Corinthia*. "The radioman reports a lot of U-boat radio traffic, sir."

"Uh-oh," Scott said, not removing the binoculars from his eyes. "They've probably found us again."

Scott scanned the water, looking for the sinister shape of a U-boat. He expected that Captain Forester was aware of the U-boat radio traffic and would order a change of course again.

The horn on the bridge gave two short blasts. Scott reached behind him and picked up the ship's phone. "Captain speaking."

"Sir, this is Darby," said the radar operator excitedly. "I've got a blip on my screen!"

"Bearing?"

"One hundred twenty degrees, sir! Range two thousand yards!"

"Keep an eye on it."

"Yes, sir!"

Scott hung up the phone. "Steer one hundred forty degrees! All ahead full! *Battle stations!*"

The howler went off as the *Corinthia* changed course, heading for the blip that Darby had reported. Men poured out of the hatches, fastening helmets and life jackets, running to guns and depth-charge equipment. Scott ordered that messages be sent to the convoy and escort commanders, notifying them that the *Corinthia* was tracking a suspicious blip on the radar screen. Then Scott moved to the bridge rail, leaned against it, and looked through his binoculars at the sea ahead.

He couldn't see a damn thing. He hoped the radar wasn't acting up again.

Ensign Hagen was the first to see the destroyer bearing down on them. "Enemy destroyer dead ahead!" he cried.

Grunberger's jaw twitched as he strained his eyes and saw through the lenses of his binoculars a dark, ominous form on the near side of the convoy.

"Hard right rudder!" he yelled.

"Hard right rudder!"

U-435 pivoted in the water, turning away from the convoy.

"Marcks!"

"Yes, sir!"

"Notify headquarters that we've been spotted by an enemy destroyer and are taking evasive action!"

"Yes, sir!"

"And give them the convoy's last position!"

"Yes, sir!"

Marcks dropped down the ladder as U-435 turned away from the enemy destroyer. Grunberger looked back at it, wondering how it had seen U-435 from such a great distance. "Rudder amidships! Both engines full ahead!"

"Rudder amidships — both engines full ahead!"

The U-boat gathered speed and pushed through the water. Grunberger looked back at the destroyer through his binoculars and thought he'd try to outrun it. At any rate, he'd already passed the message on. The other U-boats would continue to zero in on the convoy.

They would not let it get away.

"I see it, sir!" said a seaman on the bridge of the *Corinthia*.

"Where?" asked Scott.

"Over there!" The seaman pointed straight ahead.

Scott squinted through his binoculars and saw the dagger-like shape of the U-boat in the gray waves.

"Send up a snowflake!"

There was a puffing sound as the rocket shot into the air. It exploded and night became day. Scott looked at the U-boat through his binoculars. "Forward battery open fire!"

There was an explosion as the forward battery fired its first shell, which landed to the right and far ahead of the U-boat. Scott determined that he was gaining on the U-boat and it most probably would dive soon. He wished he had one of those new depth-charge launchers that he'd heard about, the ones that shot depth charges ahead of the destroyer instead of having to be dropped off the stern. Experimental models had been installed on a few destroyers, and Scott wanted one now, because he'd lose Asdic contact with the U-boat when he passed over it to drop depth charges. The new device would have permitted him to maintain contact.

The horn gave two short blasts. Scott picked up the telephone. "This is the captain."

"This is the radio room. The escort commander advises that he's sending the Digby to assist."

"Send my thanks to the escort commander."

"Yes, sir."

"Asdic?" Scott asked on the intercom.

"This is Asdic," replied a low, disembodied voice.

"The U-boat will dive any minute now. Stay on your toes."

"Yes, sir."

The U-boat was zigzagging as the forward battery fired again. The shell threw a fountain of water into the air to the left of the U-boat. Scott could see the U-boat without his binoculars now. The *Corinthia* was closing fast, and the U-boat would submerge at any moment.

"Depth-charge crew stand by!" Scott said into the voice tube.

"Yes, sir!" said the hollow voice inside.

Grunberger looked back at the destroyer and frowned. It was gaining steadily on U-435, and he wouldn't be able to outrace it.

"There's another one coming, sir!" said Ensign Hagen, pointing to the port side of the destroyer.

Grunberger raised his binoculars and spotted the second destroyer immediately, plowing through the waves. He realized that his boat would be in for a difficult time, but it shouldn't be too bad if he brought her down to maximum depth quickly.

He hesitated a moment, wondering if he should try to fire a torpedo at the lead destroyer, but decided he didn't have enough expertise as a U-boat commander for something fancy like that. He'd never worked with Marcks on a real surface attack before. He only had one alternative, and he thought he'd better take it right away.

"Down to the cellar!" he shouted.

"To the cellar!" repeated Wencke, his chief engineer.

The howler went off, and the men scrambled down the ladder into the U-boat. In every compartment men turned cranks that closed valves. Hydroplane operators pushed their wheels to the extreme dive position. Ballast operators opened valves that flooded the ballast tanks.

A U-boat could become totally submerged in only thirty-eight seconds. U-435 was going down fast. The ocean roared over her decks and smashed against the bridge. Grunberger steadied himself against the periscope in the conning tower and watched the needle on the depth gauge. The bridge slipped under the waves, and all was silent on the U-boat.

"It might be rough for a few moments," Grunberger told the men in the conning tower, attempting to mimic the cockiness Kruger always displayed in times like this, "but we'll be all right after that."

He looked at Marcks, Hagen, and Schreiber, imagining that they saw him as he used to see Kruger: the man who could get them through anything. Grunberger grinned confidently so that they could see that he wasn't afraid, but deep in his heart he wished Kruger were there.

"She's diving!" somebody shouted.

Scott saw the U-boat slow and dip her snout beneath the waves. He grabbed the ship's intercom and said: "Asdic!"

"Asdic, sir," said the voice in his ear.

"She's diving. Let me know when you make contact."

"Yes, sir."

"Radio room!"

"This is the radio room, sir."

"Connect me with the *Digby*!"

"Yes, sir!"

Scott heard static in his ear, then a human voice. "Leftenant Hall here."

"Commander Scott here. Let me speak with your captain."

"Yes, sir!"

There was a pause, then a new voice came through the earphone. "Commander Prudhoe here."

"This is Scott. The U-boat is submerging directly in front of me. Can you see her?"

"Yes, we can."

"Good. I'm going to pass over and give her some depth charges as soon as I can. I want you to pick her up on your Asdic and hold her for us."

"Will do."

"Over and out."

The *Corinthia* plowed to the spot where the U-boat had submerged. Scott braced himself against the bridge rail and held the phone tightly to his face.

"Prepare to drop a pattern of ten depth charges!" he shouted.

The order was repeated by the commander of the depth-charge crew as the *Corinthia* thundered closer to the swirling bubbles left by the U-boat. The *Corinthia* passed over the bubbles. Scott looked back at the stern of his ship. "Turn 'em loose!"

Barrels of TNT rolled down their tracks and over the stern of the *Corinthia*. In twos they splashed in the water and began to sink. Scott had compensated for his calculation that the U-boat would try to sneak away at top speed underwater, moving more or less in the direction it had been moving when it dived so it could maintain momentum.

He looked back at the wake of the *Corinthia* and waited for the depth charges to explode.

On U-435 they heard the pinging of the Asdic, then the rumbling engines of the destroyer as it passed overhead.

"Hang on!" said Grunberger.

They heard splashing sounds of depth charges and waited, looking up, holding on to whatever was nearby. Grunberger struggled to keep his face impassive while he tried furiously to outfox the destroyer above.

"There's another ship coming, sir," said the sound man.

Grunberger made a decision. "Hard left rudder!"

"Hard left rudder!" repeated the helmsman, pressing his port steering button.

The U-boat swung to the side as the first two depth charges exploded to the starboard rear of the U-boat, making it twist and shudder.

"Not even close," sneered Grunberger, looking at the depth gauge. U-435 was down to 100 meters. The destroyer moved to the U-boat's starboard side.

More depth charges exploded. The U-boat trembled, lights flickering. When the water became still again, the men looked at each other and grinned. The Tommies didn't know where they were.

"Rudder amidships!" Grunberger said.

"Rudder amidships!"

"Both motors ahead full!"

"Both motors ahead full!"

The ping of Asdic hit the hull. Grunberger heard the destroyer turning to make another pass. The second destroyer sounded farther away evidently circling slowly. Grunberger knew the game they were playing. One destroyer was holding him on Asdic while the other came in for the kill. He looked at the depth gauge: down to 200 meters. He'd be out of their range soon.

"What bearing is the closest one on?" he asked the hydroplane operator.

"One hundred sixty degrees, sir."

"Hard right rudder!"

"Hard right rudder!"

The U-boat turned as it descended, presenting its rear end to the onrushing destroyer. It was a trick Grunberger had learned from Kruger: it gave the Asdic beam the smallest possible target to work on.

"Time?" asked Grunberger.

"Oh-three-thirty hours, sir," replied the navigator.

The thrashing, whining sound of the destroyer's propellers came closer. Grunberger bit his lower lip, then checked himself because he didn't want his crew to see him doing that. The destroyer came directly overhead; Asdic continued to hit the hull like tiny pebbles. Grunberger couldn't hear if depth charges were being dropped. The destroyer was moving too quickly, the U-boat too far down. He straightened his head and looked at the depth gauge. They were at 220 meters. It wouldn't be long before they were below the range of the destroyer's depth charges. The next ten minutes would be crucial.

There was a crashing, exploding roar. The U-boat lurched to the side, lights blinking out.

"Emergency lights!" shouted Grunberger.

The emergency lights came on, showing men holding on to pipes and bracing their legs. A new explosion rattled the U-boat and pushed the bow down. Another depth charge exploded underneath the U-boat, shaking it as though an enraged giant held it in his fist.

"Damage report?" Grunberger asked calmly.

The U-boat's compartments reported, from aft to forward. No serious damage anywhere. Grunberger pushed his white cap toward the back of his head and looked at the depth gauge. They were at 250 meters, the maximum operating depth as guaranteed by the builders. The compartments reported no damage. So far, so good. He looked at Marcks and smiled.

"They don't know where we are," Grunberger said.

Marcks smiled back jauntily.

A mighty thunderclap smashed the U-boat. Emergency lights went out. Grunberger heard a gush of water as he struggled to regain his footing.

"We're taking water!" someone shouted.

"Remain calm," Grunberger said, forcing his voice to become even. He opened an emergency locker and took out a flashlight. Someone turned on another flashlight. A jet of water shot straight across the conning tower from a spot somewhere behind the depth gauge.

"Someone get that, please," Grunberger said.

Hagen reached up and turned a knob. The jet of water slackened and stopped.

"Can someone fix the lights?" Grunberger asked.

The electrician's mate scrambled aft. Grunberger focused his flashlight on the depth gauge. They were at 275 meters. He smiled. They were far below the designated limit.

"Damage report?" he asked.

Reports came in: the intake diesel flanges were leaking, but not too badly. Grunberger decided not to turn on the pumps because the sound would give them away to the destroyers. Emergency lights came on. The maddening sound of the Asdic continued to ping against the hull.

"Time?" he asked.

"Oh-three-fifty hours, sir."

"Bearing?"

"Two hundred ten degrees, sir."

"Hard right rudder."

"Hard right rudder."

"Steer twenty-five degrees."

"Steer twenty-five degrees."

Grunberger heard the destroyer approaching again as Asdic scratched across the U-boat's hull. The depth gauge read 300 meters. Grunberger relaxed. The worst was over. He looked up, heard the destroyer coming closer, and imagined the depth charges splashing down and falling through the blue water, trailing bubbles.

A sledgehammer blow knocked him to his knees, and the emergency lights went out again. He felt stunned, and frightened for the first time: the depth charge should not have come this close at his present depth. He checked the gauge again — the U-boat was at 300 meters!

"Hard left rudder!" he shouted.

"Hard left rudder!"

Grunberger heard another violent explosion, this one underneath the U-boat. He began to perspire, realizing that evidently the Tommies had new depth charges set to go off deeper than their previous ones.

"Steer eighty degrees!" he ordered.

"Steer eighty degrees!"

"Damage report?"

Before the reports could begin, the U-boat received another terrible whack against its hull, then another. Grunberger became confused. The standard tactic against depth charges was to drop as quickly as possible below range and stay there until the destroyer went away.

"Sir," said the engineering officer, flashing his light on the depth gauge. "We're far below our maximum depth."

Grunberger looked at the gauge and saw that the needle was indeed creeping lower.

"Bow up!" he said. "Level her off!"

The hydroplane operators turned their wheels. Grunberger felt the boat move to an even keel.

"Let's have that damage report!" Grunberger said.

Voices came over the loudspeaker, reporting leaks throughout the boat, but nothing serious. Another hard blow jolted the U-boat, and Grunberger's ears rang from the sound. A loud crackling could be heard throughout the boat. In the glare of the flashlights Hagen looked at Grunberger in alarm.

"It's only the woodwork," Grunberger said calmly. "Why can't the lights be fixed?"

"Working on it, sir," said the electrician's mate over the loudspeaker.

Another explosion rattled floorplates. Grunberger took off his hat, wiped his forehead with the back of his sleeve, and tried to think of something to do, but no promising course of action came to mind. He couldn't go deeper because the pressure would cave in the hull. If he went higher, the depth charges surely would get him. All he could do was try to outmaneuver the destroyers, although they had their infernal Asdic. He heard it rattle against the U-boat's hull.

"Both motors half ahead!" he shouted. "Hard left rudder. Steer 200 degrees!"

The helmsman repeated orders and pulled on the wheel. U-435 began to turn around; Grunberger's plan was to double back on his tracks. There was another explosion, followed by a roar and a crackling. Water gushed into the control room.

"Stop that leak!" Grunberger screamed, flashing his light on to it.

It was a geyser thick as a man's wrist, shooting straight down from a pipe above the ballast controls. Its force knocked one of the ballast-control operators against the bulkhead. Marcks jumped up and clawed at the pipes, turning valves. Hagen joined him along with the other ballast control operator.

Finally they found the right valves, and the geyser diminished to a trickle.

"Where are the lights?" Grunberger shouted.

"Working on it, sir!" replied the electrician over the loudspeaker.

"You've been working on it long enough! You should have it fixed by now!"

"Another few minutes, sir."

Grunberger wrinkled his nose. "I smell oil! Everyone look for an oil leak!"

Flashlights were beamed in all directions. Grunberger aimed his at the depth gauge; they were still at 300 meters. He could hear the destroyer moving away. Was it going away for good, or preparing for another pass?

Grunberger took off his hat and ran his fingers through his hair. The sensation of his fingers against his scalp felt odd to him, reminding him of his body at a time when his mind was focusing on abstractions: What course would take U-435 to safety, how could he elude depth charges? When would the destroyers give up and go away?

The lights came on. Grunberger looked around. Two seamen charged toward the spot where black oil was squirting. They turned handles but couldn't stem the oil.

"Get a can under it!" Grunberger ordered.

One of the seamen ran back to the galley and returned a few moments later with an empty can, which he placed underneath the leak.

"Bearing?" Grunberger asked.

"One hundred degrees exactly," the hydroplane operator said.

Asdic rattled against the hull of the U-boat. Grunberger's only hope was that the rest of the wolf pack would attack the convoy, drawing one of the destroyers back for additional protection. Grunberger thought he might have a chance in eluding one destroyer with Asdic, but not two.

"He's getting closer," said the hydroplane operator.

"Everybody hang on to something," Grunberger replied.

Grunberger heard the destroyer advance. He wished he had a torpedo that could be launched from the deck of the U-boat, aimed electronically so that it climbed straight up and exploded through the bottom of that destroyer. What a surprise that would be for the Tommies.

"He's dropping his charges," the hydrophone operator said.

"Let him drop them," Grunberger snarled defiantly.

The Asdic pinged against the hull as the depth charges fell through the water. Grunberger's mouth was dry, and he felt a sharp pain in the center of his chest. He thought of his wife and son in Breslau, feeling guilty about his escapades in Lorient. Now, frightened by the depth charges, he wished he'd been more loyal to Marika.

The boat was shaken by a powerful explosion. The glass plate in front of the depth gauge burst to pieces, and Grunberger nearly thrown off his feet. He held on to a pipe, a trail of perspiration working down his stubbled cheek. Another explosion knocked him off balance again. The hull clattered from front to back.

"Calling the captain!" said a tense voice.

"What is it?" Grunberger replied.

"Diesel exhaust valves leaking considerably."

"Fix them."

"I might not be able to."

"Of course you can fix them!" Grunberger said angrily. "Get going!"

"Yes, sir."

"Any other damage?"

Before anyone could answer, the U-boat was racked by another explosion. Two seconds later came another. Lights went out again. Grunberger heard water squirting everywhere.

"Stop those leaks!" he yelled.

"Sir, the forward batteries are flooding!" someone reported. "Should I pump out the bilge?"

Grunberger gritted his teeth in the dark. If he turned on the pumps, the destroyers would be able to locate him more easily, and if he didn't he might lose power and speed.

"Sir," said another voice, "we're sinking."

Grunberger looked at the depth gauge, and sure enough they were down to 325 meters, 75 below the manufacturer's danger level for the hull.

"Forward up twenty," Grunberger said.

He heard the hydroplane operators grunting as the bow of the U-boat tipped upward.

"Both motors ahead full!" Grunberger said.

"Both ahead full!"

"Hard right rudder!"

"Hard right rudder!"

The lights flickered, then came on at full intensity. Grunberger looked around and saw stark terror on the faces of his officers and men. A depth charge exploded beside the conning tower, knocking Grunberger to the deck. His ears ringing, he tried to haul himself up again as another depth charge blasted the bow of the U-boat.

"Sir!" said a voice over the intercom. "Leak in the forward torpedo room!"

"Fix it immediately!"

"It's too big."

"Drive a plug into it!"

"We'll try."

Grunberger noticed that everybody was looking at him. He tried to make himself appear confident, but was quite frightened. He considered surfacing, but as soon as he broke through to fresh air, the Tommies would blow him out of the water. If he and his men tried to abandon ship, the Tommies would machine-gun them and make the water run red with blood.

"Hard left rudder!" he said.

"Hard left rudder!"

"Bring her up to two hundred!"

"To two hundred."

"Sir, the forward hydroplane is out of action," reported one of the operators.

"Rig for manual," replied Grunberger.

"Yes, sir."

A depth charge exploded so close Grunberger felt he'd been hit in the head with a brick. He saw a white flash before his eyes and felt the U-boat lurch. The lights went out again.

"Sir!" said the intercom. "The motor room is taking water!"

"Plug all leaks immediately!"

"Can't, sir. Seams ruptured in the hull."

"That's impossible!"

"Come see for yourself, then."

Grunberger's jaw began twitching. "What was that? How dare you speak to me that way? Who just spoke!"

Two depth charges blew simultaneously, with an ear-splitting roar. Grunberger was thrown across the conning tower and banged his head against a network of pipes. Dazed, he fell to his knees and realized the deck was covered with water; he could hear it gushing from someplace. Sailors screamed, their feet splashing in the rising water.

"Remain at your stations!" Grunberger screamed, trying to stand.

"We're sinking!" somebody yelled.

"Please, God, save me!"

Pandemonium broke loose on the U-boat as it turned on to its side like a great wounded beast. Grunberger heard the slosh of water amid the cries of the men. "Stay calm!" he screamed.

"We're all going to die!" a voice yelled.

A depth charge exploded underneath the U-boat. Grunberger heard the roar of water through a rupture in the hull. The U-boat was sinking, out of control. He couldn't surface now if he wanted to. Looking from side to side, he could see nothing in the darkness. Nearby, Ensign Hagen was crying. Someone else was slobbering about God.

Grunberger knew he was going to die. He guessed the U-boat would continue to sink until the water pressure buckled its hull. Gritting his teeth, he wished there were something he could do. But there was nothing.

Men scrambled through the water in the ship, clawing at the bulkheads, screaming and wailing as the U-boat tumbled into the depths, completely out of control. Grunberger thought of Marika and little Franz. *Oh, God,* he thought, *I'm sorry for everything.*

Water rose to his knees, and the spin of the U-boat pitched him into it. In the darkness he tried to grab on to something. His hand landed on a pipe. He pulled himself out of the water, feeling panic rise within him. He imagined himself drowning under tons of water, with nothing he could do about it. Someone bumped into him and screamed. The voice was Marcks's. Grunberger was surprised that his taciturn exec was going mad with the rest.

"Calm yourselves!" Grunberger bellowed. "We can die like good Germans!"

"Fuck you!" someone shrieked.

The hull of U-435 finally buckled, and tons of water rushed in. Grunberger held out his hands to stop it, but in seconds he was engulfed. He struggled wildly against suffocation, but the water collapsed his lungs and crushed his bones. He went limp as rolling wreckage of U-435 dropped into the deepest recesses of the sea.

CHAPTER 14

The wolf pack made contact with convoy HX 167 the next day, and this time the destroyers did not detect the U-boat who'd made the first sighting. The other U-boats swarmed toward the convoy and got into position. As soon as the sun went down, they attacked.

U-112 was part of the wolf pack, and it sank three ships at the expenditure of seven torpedoes. One of the ships was a tanker. The U-boat was depth-charged once, but no extensive damage because the destroyer hunting her had to return to the stricken convoy to pick up survivors.

The next day, as the convoy neared England, more destroyers arrived, forcing the U-boats down. Several were depth-charged, and two were sunk. U-112 emerged unscathed from this encounter, but Kapitänleutnant Kruger knew that if there had been more destroyers, one of them might have bagged U-112.

A few days later U-112 was part of a wolf pack that intercepted convoy HX 168 in the middle of the Atlantic. Kruger sank two more ships and missed a third, using up all his torpedoes. He was attacked by a destroyer, but the Asdic was foiled by a layer of warm water. The U-boat got away with only minor damage, and the next day it began its long journey back to Lorient.

Awaiting them was the usual welcoming celebration at the Prefecture. Admiral Dönitz congratulated them and shook their hands. After the ceremony, Flotillenkapitän Weisacker asked Kruger to come to his office for a few moments.

Weisacker and Kruger marched across the square side by side as the crew of U-112 dispersed toward their favorite brothels and cafes. They entered the old stone mansion that was now headquarters for the Twelfth U-boat Flotilla and made their way to Weisacker's office.

Weisacker hung his hat on a peg and sat behind his desk. On the wall behind him was a large signed photograph of Admiral Dönitz, and on his desk were photographs of his wife and children. Kruger sat on one of the chairs in front of the desk, wondering why Weisacker was being so solemn.

Weisacker lit a cigarette. "I'm afraid I have bad news." He puffed his cigarette and looked Kruger in the eye. "U-435 is missing at sea."

"Grunberger," Kruger whispered, closing his eyes.

"Yes."

Kruger covered his face with his hands. "Oh, my God."

"His first command," Weisacker said sadly.

There was silence in the office for a few seconds, then Kruger removed his hands from his face. "What happened?"

"First he reported that he had sighted convoy HX 167, then that two destroyers were closing in on him. That's the last we heard from him."

"They must have got him," Kruger said hoarsely.

"Yes."

Kruger closed his eyes and saw Grunberger drowning in his new U-boat. Kruger shuddered, because he knew the same could happen to him.

"I know that you two were very close," Weisacker said.

"Yes. He was my exec for two years. He was a very capable and dedicated officer."

"I'm sorry," Weisacker said softly.

Kruger was dazed as he stepped into the summer sunlight outside the headquarters building of the Twelfth U-boat Flotilla. He'd known other U-boat officers who'd died in the Battle of the Atlantic, but never been as friendly with any of them as he'd been with Grunberger. They'd had a great many glorious days together, days of victory and rejoicing, but now that was all over. Grunberger and his crew lay in death many fathoms down.

The only thing to do now was notify the other officers of U-112. Kruger looked at his watch and decided they still might be at the hotel, getting drunk before their customary foray to the Crescent Palace. He walked the few blocks to the hotel and went to the rooms of Feiler and Blohm, but they were gone already. Catching a cab in front of the hotel, he rode it to the Crescent Palace.

He knocked on the door, and it was opened by Cecille, who embraced him warmly.

"Kapitänleutnant Kruger!" she said happily. "So good to see you!" She realized he wasn't drunk and smiling. Examining his face, she saw that he was solemn, his brow furrowed. "Why are you unhappy, Kapitänleutnant Kruger?" she asked.

"Are any of my men here?" he asked.

"Yes, of course. They just arrived."

"Take me to them, please."

"Right this way."

She led him to the big room and pointed to a table. Kruger peered through the smoke and saw Feiler and Blohm with Leutnant Fritz Seldte, his new chief engineer. Feiler had been promoted to Oberleutnant and was now his executive officer.

Kruger walked to the table, feeling numb from head to foot. He'd enjoyed many celebrations in this room and always looked forward to coming here, but today it seemed as though the dancers and drinkers were actors on a stage. He sidestepped between tables and brushed against people as he approached the table. His three officers were sitting with girls; all appeared well along the path of inebriation.

Blohm spotted him first, his arm around Julie's waist. "It's the captain!" he said, pointing his stein of beer at Kruger.

"The captain?" asked Feiler. "Where?"

"Over there!"

Seldte, a moon-faced, pot-bellied young officer, removed his arm from his girl's shoulder and stood up. "Have a drink with us, Captain!"

Kruger stood at the edge of their table and looked down at them sternly. "I'm afraid I have bad news. Grunberger has been sunk."

Their jaws dropped and their faces drained of color. Blohm remembered Grunberger at the TBT, taking aim and firing torpedoes. Seldte, who'd only met Grunberger briefly, felt like an interloper. One by one they pushed their drinks away, took their hands off their women, and stood up. Blohm didn't know whether he wanted to cry or vomit, but fought to keep himself under control.

Kruger turned and walked toward the front door of the Crescent Palace, his three junior officers following close behind. Cecille didn't try to stop them.

Back at the table, the three prostitutes looked at each other, shrugged, and dispersed, looking for other officers to lure to their beds.

CHAPTER 15

It was December 1941, and the German army was stalled on the outskirts of Moscow. The temperature had dropped to twenty-five degrees below zero, and the roads were impassable. There were rumors that the Russians were planning a massive counterattack, and for the first time since war broke out in September of 1939, the German commanders were afraid.

On a Sunday evening in that December, Adolf Hitler was dining at his eastern headquarters in Rastenburg with Martin Bormann, an adjutant named Heinrich Heim, and Walter Hewel, the diplomat. Hitler's plate contained simple vegetarian fare, while his companions were feasting more heartily.

"It's really a disgrace," Hitler complained, spiking a piece of boiled potato with his fork. "The degree of ineptitude is almost incomprehensible. We attack the Soviet Union and no one makes certain that there is adequate winter clothing for my troops. Am I supposed to take care of every little detail myself?" He placed the potato in his mouth and chewed forlornly.

"The party will take up the slack as always," Bormann said. "Even as we speak, warm clothing is being collected throughout the Reich. It will be on the way to our soldiers in days. We must be thankful that the error is not so serious that it cannot be rectified."

"I really can't understand how this could happen in the first place," Hitler said, scowling. "It is as though there are saboteurs in the highest levels of the army, because such a turn of events cannot simply be an oversight. It has to be treason; there is no other conclusion that can be drawn."

"You must order a complete investigation, *mein Führer*." Hewel was a tall, portly bachelor with a reputation for chasing women.

"It's already under way," Hitler snapped.

The door burst open, and Heinz Lorenz, a press officer, charged into the dining room. *"Mein Führer!"* he said, waving a piece of paper. "An important message!"

Hitler looked up. "What is it?"

"An American station has just reported that the Japanese have mounted an apparently successful attack on the American fleet at Pearl Harbor!"

Hitler laid his fork on his plate and stared into space. The Japanese were his allies, and if they could defeat the Americans, England would not be able to hold on alone. If England collapsed, Hitler could direct all his resources toward Russia and utterly crush her despite the minor setback at Moscow.

Everyone looked at Hitler to see how he'd react. After a few seconds he smiled. "This is marvelous news," he said, "and it arrives just in time. Once again God smiles on us Germans. Now it is impossible for us to lose the war, for we are allied with a nation that has never lost a war in three thousand years." He chuckled. "Of course, we are also allied with Italy, which has been vanquished many times, but we must bear in mind that Italy always wound up on the right side in the end."

Everyone at the table acted as though they were amused. Hitler wondered how he'd phrase his declaration of war against the United States.

Three days later Admiral Dönitz arrived by plane at Rastenburg, accompanied by several of his aides and huge scrolls of maps depicting the Atlantic Ocean. The ground was covered with snow. Dönitz found the headquarters compound bleak with its dull gray military buildings and few sickly trees devoid of foliage.

He and his staff were shown to their quarters and given time to unpack and refresh themselves. Then they were ushered into the main conference room, where Hitler, General Jodl, and Field Marshal Keitel were poring over maps. They all saluted and greeted each other warmly. The war had evidently reached a major turning point with the victory of Japan over the United States.

"What have you here?" Hitler asked Dönitz, looking at the huge scrolls.

"Charts, *mein Führer*, to show you our new campaign."

"I see. Well, lay them out on the table."

Dönitz's aides laid the maps on the table as Keitel and Jodi watched.

Hitler turned to Dönitz. "I understand you passed through Berlin on your way here."

"I did, *mein Führer*."

"How was it?"

"Some bombing last night."

"A lot?"

"I wouldn't say a lot."

"How were the people taking it?"

"Quite well, I believe, but of course it was hard for me to tell. I didn't have much time for leisurely observations."

"I understand." Hitler looked at the chart table and saw the Atlantic Ocean spread out. "I think we can begin now."

"May we speak alone, *mein Führer*?"

"Alone?" Hitler asked, raising his eyebrows.

"Yes."

"I suppose so." Hitler turned to the others. "The admiral and I would like to be alone."

The officers obediently left the room. Hitler approached the chart of the Atlantic Ocean and looked down at it. It had many red dots painted on the pale-blue water.

"What do the red dots mean?" Hitler asked.

Dönitz joined Hitler at the table and crossed his arms. "U-boats sunk within the past five months."

Hitler raised his eyebrows. "That many?"

"Yes."

"What is the reason for this great loss of U-boats?"

"At first we had no idea," Dönitz explained, "but now we think we know. During the early days of the war, allied depth charges were set for no deeper than two hundred meters, so our U-boats simply submerged beneath that level. Now, however, the British have evidently been setting their depth charges to our maximum depth."

Hitler scowled. "They've learned that our U-boats can go deeper than they thought."

"It appears that way, *mein Führer*."

"I wonder how they found out?"

"The knowledge is common in the U-boat arm, and the enemy has spies just as we do. I'm surprised they didn't find out sooner."

Hitler looked coldly at Dönitz. "It's too bad you weren't aware of this earlier. You might have saved a great many U-boats."

"We weren't aware of the pattern until quite recently, and anyway I have a new plan."

Hitler's ears perked up; he loved new plans. "What new plan?"

Dönitz pointed his finger to the center of the Atlantic Ocean. "We're losing too many boats in this area, as you can see, and until we can work out a strategy to outwit the British, I propose we move the focus of our operations here." He pointed to the eastern coast of the United States and Canada.

"There?" Hitler asked, surprised. "That's awfully far away. Can we refuel our U-boats there?"

"Yes, with other U-boats refitted as fuel ships."

Hitler nodded. "I see. And you want to stop the convoys at their points of origination instead of in the middle of the Atlantic?"

"Yes, because cargo ships are poorly protected along the coast of America. They don't even use the convoy system."

Hitler was aghast. "You mean the ships just sail from port to port by themselves?"

"Yes, *mein Führer.*"

Hitler's face expressed disbelief. "Why don't they guard their ships?"

"I don't know, *mein Führer,*" Dönitz replied. "When they reach Nova Scotia, they form into convoys for the passage across the Atlantic, but until they get there they're more or less on their own."

"Even the tankers?"

"Even the tankers."

"Well," Hitler said, rubbing his palms together, "I think you ought to direct your wolf packs to that area without delay."

"I'm so glad you agree with me, *mein Führer,*" Dönitz said. "But there's one more thing."

"What?" Hitler asked impatiently, looking at his watch.

"I need more U-boats."

Hitler sighed. "Everyone needs more of what they have. Listen, Admiral, we're dealing with finite quantities. I don't have enough resources to give everyone everything he claims to need. We cannot build more U-boats than we're building at present."

"Can you give me some of the ones you're using in the Mediterranean?"

"Of course not. I need them to keep the Allies away from the Afrika Korps. You'll have to do your best with what you have."

"But, *mein Führer*," Dönitz pleaded, "I know that if I had just ten more U-boats, I could cripple the Allied war effort!"

"I'm sorry," Hitler said, "but you'll have to cripple them with what you have."

CHAPTER 16

On the Monday before Christmas Blohm was promoted to Leutnant while U-112 was being refitted for her next patrol. Blohm and the rest of the officers and crew were granted a one-week leave. He travelled by train to Berlin, where the Propaganda Ministry sent him on a morale-building public relations tour. He was photographed by the newspapers and *Signal* magazine, and delivered a speech to his old Hitler Youth unit.

"Really, Father," he said one day, "I don't deserve all this. I'm just an ordinary officer, not a U-boat ace or anything like that." They were sitting in his father's office in the Propaganda Ministry.

"But you will be one day, my boy," said his father, a stout man with thinning gray hair and a Hitler-style mustache.

The young officer didn't want to argue with his father, so he smiled and nodded like a dutiful son. His father imagined all U-boat men, and all military men of the Reich, as pure-hearted National Socialist heroes, and would never believe that such a place as the Crescent Palace could exist, and that U-boat officers went there to get drunk and carouse with French girls — and that his son did, too.

One night there was an air raid. Blohm had to go to the cellar of his home with his father, mother, and twin sister Wilhelmina. They sat on comfortable old furniture in the dank area near the furnace, a kerosene lamp providing illumination.

"I imagine this is something like getting depth-charged," his father said with a smile as the sound of bombs could be heard exploding in the distance.

Blohm wanted to say that bombing was nothing like getting depth-charged, because you couldn't be drowned in the cellar of your home, and the odds were against your home ever taking a direct hit, whereas U-boats were being sunk fairly regularly in the North Atlantic. But Blohm didn't want to disturb his father's illusions.

He himself had few illusions left. He'd found out that the U-boat war was much more dangerous than he'd thought, and the death of Grunberger had made him understand how easily he might be killed. His love of life made him wonder about the necessity of war, and whether it was truly necessary to risk the lives of so many good men. This made him question the validity of National Socialism and the Führer, who envisaged war as the only way out of Germany's predicament after the treachery of 1919 and the Versailles Treaty. Sometimes Blohm thought that Germany would be better off if it had relied on diplomacy instead of guns after the annexation of Czechoslovakia in 1938.

"Well," said his mother, a simple-minded woman who giggled when she became nervous, "at least so far we haven't suffered much damage."

"Let's hope we never do," Blohm's father said jovially, always the confident party official.

Blohm looked at his sister, seeing himself in her face. They were twins, but her features were more delicate than his. She worked in the Propaganda Ministry as a stenographer. She was looking at the ceiling and appeared more disturbed than the others by the bombing, as though she knew Germany was in danger. Blohm suspected that she was still a virgin, a good girl who believed in all the old virtues inculcated by her mother, who was a clandestine Catholic, although she publicly denounced the Church when in the presence of her National Socialist friends.

It occurred to Blohm that girls in the Crescent Palace probably had been much like Wilhelmina once, with families who loved them, and then, through circumstances caused by the war, had become harlots. He tried to imagine Wilhelmina in a brothel and felt a twinge of pain.

"Anything wrong?" his mother asked, for she noticed everything that happened to her children.

Blohm shifted position. "I guess I'm getting a cramp in my leg."

"Well," his father said heartily, "the bombing will soon be over. They never stay too long."

Wilhelmina looked fearfully at the ceiling. "But they always come back," she said, "and each time they stay a little longer."

Blohm returned to Lorient the day after New Year's and checked the bulletin board in the lobby of the Hotel Beau Séjour before going up to his room. Sure enough, there was a notice posted by Kapitänleutnant Kruger. There would be a muster aboard U-112 at 0800 hours the next morning.

Blohm carried his luggage to his room, then came back downstairs for dinner. None of the officers from U-112 was there, so he sat with other officers whom he knew vaguely. They spoke about U-boats, tactics and the girls at the Crescent Palace, and after the meal Blohm went up to his room.

He sat in his chair next to the window and looked down at the square. Dusk was falling, and people strolled around casually, most of them officers with local girls. A steady stream of cabs pulled up in front of the hotel, disgorging officers and taking on new ones.

Blohm felt unsettled and didn't know what to do with himself. Normally he'd go to the Crescent Palace and get drunk, but didn't feel like doing that tonight. Actually, he hadn't felt like doing that in a long time. He was tired of hangovers, headaches, and vomiting, and the sex didn't interest him as much as it did at the beginning. He smiled ruefully as he remembered how he'd loved Julie so desperately, but had become accustomed to her after a while, and curious about some of the other girls, such as Beatrice with the enormous breasts. Finally he went upstairs with Beatrice, then Lisette the blonde, and Marie who was reputed to give the best blow jobs in the house (Blohm had to agree after she'd given him one), and now Blohm was like all the other officers, screwing whichever one struck his fancy in the moment, and never really thinking too much about it.

"I knew you really didn't love me," Julie had chided him one night.

"Evidently you were right," he admitted, then saw her eyes cloud over. He thought she was hurt by his nonchalance, and had no way of knowing she was thinking about Armand, with whom she was now involved in a passionate bittersweet romance, and who also claimed to love her. Could she believe him after so many others had lied?

Blohm lit a cigarette and paced back and forth at the foot of his bed like a caged tiger. He felt like running and screaming at the top of his lungs. He wanted to do something, but didn't know what. He put out his cigarette in an ashtray, lit another, and continued pacing. His cheek became itchy and he scratched it. There seemed to be no place he could go for solace and understanding. The only people he knew were U-boat officers who were as crazy as himself, and prostitutes at the Crescent Palace who wanted his money.

He wished he had a wife and family; maybe that would comfort him. He remembered that sweet little nurse he used to like, Christina — but he hadn't seen her for a long time, and he couldn't call on her now. She had been a nice girl, and you just didn't force yourself into the lives of nice girls that way.

Blohm realized that he only had one place to go: the Crescent Palace. His cigarette dangling out of the corner of his mouth, he straightened his tie and put on his hat. Noticing the Iron Cross dangling from his jacket pocket, he shrugged sadly, puffed his cigarette, and left the room. In the lobby he met some other officers on their way to the Crescent Palace and shared a cab with them.

In the morning Blohm reported to the pen of U-112. He arrived fifteen minutes early and boarded via the catwalk, joining the men already there. He was the first officer to arrive, but Feiler showed up a few minutes later, then Leutnant Seldte, his eyes bloodshot and face puffy. The men arrived in twos and threes, then Kruger showed up a few minutes before eight. He nodded to his crew, climbed the ladder to the bridge, and went below. Eight o'clock arrived and he didn't return to the deck. A few minutes after eight Leutnant Mohlmann, the first watch officer, came running toward the U-boat, leaped across the catwalk, and joined the other officers who were congregating around the deck gun.

"I'm late," he said, looking at his watch. He was tall and stoop-shouldered, and had mournful eyes. "Did he say anything yet?"

Feiler pointed his thumb downwards. "He's still below."

Mohlmann breathed a sigh of relief. "Thank God."

After a while Kruger returned to the bridge and ordered them to fall into formation on the deck. The roll was called by Chief Petty Officer Schaap. The entire crew was present except for one seaman who was in the hospital with appendicitis. Kruger told them all to go below to the control room, where he would speak with them.

The officers ascended the ladder to the bridge and then down into the U-boat. The men followed, all congregating around Kruger, who stood in the corner near the ballast controls, leaning against the bulkhead. When they were all there, he stood erect and placed his hands in his pockets.

"On Friday we're going out on patrol again," Kruger said, then paused for their reaction, but didn't receive any. The days had long since passed when men cheered and threw their hats into the air upon hearing they were going on patrol. "This time we're going to a place quite different, a place that will be warm for a change, and we won't be operating within the constrictions of a wolf pack. Admiral Dönitz has decided to send us deep into the heart of the enemy camp — to the very shores of America. We will actually operate within sight of American cities and sink cargo ships before they form into convoys. Our information is that cargo ships are not guarded very well near the American coastline, and the good old happy days will be back again. At any rate, after this meeting all of us will move back into U-112. We'll begin taking provisions and fuel, and then we'll go out into the bay for a final check of our equipment. On Friday we'll leave for America. From this moment until then there will be no more passes into town. Any questions?"

No one raised his hand.

"Good," said Kruger. "You may all return to your quarters, settle your affairs, and return here by no later than twelve noon. You are dismissed until then."

On Friday morning U-112 sailed from Lorient with the usual ceremony. Nurses tossed flowers on to the deck, the band played, and Flotillenkapitän Weisacker saluted. The U-boat backed out of its pen, turned around, and headed for sea. It was all routine for Blohm now. As the pier receded in the distance, he wondered if he'd return from this patrol.

Electrician's Mate Steiner came to the bridge with a new piece of equipment, an aerial called a Biscay Cross that signaled the presence of British radar long before the British ship or airplane could be seen. Steiner affixed the aerial to the periscope shears and then went below to put on the headphones and listen.

Kruger looked at the aerial and frowned. "Ugliest thing I ever saw," he said. "Let's hope it works."

The seamen threw the flowers overboard, and the U-boat entered the Bay of Biscay. Its voyage was uneventful until five o'clock that evening, when half the crew was having dinner. Steiner, who had been sitting with his headphones on, contemplating the chicken being served, when he heard a buzz in his ears, indicating that enemy radar was in the vicinity.

"Enemy radar!" he shouted, jumping to his feet. "Enemy radar!"

Kruger was in the wardroom eating his roast chicken when he heard the shouts. "Take her down!" he screamed.

Simultaneously, Feiler on the bridge heard Steiner's alarm. "To the cellar!" Feiler waited impatiently for men on the bridge to crowd down the ladder. He looked around but could see nothing in the air or on the sea. One of the seamen grabbed the aerial and carried it down with him. Blohm dropped down the ladder, and finally Feiler descended, dogging the hatch above him.

They all gathered in the control room as waves crashed against the conning tower of the U-boat. The boat was inclined downward, both hydroplane operators holding their wheels at the hard dive position. Kruger glanced at the depth gauge; they were already at ten meters, but would need to go a lot deeper if they wanted to be invisible from the air.

Kruger turned to the sound room. "Hear anything?"

"Nothing, sir."

Kruger grunted. If it was a ship, they'd be able to hear it by now, but maybe it wasn't a ship, because the Biscay Cross was supposed to be accurate for extremely long distances. If it had been a plane, they wouldn't be able to hear it at all. It might be up in the sky right now, wondering where the U-boat had disappeared to.

It occurred to Kruger that if he hadn't had that funny-looking aerial, a British plane might have dived suddenly out of the sun and dropped a bomb on U-112. They all might be sinking to their graves right now instead of to safety.

Kruger looked at the Biscay Cross leaning against a bulkhead and decided that maybe it wasn't so funny-looking after all.

After twenty minutes Kruger brought the U-boat to periscope depth and took a quick look through the sky scope. He couldn't see any airplanes, so gave the order to surface. The ballast tanks were blown, and the hydroplane operators turned their wheels to the hard rise position. U-112 broke through the surface, and Kruger went up the ladder. Feiler followed him, carrying the Biscay Cross.

Kruger opened the hatch and stepped on to the wet bridge. He raised his binoculars and looked around as Feiler fastened the Biscay Cross to the periscope shears.

"Enemy radar!" Steiner screamed.

"All the way down!" Kruger yelled.

Feiler pulled the Biscay Cross down from the periscope and went down the ladder. Kruger followed, closing the hatch and thinking that it would take longer for them to get down this time, because the boat hadn't been going very fast. He descended the ladder to the control room, imagining a Sunderland diving at U-112 and dropping bombs.

"Any sound?" Kruger asked.

"No, sir," replied the hydrophone operator.

Kruger watched the needle on the depth gauge drop. When it went past ten, he breathed more easily, because the U-boat completely underwater. At fifty meters he knew it would be difficult to see the U-boat from the air.

"Both motors ahead one-third," Kruger said. "Steer previous course."

"Ahead one-third — steer previous!" replied Leutnant Seldte, the new chief engineer.

"Level her off at two hundred meters, Chief."

"Level at two hundred."

"All right," Kruger said, looking around. "Everyone might as well return to whatever he was doing before, because we're going to stay down for a while this time."

Kruger walked forward to the officers' wardroom. The rest of the crew dispersed throughout the U-boat.

Kruger brought U-112 to the surface after dark and charged its batteries as he proceeded west toward the United States. Shortly before dawn he submerged again and looked through the periscope to make sure no British ships or planes were about. Then the U-boat surfaced again. Kruger went up first, carrying the Biscay Cross.

"Hear anything?" Kruger shouted into the U-boat.

"Nothing, sir!" came the answer.

Kruger handed the cross to Blohm, who affixed it to the periscope. The morning watch took positions around the bridge, holding binoculars to their eyes.

"Both engines ahead two-thirds!" Kruger shouted.

"Ahead two-thirds!" echoed Leutnant Seldte.

It was a cloudy and windy winter day. Kruger could see a storm forming ahead of him. He considered it a mixed blessing, because it would keep enemy aircraft out of the sky.

The waves became higher as the day progressed, and at noon they were smashing over the bridge. The men on watch tied themselves to the bridge rail to keep from being swept away. They continually had to wipe their binoculars clean so they could see through them.

Blohm came off watch feeling more dead than alive. He was soaked to his skin, his eyes were red and stinging, and he felt disoriented from the steady pounding of waves. Descending into the U-boat, he could smell the rancid odor of vomit. Everyone in the control room looked green. Blohm made his way forward to the officers' quarters, watching the sausages and sacks of food, suspended from pipes and fixtures on the ceiling, swinging back and forth as the U-boat swayed from side to side in the heavy seas.

In the officers' quarters Mohlmann vomited into a bucket. "I can't take much more of this," he muttered, lips dripping with bile.

Blohm took off his wet clothes, hung them from pipes, and put on dry clothes. Wearing a knit sweater and his visorless black cap, he made his way to the wardroom, where he was surprised to see Kruger seated at table, holding a chewed-down sausage in one hand and a book in the other. Leutnant Fischer, the second watch officer, held a cup of coffee with two hands and stared into it. Blohm poured himself a cup from the gimballed pot on the hot plate and sat at the table.

Kruger looked up from his book. "What's it like on the bridge?" he asked Blohm.

"Pretty bad." Blohm looked at the spine of the book and saw that it was *The World as Will and Idea* by Arthur Schopenhauer.

Kruger noticed him looking at the book and held it up. "You ever read this?"

"No, sir."

"I didn't think so. You young people these days don't receive much of an education." He motioned with his chin toward Fischer. "He hasn't read it, either. When I was a student, we *had* to read things like this, and I'm glad we did."

Blohm shrugged. "It's good for the mind, I suppose. What does it say?"

Kruger raised his eyebrows. "You expect me to boil it all down into a sentence or two for you?"

"No, sir, but I thought maybe you could give me the general gist."

Kruger leaned toward Blohm. "Do you know what's wrong with your generation?"

"What, sir?"

"You're more interested in the general gist of things than the real meaning. Maybe that's because the example for you is being set by our beloved Führer, who is such a dilettante himself."

Blohm shrugged. "Maybe." He raised his coffee to his lips and took a sip.

Kruger looked at Blohm for a few seconds, then placed his hand on Blohm's shoulder and shook him gently. "You know, Blohm, you've really changed a lot since you've come aboard this U-boat. If I'd said that when you'd first come aboard, you would have jumped out of your skin, but now it doesn't bother you at all. I'm afraid I must attribute this to the good influence that I have had upon you."

Blohm grinned. "Unquestionably that's true, sir."

"You'll probably make an excellent U-boat captain someday. You have all the qualities except a good education, but that really doesn't matter so much out here. If the war lasts much longer, you'll get your own boat. Just be patient."

"If I ever got my own U-boat I'd have very mixed emotions, sir," Blohm said, "because on one hand I'd want my own boat, but on the other hand I'd hate to leave your command."

Kruger stared at Blohm for a few moments, then burst into laughter. "Now I know you'll be a good U-boat captain, because you've also learned to be a good liar."

"Everything I am, I owe to you, sir."

"Oh, you're really something, Blohm. You'll go far in this navy."

"That's what everybody tells me," Blohm replied, wondering how far he really wanted to go in the navy now that he knew what it was really like.

Blohm returned to the bridge at nightfall and the seas were boiling around U-112. Sheets of water whipped the men on the bridge, who struggled to maintain their footing and look through binoculars at a horizon they barely could discern. The bow of the boat dipped into the waves and appeared as though it would never come up, but then finally, with shudders that passed throughout the entire boat, it rose.

Blohm raised his binoculars, but the lenses became wet before he could see through them. He wiped them off and took a quick look at the horizon, but the lenses clouded again. The wind howled around him and the huge waves surged at the bridge like mountains. Water fell on him and nearly knocked him down. It entered his sleeves and the openings around his neck, soaking him to his skin. He wished Kruger would submerge the boat and take it to the serenity of deep water, but there'd be no point to that because winter storms in the Atlantic could last for days. They'd never make it to their station if they made a habit of submerging in bad weather and depleting batteries.

Blohm held the bridge rail with one hand and raised binoculars to his eyes with the other. He couldn't see anything, but he was sure the British and Americans couldn't either.

The weather changed dramatically four days later when U-112 entered the Gulf Stream. Within the space of a few hours, the sun came out and the seas went calm. Bleary-eyed men with green complexions climbed to the bridge and raised their faces to the sun.

"Keep your eyes peeled, gentlemen," Kruger warned them. "We're not very far from America now."

The next day a lookout spotted land. Kruger called Mohlmann, who was also navigation officer, to the bridge to take a fix and find out what it was. Mohlmann shot the sun through his sextant, took a bearing on the land, and went below to his computations. Several minutes later he returned to the bridge.

"It's one of the Bahamian Islands, sir," he said. "I can't tell which one because there are so many."

"Ah," said Kruger. "That means we'll be on station sometime late today. From now on we double the watch. Strange that we haven't seen any American patrol planes yet. Steiner!"

"Yes, sir."

"Are you sure your equipment is working properly?"

"Yes, sir."

"Stay awake and keep your ears open. We're only a few hours from the American coast."

"Yes, sir."

Kruger doubled the watch on the bridge as U-112 made its way toward the coast of Florida. He was surprised that he still hadn't encountered any American patrol ships or planes. Didn't the Americans know they were at war with the Reich?

At 1700 hours Blohm was on the bridge again, and he was the first one to sight the coast of Florida. "Land straight ahead!"

Kruger and Feiler scrambled up the ladder to the bridge and looked at Florida through binoculars.

"Well," Kruger said, "it looks like we're finally on station, gentlemen."

Kruger's orders were to patrol the coast of Florida and sink whatever ships passed by. It was anticipated that he'd have many targets, because tankers filled with oil would pass on their way from the gulf ports of Texas and Louisiana to Nova Scotia, where they would form into convoys. Freighters from Central and South America would use the same route.

As dusk fell on that first day, U-112 stayed on the surface, its crew standing watch and looking for ships to sink. They were amazed at how good the visibility was, with Florida's lighted cities silhouetting any passing ships.

At two o'clock in the morning, a freighter was sighted. Kruger climbed to the bridge, sighted the ship in his binoculars, and thought it too easy to be real. Feiler took Grunberger's old post at the TBT as Kruger maneuvered the U-boat for the kill. He issued the firing order, and Feiler turned loose only one torpedo, which sank the *Parma*.

No more targets presented themselves that night. At dawn U-112 submerged, because Kruger knew the Americans could see him from shore in daylight, and he thought they'd be looking after what had happened last night. Underwater he moved south down the Florida coast, remaining at periscope depth and maintaining a steady watch at the periscope.

At three o'clock that afternoon, off the coast of Miami, Leutnant Fischer was on the periscope and spotted a tanker which he estimated to be fifteen thousand tons. He sounded the alarm, and Kruger soon appeared in the conning tower. Kruger looked through the periscope and saw the big tanker sailing peacefully along under the tropical blue sky. It was big, fat, and in perfect position.

"Battle stations!" Kruger shouted.

Four miles away, at Lummus Park in Miami Beach, Commander Mulford of the Royal Navy wore a blue bathing suit and reclined on a beach blanket, the sun making his body pleasantly warm. Beside him lay Helen McCrary in a maroon one-piece bathing suit. It was Saturday, and they'd come to the beach together because he had no classes to teach on weekends.

Also on the blanket, folded under one of Mulford's shoes, was a copy of the morning's *Miami Herald*, with the front-page story of the *Parma* being sunk by a German U-boat off the coast of Palm Beach. Admiral Rufus Dexter, the chief of operations for the US Navy, had promised prompt and decisive action to rid American waters of the U-boat menace, but Mulford knew that America's efforts to stop the U-boats would be useless unless they adopted the procedures implemented by the Royal Navy.

He'd been trying to sell the Royal Navy's hard-won knowledge to all the American naval officers he'd met, and many agreed, but Admiral Dexter and his staff had not budged from their earlier contention that the convoy system was of dubious value.

Mulford was becoming more discouraged with every passing day, and wanted desperately to return to England. He felt as if he was being wasted in Miami when there was important escort work to be done in the North Atlantic.

Helen rose to a sitting position on the blanket. "I want some ice cream," she said. "Would you like some?"

"No."

"Then I'll get some for myself."

She opened her purse, took out some coins, sauntered toward the ice cream stand, and Mulford admired her shapely figure, but felt little passion. He'd made love to her too many times, even as recently as this morning, and had grown accustomed to her beauty. Now he was more aware of her deficiencies, such as her immaturity and vindictive temper. She was gaining weight because she ate too much ice cream and fatty foods. She seemed to have no willpower whatever, no sense of culture, and became sloppy when drunk. Yet Mulford didn't think he could live without her, because he knew he was growing old, and she made him feel youthful.

He felt uncomfortably warm and decided to go for a swim. Standing, he placed his fists on his hips and looked out to sea, seeing a big tanker on the horizon, steaming north. *I wonder if that one will make it?* he wondered as he walked toward the water.

He passed people lying on blankets getting suntanned or drinking soda pop out of bottles. Palm trees leaned lazily toward the sun, green coconuts hanging in huge clumps beneath long, willowy leaves. Mulford's feet touched the wet sand and he felt a chill; the water was surprisingly cold in Florida during the winter.

There were few people in the water. Mulford waded in to his knees, inhaling the salty air, and the sun beat down on him, making him feel healthy. Taking huge steps, he bounded deeper into the water and dived. He splashed down and dropped beneath the surface, the water chilling his skin, and he swam underwater for ten feet, then angled upward, his head breaking through the surface. Standing, he wiped the saltwater from his eyes and looked straight ahead at the tanker. Suddenly, as he was gazing at the tanker, it exploded before his eyes.

Jets of flame shot into the sky, and people on the beach started shouting. Then the sound wave reached land, and he heard the big, booming roar. Stunned, stumbling in the sand, he saw the tanker explode again in a fiery red burst. When the smoke cleared, the tanker was listing to seaward and going down quickly. It was too far away to see specific details clearly, but he could imagine sailors abandoning ship and jumping feet first into burning oil that would fry them to death.

His jaw hanging open, his lungs gasping for air, he remembered the day the *Centurion* was sunk. The war had become a distant phenomenon during his past several months in sunny Miami, but now it was brought home to him with full force.

Behind him on the beach, people were screaming and pointing at the tanker, the foredeck of which was dropping beneath the sea. Mulford clenched his teeth and balled up his fists. *Somehow I've got to get back to England.*

Hitler sat behind the desk in his office at Rastenburg, reading his correspondence. His wire-rimmed glasses were perched low on his nose and he wore his customary tan military tunic with the swastika on the sleeve and his Iron Cross hanging from his pocket. There was a knock on the door.

He looked up from the letter he was reading. "Come in."

A young SS aide entered the room, carrying an envelope. He approached the desk, raised his arm in the air, and shouted: *"Heil Hitler!"*

Hitler showed the palm of his hand and looked at the envelope. "What do you have there?"

A message from Admiral Dönitz, *mein Führer.*"

"Give it here."

The aide handed over the message and marched out of the office, closing the door behind him. Hitler held the message under the light of the lamp on his desk.

Mein Führer:
Reports from the coastal waters off North America indicate that the U-boat campaign there will be successful for much longer than anticipated. All U-boats in the area signal they have achieved results far above expectations. Over one million tons sunk so far this month. My best wishes to you.
Admiral Karl Dönitz

CHAPTER 17

It wasn't until February 1942 that Mulford was able to extricate himself from his odious instructor's duty in Miami. He'd written imploring letters to every high-ranking British officer who'd ever shown any interest in him and pulled every string he knew. Finally the orders came down posting him back to Liverpool.

He was flown up the North American coast to Nova Scotia, then across the North Atlantic to Greenland. He made a short hop to Iceland and finally to Liverpool. He traveled without Helen, who was supposed to follow later. They'd had a melancholy farewell in Miami, after which she took a train north to visit her family in Washington, DC.

Mulford was happy on the day he reported for duty at Western Approaches Command Center. He stepped briskly down the corridor, pipe sticking out of his mouth, old leather briefcase in hand. The officers and Wrens he passed in the corridor spoke English in the accent he was most accustomed to, music to his ears. The people moved about smartly, with a sense of purpose, unlike the confusion he'd witnessed on naval bases in America. The Americans didn't know what to do yet, but they'd learn, just as the British had. It might take a little longer, but sooner or later they'd wake up.

"Commander William Mulford to see Admiral Noble," he told the girl at the desk.

"Go right in," she replied with a smile. "He's expecting you."

Mulford passed through the two doors, entering Admiral Noble's office. The admiral stood, uniform fitting him impeccably as usual, and held out his hand. "William, so good to see you again."

"Good to see you, sir."

"Have a seat."

Mulford sat in front of the desk, puffing his briar. Noble lowered himself into his chair and folded his hands on the desk, looking at Mulford and smiling, obviously pleased to see him. "So you didn't like America very much?"

"Dreadful place, and you simply can't deal with their navy people."

"Yes, they're losing a lot of ships. Their Admiral Dexter is stubborn as a mule. I've been in touch with him through intermediaries, but he still won't adopt the convoy system."

"He will eventually. His losses are becoming unacceptable."

"Let's hope it's not too late."

"Well, at least there have been benefits for us. The U-boats aren't very active in the North Atlantic these days, but they'll return once the Americans come to their senses."

"I agree. Then the U-boats will make life hell for us again."

Noble leaned forward. "They've countered our radar, you know."

Mulford removed his pipe from his mouth. "They have?"

"Yes. Evidently they have a detection device of some kind, but our technicians are working on a way to circumvent it. We have some other gear coming, also: a device that can fire depth charges nearly a hundred yards or more in front of our destroyers, and a radio direction finder that will enable us to home in on U-boats sending messages."

Mulford smiled. "Sounds wonderful, sir. I'm glad things haven't been static while I was away."

"We've also been making some progress in cracking their codes, but we haven't got one of their cipher machines yet.

That's still top priority, you know. When we get one of those machines, we won't be on the defensive anymore. Then we'll know what they're going to do before they do it."

Mulford shrugged. "I wouldn't count on getting one if I were you, sir. German officers are trained to scuttle their U-boats, just like our own submarine forces."

"I know but they'll make a mistake one of these days, and I hope my commanders will exploit the opportunity."

Mulford changed position in his chair. "Where do I fit into the picture, sir?"

Noble smiled. "You're getting a new destroyer, William — and command of the Eighth Escort Group."

It took Mulford a few moments to realize that the dream he'd nurtured throughout his months in Miami was coming true. "When do I start, sir?"

"I thought you might want to go home to see your wife for a week. So why don't you report back here on the eleventh for duty? Does that agree with you?"

"Sure does, sir. What's the name of my new ship?"

"Just a moment — let me look." Noble shuffled through the papers on his desk and held one up. "The *Pembroke*."

"Lovely name."

"It's a lovely ship, and quite deadly."

Carrying a huge bouquet of flowers, Mulford walked up the steps of his Mayfair home and rang the bell. He waited several seconds and nothing happened, so he rang again. This time he heard footsteps, then the door was opened by Agnes.

"Commander Mulford!" she exclaimed, placing a hand over her breast.

"Agnes, my love," he replied with a big grin.

"You're back!"

"Indeed I am."

She took a deep breath. "Sir," she said sternly, "you really ought to give a body advance notice when you're coming home. You're liable to give someone a stroke coming home so suddenly like this after being away so long."

"I wanted to surprise everyone."

"You're liable to surprise someone into a grave someday, sir."

"Sorry," Mulford said, realizing Agnes was getting on in years and surprises probably weren't good for her. "I'll call next time. Now let me kiss your cheek because I'm so happy to see you."

He bent and kissed her cheek. She wrinkled her nose, enjoying the bit of affection.

"How long have you been back in England, sir?"

"I arrived the day before yesterday. Is milady in?"

"I'm afraid she's still in bed."

Mulford looked at his watch; it was nearly one o'clock in the afternoon. "I trust she's well?"

"As a matter of fact, she hasn't been well lately, sir."

Mulford entered the vestibule, taking off his coat and hat while Agnes held the flowers. "What's wrong with her?"

"Don't know, sir."

"Has the doctor visited?"

"She's not sick in that way, sir. She's just been awfully down at the mouth, if you know what I mean."

"Do you know why?"

"I think I do, but maybe she'd better tell you herself, sir."

Mulford walked up the stairs, carrying the bouquet of flowers. Approaching Vanessa's door, he wanted to barge in and awaken her with a kiss, but he remembered her anger the last time he'd done that, so he knocked on the door instead.

There was no answer.

He knocked louder, and still she didn't answer. Finally he pounded on the door with all his might.

"Who's there?" she screamed.

"Your husband!"

"My husband?" she asked, on the other side of the door. "But I don't have a husband."

Mulford opened the door and held out the flowers. "Of course you do!"

Vanessa sat up in bed and held out her arms. "You're back!"

He rushed toward her. "Indeed I am."

Laying flowers beside her, he bent over the bed and kissed her lips. She clasped her arms around his neck and pulled him down on top of her. They hugged and kissed for a few moments.

"When did you get back?" she asked after a while, when they were lying side by side.

"Day before yesterday. Arrived in London just now."

She pouted. "You should have written to say you were coming. I could have had a little welcoming party to celebrate your return from the war."

Mulford sat on the edge of the bed. "I haven't been to war at all. I've been trying to talk sense into the thick skulls of Americans, without much success."

"Well, you know what they're like."

"I certainly do." He lit a cigarette and took a puff. "But anyway — here I am. How have you been?"

"Oh, all right."

Mulford looked at her and didn't think she looked well. She had lines around her eyes, and she seemed older. "You look tired. Have you been getting enough rest?"

"Plenty of rest."

"How's Jeremy?"

Her eyes closed and all the strength seemed to drain from her body. "He's dead."

"Oh." Now Mulford understood what was wrong with her. "When did it happen?"

"Three months ago. He went out on a mission and never came back. You know how it is."

"Yes, I do. He was such a nice young man. Probably had a brilliant future in front of him. What a pity."

She looked at him harshly. "You're not being facetious, I hope?"

He shook his head. "Death is nothing to be facetious about. I've seen it many times myself. In fact, it might claim me one of these days — who knows?"

She leaped on to him and hugged him tightly. "No, don't say that! If anything happened to you, I don't think I could go on!"

He chuckled in an effort to dispel the funereal atmosphere that had descended on the bedroom. "Sure you could."

She rested her cheek against his shoulder. "No, I honestly don't think I could."

"Would you like me to take you to a restaurant for lunch?"

"I can have Agnes bring something up. I'll call her." She reached to the side and pulled the cord. "I don't like to go out much anymore. Life's so sad."

"You're just finding that out?"

She looked at him with doleful eyes. "I used to think life was a big party, but this war has ruined everything."

CHAPTER 18

It was July 1942. A Ford sedan stopped in front of the White House, and a young ensign named McCrary in a starched white uniform stepped out of the front seat on the passenger side, ran around the front of the car, and opened the rear door.

Admiral Rufus Dexter placed his big foot on the ground and got out, smoothing the front of his white uniform. Ensign McCrary reached into the car and pulled out the admiral's briefcase, handing it to him. The ensign closed the door of the car, and it rolled away.

Ensign McCrary ran up the steps of the White House and opened the door. Admiral Dexter marched into the White House. The crew of Secret Service men in the vestibule recognized him and let him pass.

Dexter made his way through seemingly endless corridors, passing portraits of former presidents and first ladies. Ensign McCrary walked respectfully several paces behind.

Finally they came to the Oval Office. The pretty secretary told Admiral Dexter that he should go right in. McCrary stayed behind to wait for the admiral's return and perhaps flirt a bit with the secretary.

Admiral Dexter entered the office of President Roosevelt and saw him sitting behind his desk, smoking a cigarette in his long, elegant cigarette holder. Next to him was his secretary of commerce and principal adviser, Harry Hopkins.

"Come in and have a seat, Admiral," President Roosevelt said.

Dexter walked to the nearest chair and sat, placing his briefcase beside his chair. He knew he was in for a bad time and felt uneasy. Looking over the president's head, he could see the dome of the Capitol Building in the background.

"Well," said President Roosevelt with a smile, removing the cigarette holder from his mouth, "I guess you know why I've asked you here, Admiral."

"I believe I do," Admiral Dexter replied, his shaved head and large ears making him look like a guilty little boy.

"We can't afford to lose any more ships," Roosevelt declared. "If we continue losing them at our present rate, England will be out of the war and we'll have to carry on alone. I don't think that would be a very happy eventuality, do you?"

"No, sir."

"I've been in contact with the prime minister of Great Britain. He's advised me to adopt the convoy system plus the strategy of concentrating all our anti-submarine forces in defense of convoys. This is the system that the British use. It has been reasonably successful, certainly more successful than the system presently employed by the US Navy. It is my understanding that you have opposed both British approaches to dealing with the U-boat menace."

Dexter looked back and forth between Roosevelt and Harry Hopkins and thought Hopkins looked like a small-town undertaker. "That's true, sir, but even I think we ought to try them now."

Roosevelt smiled. "Good. I'm glad you agree because I'd like you to implement them immediately in all commands of the United States Navy."

"Yes, sir."

"A written order to that effect will arrive on your desk tomorrow morning, but I want you to get to work on it right away."

"Yes, sir."

"Any questions?"

"No, sir."

"That is all, Admiral Dexter. You may leave."

"Yes, sir."

Admiral Dexter stood, saluted, picked up his briefcase, and marched out of the Oval Office, closing the door behind him.

Roosevelt swung around on his swivel chair and looked at Hopkins. "Well, that's that."

"I think you should have fired him."

Roosevelt puffed his cigarette holder. "No, I can't do that. It'd be bad for Navy morale. I wish I could promote him out of his job, but he's the number-one man and there's no place to send him."

Hopkins shrugged. "Well, maybe he'll retire one of these days."

"Let's hope so."

CHAPTER 19

North of the Bahamas, U-112 was lying still on calm water. It was a bright, sunny day in September, and most of the crew were frolicking on the deck and in the water, while Kruger, Blohm, and Mohlmann were on the bridge with a few crew members, scanning the sea and skies for American planes and ships as recreation continued. In another hour Kruger would replace the seamen on the bridge and those on duty below with some who were in the water, so they could all have a little swim. However, he had no intention of stripping and jumping into the water himself, because that spectacle would be damaging to the dignity and authority of a U-boat captain.

Kruger held his binoculars to his eyes and scanned the pale-blue horizon. He felt safe because he was far from American shipping lanes, their anti-submarine craft on convoy-escort duty. Since August the Americans had organized their shipping into convoys, heavily protected by destroyers and aircraft. He'd been unable to find a decent target since then, and the heat aboard the U-boat was unbearable in the tropics. So he'd devised this little party for today, and tomorrow he'd go back on station.

He heard steps on the ladder and saw the radioman come into view, carrying a message. "This just came in for you, sir."

Kruger let his binoculars hang from his neck and accepted the message. U-112 PROCEED TO BD 12 AND REPORT UPON ARRIVAL. DÖNITZ.

Kruger looked at the radioman. "Reply that we're on our way."

"Yes, sir."

The radioman descended the ladder into the U-boat, and Kruger looked at his watch. It was four o'clock in the afternoon. He saw no point in interfering with the recreational period; he'd depart at nightfall when it was cooler.

"Mohlmann," he said.

"Yes, sir?"

He handed over the message and went below.

"Where are we going, sir?" asked Blohm, who had overheard and read part of the message over Kruger's shoulder.

"Back to the North Atlantic," Kruger replied. "Wolf-pack duty again."

It was a cold, rainy day in Reykjavik as Commander Mulford climbed the gangplank of his *Pembroke*, tied up at the pier. He carried a leather suitcase because he was going to sea again.

"Morning, sir," said Boatswain's Mate Conaway, saluting at the top of the gangplank.

"Morning, Conaway," Mulford replied, returning the salute.

Mulford stepped on to the deck of the *Pembroke* and looked up at the derricks loading supplies aboard. Crossing the deck, he stood at the guardrail and gazed at the blurred outlines of the mountains ringing the harbor. Also on the pier were five other destroyers of the Eighth Escort Group, all scheduled to set sail at dawn the next day for the CHOP line southeast of Greenland, where they'd relieve an American escort group guarding convoy HX 289 bound for Liverpool.

Mulford went below decks to his cabin, set his suitcase down beside his bunk, and sat at his desk, where he filled his briar and lit it up. On his desk was top-secret information on the convoy. He looked over the names of the ships and their cargos, seeing that they were the usual international conglomeration of registries carrying everything from oil to tanks to refrigerated sides of beef, their crews consisting of an odd mixture of Swedes, Britishers, American, Spaniards, Italians, and Lascars. He wondered why such men volunteered to go to sea when they knew of high shipping losses, and considered them braver even than his navy sailors, because the merchantmen had little armament to fight back with, and some sailed in ships that should have been retired from service long ago.

Mulford didn't expect much difficulty for convoy HX 289. The U-boats had drastically curtailed their activities in the North Atlantic during the past several months.

There was a knock on the door.

"Come in."

The door opened. Yeoman Grogan stood there.

"Letter came in for you today, sir."

Mulford took it. "Thank you, Grogan."

Mulford looked at the pale-blue envelope. In the upper right-hand corner was Helen McCrary's name and address in Washington, DC. *So she's coming at last!* Mulford thought happily, tearing the letter open. Although she annoyed and disappointed him at times, he'd been anxiously awaiting her return to England since he'd been back, because in a certain way he loved her youth and beauty. Holding the letter up to the light of the porthole above his desk, he read it, his face wilting with every line.

Dear William,

I don't know how to tell you this, but I've decided not to return to England. My country is at war now and I feel I must do what I can for the war effort. My father has been able to get me a commission in the WAVES, and I'm to report for duty in about two weeks. This probably

will come as a shock to you, but it shouldn't. You persist in thinking of me as a flighty little thing, but I'm much more serious than you think. Moreover, I have gathered the distinct impression that your feelings for me are not as warm as they were when we first met. I think my decision is the best for both of us, and I hope that someday fate will bring us together again, for I shall never forget you and the love we shared.
Yours,
Helen

Good grief, thought Mulford, laying the letter on his desk. Puffing his pipe, he wondered what to do. He decided against answering her letter and wondered if she'd found another boyfriend, a young, handsome officer who was good-natured and not a drunk like Mulford. *Yes, that's it,* he thought, *she's found herself another fellow. You can't trust any of them.*

It disheartened him to think that he'd never hold her firm young body in his arms again, and he speculated that she might have been the last young woman he'd ever sleep with, for he was pushing forty and not many young women fall in love with men old enough to be their fathers.

He tried to see the bright side of the situation. Now he'd be able to spend more time with Vanessa, who herself was unencumbered by a lover these days — or that had been the case when he'd left London two weeks ago. He expected to be back in Liverpool in about ten days, then perhaps he could make a quick trip to London.

Mulford held the blue letter up, then dropped it into his wastebasket. He sighed and puffed his pipe, feeling old and tired.

CHAPTER 20

Kruger and Feiler were inspecting the forward torpedo room when Radioman Zeigler sped toward them with a message from headquarters.

U-112 PROCEED WITH MAXIMUM SPEED TOWARD
AK 26 AND INTERCEPT CONVOY HX 289 OVER
SIXTY SHIPS COURSE DUE EAST 10 KNOTS. DÖNITZ

It was three o'clock in the afternoon, the U-boat rolling in a storm. Mohlmann was on duty in the control room. Kruger walked back to him, handing him the message.

"Plot a course to this square."

The *Pembroke* pitched and tossed in the heavy seas as Mulford stood on the bridge and watched convoy HX 289 approach. It was in ten columns of six ships each, with a rescue ship in the rear and escort ships at its corners, front, and back, all ships spread out over thirty square miles of ocean.

The destroyer belonging to the American escort commander flashed a message saying that his group was disengaging and wished the British escort group luck. Mulford ship flashed back a *thank you* and said his ships were assuming their positions forthwith.

American destroyers veered away from the convoy and turned around to regroup behind it, while Mulford's destroyers moved toward positions he had previously assigned them. He would take the lead position in the center front of the convoy and communicate with the other escort ships via radio.

Mulford's Asdic and radar were sweeping the sea, a full watch on deck because this was when the convoy was most vulnerable. The CHOP line was far from Allied air bases, therefore had no cover, and the maneuvers of the transfer left the convoy open to attack. The British admiralty wanted to do away with the CHOP line and have escorts stay with convoys from the beginning to the end of their voyages, but Admiral Dexter of the American navy didn't like that idea. He wanted American ships to safeguard American territorial waters and the British to safeguard their own waters, although the arrangement increased danger to the convoys.

The *Pembroke* reached its position and turned around, leading the convoy toward England. The other ships likewise took their positions, with Commander Michael Scott's *Corinthia* on the right flank.

The American escort ships headed for Reykjavik as Mulford and convoy HX 289 drove through the heavy seas toward England.

Kruger was in the officers' wardroom drinking a cup of coffee when the next message came in.

CONVOY HX 289 SIGHTED AK 59 BEARING 95 INTERCEPT AND REPORT CONTACT.

He jumped up from the table, put on his white cap, and moved quickly toward the navigator's table in the control room. Mohlmann was there, smoking a cigarette and studying the charts. Kruger handed him the message.

"Plot this course and give it to me immediately. I'll be on the bridge."

"Yes, sir."

Kruger put on his leather jacket and climbed the ladder to the bridge. The sky was gray and the seas high, with waves washing the deck of U-112. Feiler and Blohm were on duty there along with some seamen.

"The convoy has been sighted," Kruger said. "It's not more than a day's run away."

Feiler and Blohm smiled, eager to get into action again. Kruger raised his binoculars and swept the horizon. British planes didn't fly in weather like this; he expected an unimpeded voyage to the convoy.

Next to him, Blohm wondered why he felt so excited by the prospect of a good fight, because he no longer believed in the war with the fervor of his first days on U-112. Perhaps it was the prospect of a life-or-death struggle that stimulated him.

Mohlmann came to the bridge with the new course, and Kruger read it.

"Hard left rudder!" he ordered. "Steer three hundred fifty degrees! Both engines ahead two-thirds!"

Mulford stood on the bridge with the second watch when his executive officer, Lieutenant Commander Peters, approached. "Sir, the radio shack reports heavy U-boat traffic."

Mulford gazed out to sea and frowned. The convoy must have been spotted by a U-boat, which had reported its position and was now shadowing from behind. The best response would be to force the trailing U-boat down and have the convoy change course.

"Dispatch the *Westminster* to the rear of the convoy," Mulford said, "and have it join the *Leamus* in a radar search for U-boats."

"Yes, sir."

Peters returned to the bridge house and transmitted the orders to the *Leamus* and the *Westminster*. *Leamus,* already at the rear of the convoy, turned around and steamed west, its radar antenna spinning. A few minutes later the *Westminster* arrived from the port side of the convoy and also began a radar sweep to the rear.

The trailing U-boat was U-361, commanded by Kapitänleutnant Gerhardt Schmidt, who stood on the bridge, observing through his binoculars the convoy far in the distance. His U-boat was trimmed low in the water. The electrician's mate had reported the presence of radar for some time, but Schmidt decided he would track the convoy until one of the escort ships actually threatened him.

"Sir!" said Leutnant Zeissler, his executive officer. "I think there are ships headed this way!"

Schmidt squinted his eyes. "I don't see anything."

"I think I see them too, sir!" said Leutnant Kolbe, the second watch officer.

"I think you're both having hallucinations," replied Schmidt dryly, continuing to scan the rear of the convoy through his binoculars, but then he noticed two dark shapes that had separated themselves from the convoy.

"Hard right rudder!" Schmidt called out.

"Hard right rudder!" replied his helmsman.

The U-boat responded instantly to its twin rudders and began to turn in the high seas. Schmidt shifted his position so he could see the convoy, then spun around to watch the progress of his boat.

"Rudder amidships — both engines full ahead!" he yelled.

"Rudder amidships — both engines full ahead!"

U-361 accelerated through the water and raced away from the convoy.

"Take the bridge," Schmidt said to Zeissler.

"Yes, sir."

Schmidt descended the ladder into the U-boat and made his way to the radio room. "Send a message to headquarters that we're being pursued by two escorts and have had to break off contact," he told the radioman.

"Yes, sir," replied the radioman, turning toward his key.

At U-boat headquarters in Kerneval, Admiral Dönitz frowned as he read the message. It was happening again — Allied ships chasing away his contact boat. The cursed radar was ruining the tactics he'd developed so carefully over the years, but he wasn't ready to give up yet.

He looked down at the big chart of the ocean. He had ten U-boats in this wolf pack, and the convoy would not get away no matter how much radar it had. Bending over the table, he decided to deploy his U-boats in a wide skirmish line directly in the path of the convoy. Even if the convoy changed course, which he fully expected it would, it would not be able to escape this wolf pack deployment.

He pointed to the chart table. "Direct the boats to deploy themselves in this manner," he said to his chief of staff. "And tell them to attack as soon as they sight the convoy."

"Yes, sir."

Dönitz folded his arms, looking at the chart table. He would have preferred his wolf pack to attack en masse, but enemy radar no longer permitted that. His only hope now was to attack the convoy in any way he could, sinking ships wherever possible and slowing the convoy down enough for the other U-boats to home in on it.

Then the mass destruction would begin.

On the bridge of the *Pembroke*, Mulford stood with the telephone to his ear and stared at the sea as he listened to Commander Rowland of the *Westminster*.

"We have sporadic contact with the U-boat on our radar, sir," Rowland explained, "but the seas are high and we can't get a good fix on her. Would you like me to go after her anyway?"

Mulford thought for a few moments, then said, "Yes, keep after her for ten more minutes, then return to the convoy in such a way that the U-boat won't know where we are by your direction, understand?"

"Yes, sir."

"The same for you, too, Woodcock." Mulford was referring to Commander Woodcock of the *Leamus*.

"Yes, sir."

"Over and out."

Mulford walked back to the bridge, raising his binoculars and scanning the sea once more. If he had more escort destroyers he could leave the *Leamus* and the *Westminster* back there to sink that U-boat, but a commander never could get all he needed to fight a war, and had to make the best of what he had.

The convoy zigzagged though high waves as Kapitänleutnant Schmidt of U-361 maneuvered full speed ahead on the surface to somehow get in front of it. The ocean was vast and it would be easy to miss the convoy altogether, but luck and fate were components of every battle.

At 1630 hours Kapitänleutnant Schmidt was astonished to see the convoy directly in front of him. "Navigator to the bridge!" he shouted.

The navigator scrambled to the bridge with his pelorus hanging around his neck. Schmidt pointed straight ahead. "Give me a bearing and course on the convoy and radio the information to headquarters immediately. Notify me when you've accomplished that."

"Yes, sir."

The navigator went down the ladder and Schmidt studied the convoy. He thought it might be a good idea to move to its side so he could get broadside shots. "Hard right rudder!" he shouted Schmidt.

The U-boat veered to port as the radio message went to Admiral Dönitz.

"Radar shack calling the captain!"

Mulford lifted the phone off the hook. "This is the captain."

"I have an unidentified craft bearing sixty-eight degrees, distance four thousand yards, course one hundred and sixty degrees."

"Stay with her." Mulford moved the phone a few inches from his face. "All ahead full!"

"All ahead full!" replied the helmsman.

The *Pembroke* picked up speed and charged through huge waves. Mulford told his watch to look for the U-boat, then radioed the rest of the convoy and ordered a change in course.

The convoy swerved in a northeasterly direction as Mulford continued due east, his officers and men scanning the ocean ahead through their binoculars for the low, dark silhouette of a U-boat among the waves.

"Are you there, Captain?" asked the radar operator.

"I'm here," replied Mulford.

"I just lost her, sir."

"What was her range when you lost her?"

"Three thousand yards, sir."

"Report any new contacts right away."

"Yes, sir."

Mulford hung up the phone and lit a cigarette, cupping his lighter with his hands. The U-boat had evidently dived too far away for his Asdic to pick it up. He could go to the spot where it had dived and conduct a search for it there, but by then it would probably be out of range.

The only thing to do was return to the convoy.

"Hard left rudder!" Mulford said.

The *Pembroke* began to turn, as Mulford puffed his cigarette, looking at the darkening sky. He knew that U-boats were zeroing in on the convoy and it wouldn't be long before another made contact.

Through his periscope Schmidt saw the convoy turn away. "Damn!"

"What is it, sir?" asked his exec.

"They must have seen us. They're turning away. Send this new information on the convoy to headquarters."

Admiral Dönitz read the message from Kapitänleutnant Schmidt, then looked down at his chart. He smiled as he saw his wolf pack converging on the convoy. It couldn't get away from him now unless it turned around and went back to America, which it would not do.

"Send this new position to the wolf pack," Dönitz said, handing the message to his chief of staff, "and reiterate that I want them to attack immediately upon contact. Tell them to be bold, and I will accept no excuse for failing to conduct a decisive attack at close range once the convoy is sighted."

"Yes, sir," said the chief of staff, taking the message and carrying it to the radioman.

Shortly after dusk Kapitänleutnant Hans Loesser in U-381 saw the convoy loom up before him out of the sea. He blinked: he couldn't believe his good fortune, but there it was, moving eastward.

"Battle stations!" Loesser shouted. "Oberleutnant Zech to the bridge! Radio shack — notify headquarters of the sighting!'

Oberleutnant Rolf Zech arrived on the bridge and looked at the convoy through the TBT. Loesser ordered a change in course that would send him toward the port flank of the convoy. He assumed the escort ships probably had him on radar, but he was an experienced U-boat commander and thought he could speed in, sink a ship or two, and speed out before any damage could be done to him.

U-381 raced toward the convoy, wind flapping the coats of the men on the bridge. Loesser examined the convoy through his binoculars while Zech held it in the sights of his TBT. The other men on the bridge watched for threats from other directions.

The convoy came closer, and Loesser could see the emerging outlines of individual ships. He wondered how long it would be before they saw him.

On U-112 a new message came in from headquarters. Kruger happened to be standing beside the radio room, dressed in his heavy leather coat and drinking a cup of coffee. He read the message, noted the new position of the convoy, crossed the control room in long strides and looked at the chart on the navigation table.

"It's not far away at all," Kruger said to Mohlmann, who was already plotting a new course.

"Not more than two hours, I'd say," Mohlmann replied.

The *Murdock* was on the starboard side of the convoy, with Commander Quarles on the bridge, when the radar room called.

"I have a blip four thousand yards away bearing one hundred eighty-five degrees and headed this way, sir."

"Radio room!" said Quarles.

"Radio room, sir."

"Report the radar contact to the *Pembroke*."

"Yes, sir."

Quarles turned at the bridge rail and looked aft. "There's a U-boat headed this way, boys. Keep your eyes peeled for her."

The men on the bridge raised their binoculars and leaned to starboard as they peered through the night for a sign of the U-boat.

"Battle stations!" shouted Quarles. "Send up a snowflake!"

Men poured out of the *Murdock*'s hatches and manned their guns and depth-charge gear as the snowflake flare shot into the sky and exploded, illuminating the sea.

On the bridge Quarles looked through his binoculars and swept the sea, but couldn't find anything unusual. "Anyone see the U-boat?"

No one said that he had. Quarles picked up the headset and called his radio room. "Do you still have that on your screen, Hayes?"

"Yes, sir. It's still heading this way."

Quarles yelled. "Keep a sharp eye out, men! You should see the damn thing any moment now!"

Loesser and Zech were blinded for a few moments when the snowflake went up. They blinked a few times, and then they saw the convoy spread out in front of them in light as bright as day.

U-381 pounded through the waves toward the convoy. Zech crouched behind the TBT and chewed his lower lip because he knew the escorts would see them soon and start shooting. They might score a lucky shot, which was all it would take to sink the thin-hulled U-boat.

"Get ready," Loesser told Zech. "Choose your target and keep your eyes on it."

"How soon can I fire, sir?"

"We're not going to fire until we're right in there, so keep your nerve and don't let me down."

"Yes, sir," Zech said.

"U-boat off starboard bow!" shouted one of the *Murdock*'s officers.

Quarles turned and saw it, a lethal dark form speeding toward the convoy.

"All batteries open fire!"

Two seconds after he got the last word out of his mouth, the first battery fired. Shells landed surprisingly close to the bow of the U-boat. Then a second battery fired, and within seconds shells were raining down all around the U-boat.

"Steady your aim and keep firing!" Quarles shouted.

Quarles looked at the U-boat and saw the splashes of shells surrounding it. *It'll turn away any moment now,* Quarles thought. *It can't put up with this shelling much longer.*

On the bridge of U-381 Zech's teeth were chattering behind the TBT. Loesser stood erect at the bridge rail, looking at the convoy through his binoculars while shells dropped into the sea nearby and sent water splashing to the bridge.

"Keep your nerve, Zech!" he shouted. "We're almost there!"

"Yes-yes, sir," Zech stuttered.

"Chief, can you get any more knots out of this thing?"

"We're at top speed now, sir."

U-381 passed behind the *Murdock*, which was navigating to remain broadside to the U-boat. Another destroyer, the *James* toward the rear of the convoy, had spotted the U-boat and was heading toward it, too.

Loesser breathed through clenched teeth as he came within close range of the convoy. Shells rained down in his vicinity but all he could see were the ships.

"Prepare to fire!" he screamed.

"Tubes one to four ready for surface attack!" Zech replied. "Open tube doors! Target angle left ninety-five! Speed ten! Range fifteen thousand! Torpedo depth seven! Stand by!"

"Fire!" said Loesser.

"Tube one — fire! Tube two — fire!"

"Get the second one, now!"

Zech's trembling hands brought the cross hairs on to the next big ship. "Target angle left ninety—"

A shell slammed down on the foredeck of U-381, the explosion jolting the boat so severely that Zech was hurled against the TBT, gashing his head and knocking him unconscious. Loesser, thrown to the deck, scrambled to his feet and saw the bow of the U-boat sinking into the water. He realized instantly that his U-boat was finished, and all he could do was attempt the evasion procedures that had been drummed into his head for years.

"Hard left rudder!" he screamed.

His crew erupted on to the bridge, expressions of horror on their faces.

"Who's at the helm?" he demanded.

At that moment his helmsman showed his head in the hatch of the conning tower.

"What are you doing here?" Loesser screamed. "We're going down!"

His helmsman screamed back. "I'm not drowning in this sinking boat!"

"Get back to your station!" Loesser moved to kick the man in the head, but the man leaped out of the hatch and tackled him. Both of them fell to the bridge deck as machine-gun bullets buzzed over their heads and whacked into the conning tower. A sailor shrieked and dropped to his knees, blood spurting from his throat.

"Did anyone close the hatches?" Loesser demanded, looking up from his helmsman.

"Yes, sir," said Ensign Haller, huddling nearby. "All of them."

Loesser tried to think. If all the hatches were closed, that meant the U-boat wouldn't sink so quickly. "Man the guns!" he ordered.

"Man them your own goddamned self!" somebody replied.

Just then there was a huge explosion from the direction of the convoy. Loesser looked up to see what it was, and smiled as he saw one of the ships shooting bolts of fire into the sky.

"We got it!" Loesser bellowed, reflections of flames lighting his face.

He was standing in the middle of the hail of machine-gun fire, and one of the bullets hit him on the side of the face. It was a big .50-caliber bullet, and it blew his head away. Loesser's body sagged to the deck of the bridge, the men staring in horror at the blood gushing out of his neck.

"Let's get out of here!" somebody screamed.

The bridge deck was covered with Loesser's blood. Crew members jumped over the bridge rail as the U-boat was raked from stem to stern with machine-gun bullets. Another British shell landed aft of the bridge, blowing that part of the deck and a ballast tank to smithereens. Most of the men were killed before they hit the water. The conning tower of the U-boat became streaked with blood.

Trembling, Zech peeked over the bridge rail to see what was going on. His body went slack and his bladder emptied into his pants as he saw the British destroyer bearing down on the sinking U-boat, all its guns firing.

Zech crouched behind the steel wall and looked for someplace to hide.

"Prepare to ram!" shouted Commander Quarles on the bridge of the *Murdock*.

The destroyer pounded against the waves as it roared toward the U-boat. Its gun crews stopped firing because they were too close to the U-boat and couldn't get sufficient declination. U-boat survivors were jumping into the raging seas. Quarles gripped the bridge rail and braced himself. The *Murdock* slid down a wave and slammed into the U-boat, breaking it in half. The U-boat began to sink, the *Murdock* rolling right over it.

Commander Quarles flinched instinctively as he heard scraping under his hull and realized he was going to lose his Asdic module, but it was too late now. The destroyer passed over the U-boat, and Quarles looked behind him at the place where the U-boat had been, but he couldn't see it anymore.

"Hard left rudder!" Quarles said.

The destroyer turned around and went back to the spot where the U-boat had sunk. A few German heads bobbed in the water, and Quarles thought he'd pick them up.

"All engines stop!" Quarles ordered. "Boarding nets over the side!"

Sailors threw the nets as three Germans in the water swam toward the *Murdock*. They grabbed the nets and wearily climbed up, slipping a few notches as the *Murdock* pitched in the high seas, but ultimately making it to the rail, where the *Murdock*'s men pulled them on to the deck.

Zech was the last one up, and when he landed on the deck, he dropped on to his knees, exhausted and shivering from the cold. His two comrades also looked like drowned rats, teeth chattering and clothes plastered to their bodies.

"So these are the dauntless U-boat men," sneered one of the British sailors.

"Lock them in the brig!" ordered a deck officer.

A group of sailors escorted the staggering U-boat men away. When they were halfway across the deck, they heard a thunderclap in front of them. Looking up, they saw another ship in the convoy explode.

CHAPTER 21

Blohm was looking at the dark horizon through his binoculars when suddenly he saw a bright dot of light far away. He closed his eyes for a few seconds and looked again, because sometimes when his eyes were tired, he saw pinpricks of light that vanished almost immediately.

When he looked again, the light was still there. Then a few seconds later the light grew brighter.

"Captain to the bridge!" Blohm shouted.

Kruger clambered up the ladder, anticipation on his face. "What is it?"

Blohm pointed. "The convoy!"

Kruger raised his binoculars. "Yes, it's the convoy all right. And it must be in trouble, otherwise it wouldn't be lit up that way. Steer three hundred degrees! Both engines full ahead!"

The U-boat gathered speed as it headed for convoy HX 289.

On the bridge of the *Pembroke,* Mulford heard another explosion. Turning around, he saw that it was on the starboard side of the convoy. This was the third ship torpedoed so far, and they'd only sunk one U-boat — and that at a cost: the *Murdock* had destroyed its Asdic in the process.

Mulford looked at his watch and saw that it was five o'clock in the morning. Soon it would be dawn, then the U-boats would withdraw, or so he hoped. All around the convoy his destroyers were chasing blips on their radar screens, and echoes on their Asdic, but there were too many U-boats. While the destroyers were attacking some, other U-boats broke through the defenses and fired torpedoes.

Mulford felt frustrated; it was like fighting with one hand tied behind his back. His ship was well in advance of the convoy, following a radar blip, and he imagined that another U-boat might be sneaking right past him. His radio operator had counted ten different U-boat signals so far, and six escort ships simply were not enough.

He decided to have the convoy change course again. That wouldn't shake the convoy loose from the U-boats, but it might spoil the aim of some of those torpedoes.

Mulford reached for the phone and ordered the change in course. Before he could finish giving the new course, another ship in the convoy went up in flames. It was a tanker, and the water around it covered with burning oil.

At U-boat headquarters an aide brought the latest message to Admiral Dönitz.

HAVE SUNK TANKER 20000 TONS U-371

Dönitz smiled and handed the message to an aide, who read it and removed one of the convoy ships from the table. It was the fourth ship sunk so far. Dönitz looked at the clock on the wall. Daylight would come soon, but he was confident his wolf pack would send a few more ships to the bottom by then. He studied the deployment of the wolf pack, wondering if they would be more effective if he shifted them around a bit. Another aide brought him a message.

HAVE SIGHTED CONVOY 27N 58W CLOSING FOR ATTACK U-112.

Dönitz smiled; he knew that was Kruger's boat. He doubted whether it would be long before he received a victory message from Kruger.

The stiff breeze fluttered the white cloth on Kruger's hat as U-112 sped toward the convoy. Feiler stood at the TBT, taking bearings, and Blohm stood beside Kruger watching the convoy through his binoculars.

The sea around the convoy was bright as day and looked eerie in the middle of the dark ocean. Ships burned and trails of smoke were blown away by the wind.

"I think we'll go in from windward," Kruger said. "That way they won't see our wake so well, and the wind will hit them right in the eyeballs. Steer forty degrees to port!"

The U-boat angled to the side, made a semi-circle, then turned again and sped toward the convoy. As the U-boat crew drew closer, they saw that they were in front of it, on its starboard side.

"Destroyer two points off the bow, sir!" Blohm shouted.

Kruger looked and saw a tiny shadow on the water in the distance. "You have marvelous eyes, Blohm. I think I'm going to start calling you Eagle Eye. Well, we'll see what he does. If he makes the mistake of coming for us, I'll fire a torpedo right down his damned throat. Battle stations, everyone! This is it! Feiler!"

"Yes, sir."

"Sight on that destroyer, because I want to be ready for him if he comes for us."

"Yes, sir."

"I'll want to fire two torpedoes — you know how I like to do it."

"Yes, sir."

The destroyer was the *Alcestis,* and on the bridge was Commander Richard Greer. He was conducting a radar and Asdic sweep on the front of the convoy; Commander Mulford and the *Pembroke* were a few miles to port.

There was a clanging next to the phone, and Greer picked it up. "This is the captain speaking."

"This is Radarman Burns, sir. There's an unidentified vessel on my screen bearing ninety-five degrees, and he's headed straight for the convoy."

"Steer right twenty-five degrees!" shouted Greer.

The helmsman spun the wheel, and the *Alcestis* swerved toward the unidentified vessel. Greer raised his binoculars and swept the horizon for her.

"Send up a snowflake!" he ordered.

Kruger saw the flare shoot into the sky.

"She's headed right at us, sir," Blohm said.

"I can see it," Kruger replied. "Well, it looks as though we're going to have to sink the son-of-a-bitch."

Blohm gazed at Kruger, admiring his aplomb. Even in the thick of battle, Kruger was completely calm and rational — much more calm and rational, in fact, than he ever was ashore.

Blohm raised his binoculars and sighted on the destroyer. It was coming at top speed, and U-112 was moving toward it at top speed. In the background were flaming ships and the convoy ships, huddled together like frightened sheep.

"Prepare to fire!" Kruger screamed.

"Forward battery open fire!" Greer shouted on the bridge of the *Alcestis.*

The ship trembled as its heavy guns fired their first volley. Greer watched the U-boat through his binoculars. White water gushed into the air where his shells landed around the U-boat, but it kept coming, slicing through the water like a knife. It was two thousand yards away now, clearly visible in the light of the flares, but presenting a low silhouette and not much of a target. Greer thought he could see the captain in his white hat on the bridge.

"Torpedo off the starboard bow!"

Greer lowered his binoculars and saw it streaking through the water, straight at the *Alcestis*. "Hard left rudder!" he shouted.

The *Alcestis* veered to escape the torpedo. Greer watched it approach, holding his breath. It looked as though it might pass astern — yes, it would pass astern. Fortunately his lookout had spotted it soon enough.

"Torpedo dead to starboard!" a lookout yelled.

Greer swung around and saw this one headed straight for the center of the *Alcestis*'s waterline. He couldn't go backward and he couldn't speed up — all he could do was hope it was a dud.

The crew of the *Alcestis* watched in horror as the torpedo flashed toward its hull.

"Hang on!" Greer told them.

One torpedo hit the *Alcestis* amidships, sending water and flame shooting into the sky.

"You got her, sir!" Blohm shouted excitedly, pointing toward the stricken ship.

"Steer right thirty degrees," Kruger said coolly.

"Right thirty degrees!"

The U-boat swerved around the sinking destroyer, whose crew were trying to lower lifeboats amid raging fires. Kruger looked at the ship as he passed it by, and saw that it was split in two, bow and stern making a big V. "We must have hit her in the magazine," he said. "Reload torpedo tubes!"

"Reload torpedo tubes!"

Kruger looked at the convoy and could spot no more destroyers. Now he could pick targets at his leisure and sink them with careful precision.

"Prepare for firing!" he shouted.

Feiler crouched behind the TBT and twirled knobs while Blohm leaned against the bridge rail and looked at individual ships through his binoculars. Wind whistled past his ears and through his blond hair, which was partially covered by his visorless black hat. He felt mighty and powerful, and thought, *Yes, this is what war is all about, and to hell with all the politics.*

The buzzer went off next to the phone, and Mulford grabbed it. "Mulford here."

"This is the radio shack, sir. The *Alcestis* reports that it has been torpedoed and is sinking fast. I also have a bunch of messages from ships in that part of the convoy who say they can see a U-boat coming at them on the surface."

"Anything else?"

"No, sir."

Mulford hung up the phone and made his decision immediately: he must stop that U-boat. "Hard left rudder!" he shouted. "Battle stations!"

Feiler looked at the row of convoy ships in front of him. They were silhouetted by fires raging in other parts of the convoy, and while he was sighting through his TBT, another ship exploded on the far side of the convoy.

"Magnificent," muttered Kruger. "Really amazing. Just like the good old days."

The U-boat had slowed down for steady firing and was twelve hundred yards from the convoy. Strangely, there wasn't a destroyer in sight — a rare occurrence — and the convoy ships moved slowly and obediently in line.

"Fire!" shouted Kruger.

Feiler pressed the levers. "Tube one — fire! Tube two — fire!"

"Now the next target!"

"Tube three — fire! Tube four — fire!"

The U-boat rebounded as each torpedo fired away. Kruger watched the gleaming fish slip beneath the waves toward their targets.

"Reload torpedo tubes!"

In the forward torpedo room the sailors grunted as they opened the doors to the tubes and pushed the torpedoes forward on their tracks. They were an experienced, smooth-working team and accomplished their task quickly, signaling the bridge when all tubes were loaded again.

Kruger, Feiler, and Blohm looked at the ships through their binoculars. In a rapid series of explosions, each of the torpedoes struck home. The sky filled with sparks and flames, smokestacks and funnels, flying through the air along with men and parts of men.

Kruger decided to get four ships with four torpedoes this time. It would be difficult, but he was close and in excellent position. He thought it would be worth a try, imagining the diamonds that would be added to his Knight's Cross if he succeeded.

"Feiler," he said, "I want four ships this time. Prepare for firing."

Feiler peered through his TBT. "Yes, sir."

The *Pembroke* slammed through the ocean as it made its way to the last reported site of the U-boat attacking the convoy on its forward port flank. The convoy ships radioed that the U-boat was sitting calmly on the water, firing its torpedoes at close range. It enraged Mulford that a U-boat was causing such wholesale destruction without being chased or threatened in any way.

The *Pembroke* plowed toward the U-boat. Mulford thought that maybe he should have the closest destroyer assist him in trapping it.

He picked up the bridge phone. "Radio room!"

"This is the radio room," said the voice at his ear. "A message has just come in for you, sir. The *Westminster* reports that after depth-charging a suspected U-boat target, it has observed wreckage floating to the surface."

Mulford breathed a sigh of relief. "Send the *Westminster* my congratulations and direct her to return to her position in the convoy, but first contact Commander Scott on the *Corinthia* and tell him to proceed at once to the U-boat target that we're headed for right now."

"Yes, sir."

Mulford hung up the phone and returned to the bridge rail.

"Men in the water, sir!" shouted a lookout.

"Steer around them!" Mulford told the helmsmen.

The *Pembroke* swerved to the side, and Mulford looked at heads bobbing in the churning sea. They waved at the *Pembroke,* but Mulford didn't think he should stop while that U-boat was nearby, still sinking ships.

He suspected they were the survivors from the *Alcestis*, and wondered if Commander Greer was down there.

He also wondered if he'd be down there soon himself.

"Fire at your first two targets!" shouted Kruger.

Feiler pressed the levers. "Tube one — fire! Tube two — fire!"

"Prepare to fire at your next two targets!"

"Tubes three and four ready for surface attack!" Feiler said. "Open tube doors! Target angle right eighty! Speed ten! Range one thousand! Torpedo depth seven! Stand by!"

"Fire!" cried Kruger.

"Tube three — fire!" Feiler pressed the levers and sighted on the next ship. "Tube four — fire!"

Kruger pinched his lips together as he held his binoculars to his eyes and watched the row of ships. "I hope we're keeping a sharp lookout, gentlemen. We wouldn't want one of those destroyers to creep up on us, would we? Reload all forward torpedo tubes!"

"Reload all torpedo tubes!" repeated Feiler.

Kruger was watching the convoy ships when the first torpedo slammed home with an ear-splitting roar. A few seconds later the second torpedo hit the next ship in the line, and finally the fourth ship was struck slightly forward of its rudder, causing it to sit down in the water like an old cow.

"One missed," Kruger said thoughtfully as U-112 bobbed up and down in the water. "A quite remarkable performance, actually."

"Destroyer dead to starboard!" Blohm shouted, pointing in that direction.

Kruger raised his binoculars and saw the ship coming at full speed. The destroyer shot up a flare which brightened an ocean already alight with flares and fire.

"Hard right rudder!" Kruger said. "Feiler, prepare to fire two torpedoes at that destroyer in the customary pattern!"

"Yes, sir!" Feiler crouched behind the TBT and took careful aim. Like Kruger, he was intoxicated by their success — five ships sunk already — what a celebration they'd have in Lorient! "Tubes one to four ready for surface attack!" he said. "Open tube…"

"Destroyer astern, sir!" shouted one of the lookouts on the bridge.

Kruger spun around and saw it. Suddenly the picture changed. A fountain of water shot into the air beside the U-boat as the second destroyer opened fire.

Kruger excitedly looked back and forth from destroyer to destroyer and tried to think of what to do. He decided that if he sat still and tried to knock out one destroyer, the other one would be on top of him quickly. The only thing to do was make a run for it.

"Close torpedo doors! Hard right rudder!"

The U-boat turned in the water and pointed away from the convoy as shells landed in the water fifty yards away.

"Rudder amidships — both engines full ahead!"

The U-boat leaped forward and streaked away from the convoy. Kruger hoped the destroyers would be content to chase him away and not be persistent about sinking him. He never could guess what they'd do on any given day. Sometimes they'd try to kill you and other times they'd be anxious to return to the convoy.

The two destroyers stormed after him. They could do thirty knots, and he could only make seventeen on the surface, so his only hope would be to keep zigzagging and try to outmaneuver them until they returned to the convoy.

"Hard left rudder!" he ordered.

The U-boat snaked through the water, but the destroyers kept coming, gaining steadily. The situation would soon reach a point where he'd have to dive, because they were adjusting course every time he altered direction. He couldn't wait too long before he dived, or they'd depth-charge him right out of the water.

He trained his binoculars first on one of the destroyers, then the other. They were about nine hundred meters away now, flashes of orange light on their turrets as they fired at him. He thought about firing his stern tube at one of them, but didn't think he'd have time. They were gaining too quickly. He needed to dive immediately and get as deep as possible before they passed over him and dropped depth charges.

"Take it all the way down!" he screamed.

The sailors scrambled down the ladder, then Blohm and Feiler, and finally Kruger followed, closing the hatch above him. In the rear of the U-boat, diesel engines switched off and the electric motors hummed to life. Seawater poured by the ton into the ballast tanks, and U-112 dropped beneath the surface of the sea.

"He's diving, sir!" said Lieutenant-Commander Peters on the bridge of the *Pembroke*.

"I see him." Mulford watched the U-boat settling lower in the water. He picked the phone off the bulkhead. "Get me Commander Scott."

"Yes, sir."

He listened as the connection was being made. The U-boat dropped out of sight into the cold, gray waters of the Atlantic. Beyond it, on the eastern horizon, came the first faint glow of dawn.

"Commander Scott here," said the voice in his earphone.

"This is Mulford. I'm going after her, Scotty, and I want you to maintain Asdic contact for me."

"Yes, sir. Good luck."

"Over and out."

Mulford hung up the headset. "Prepare for depth-charge attack!"

On the after deck, depth-charge crews huddled around their canisters filled with Torpex explosive. Mulford guessed that the U-boat was trying to get away at top speed, but in which direction?

"Asdic!" said Mulford into his headset.

"Asdic, sir," said Electronics Mate Woolton below.

"Where is the son of a bitch?"

"Bearing one hundred twenty degrees, sir. Approximately five hundred yards away now, and moving I'd say to the north northeast."

"Advise me immediately of any change."

"Yes, sir."

U-112 was moving at its top speed of seven knots underwater, heading downward and in the north-north-easterly direction Woolton had discerned. Kruger sat on his seat at the periscope in the conning tower, looking at the depth, water temperature, and salinity gauges. Kruger had been depth-charged many times and had brought his boat back each time to Lorient. He saw no reason why he couldn't do it all again. The British Asdic scraped across his hull like fingernails.

"Hydroplane?" he asked calmly.

"Two ships headed in this direction, sir," said the hydroplane operator in his little nook below. "One is some distance ahead of the other — I'd say three hundred meters."

Kruger chuckled. "They're going to play fancy games with us, evidently. Well, we know how to play fancy games, too." He looked at the depth gauge and saw that they were down to a hundred meters.

"Hydroplane?" Kruger asked.

"Yes, sir."

"Are they headed in our present direction or toward the spot where we dived?"

"Our present direction, sir."

"You're sure?"

"Reasonably sure, sir."

"Steer right ninety degrees," Kruger said softly to his helmsman. The temperature and salinity gauges didn't show anything he could play with, so he decided to slow the U-boat to minimum speed so as to make as little noise as possible.

"Starboard motor stop, port motor ahead one-third," he ordered. "Steer right ninety degrees."

The U-boat slowed and turned in the water as the Asdic pinged against its hull. Kruger looked up as he heard the destroyer's motors drone closer. "Well, here they come," he said. "Hydroplane?"

"Yes, sir."

"Are they coming directly at us?"

"Yes, sir."

"Hard right rudder. Both motors full ahead."

The U-boat accelerated to the side, and Kruger pushed his white hat to the back of his head. "Hang on to something, gentlemen," he said. "The morning's festivities are about to begin."

"Just lost them, sir," said the Asdic operator on the *Pembroke*.

Mulford asked, "Where is he, Scotty?"

"Sounds as though he just turned to the north, sir."

"Oh, he did, did he?" Mulford pulled the phone away from his mouth. "Steer twenty degrees to starboard!"

The *Pembroke* swerved in the suspected direction of the U-boat, Mulford holding the phone to his ear again.

"You should be just about over her now, sir," said Commander Scott.

"Drop depth charges!" Mulford shouted.

The depth charges rolled off their tracks and fell into the water, sending up trails of bubbles on their way down.

The first depth charge exploded, shaking the U-boat slightly.

"Not bad at all," Kruger said, wrinkling his nose. He turned to the side, his eyes falling on Blohm. "We've been through much worse than that, haven't we, Blohm?"

"Yes, sir."

"The Tommies have no idea where we are. The lesson to be learned, I suppose, is to get down fast if two escort ships are after you. I hope you pay attention to the little things I say, Blohm, because we all know you're going to be a great U-boat ace someday."

Blohm smiled. "I doubt if I'll ever catch up with you, sir."

Kruger laughed. "You really should have been in the diplomatic service, Blohm. You could flatter the fur off a monkey."

Blohm was about to say that his words weren't merely flattery when several depth charges went off nearly simultaneously, rocking the U-boat again.

"What a waste of explosive," Kruger sighed. "Steer right ninety degrees — both motors full ahead."

They felt the U-boat swing to the side as the hum of the destroyer's propellers passed by overhead.

"I think that'll be all for a little while, gentlemen," Kruger said. He looked at Feiler. "You know, I think it's about time you had your own U-boat, Feiler."

"It's kind of you to say that, sir," Feiler replied, hanging on to a pipe.

"Your performance at the TBT tonight was really quite exemplary. They'll have to take note of it in Kerneval. They'll give you a U-boat for sure."

"But you did it all, sir. I merely pushed the buttons."

"Flatterers," Kruger said, glancing at the depth gauge. "I am surrounded by flatterers. Who among you will tell me the truth?"

Blohm smiled. "We all tell you the truth, sir."

Kruger made a mock expression of dismay. "Flatterers and liars," he said sadly. "What has the U-boat arm come to?"

The depth gauge read 250 meters as the sound of propellers receded.

"Hydroplane?" Kruger asked.

"Yes, sir."

"What's the idiot doing up there?"

"It sounds as though he's circling for another run, sir."

"You mean we have to go through all that again?"

"I think so, sir."

"How tiresome."

On the *Pembroke* Mulford spoke alternately with his Asdic operator and Commander Scott on the *Corinthia*. The *Pembroke* finished its turn and was rushing against the waves for its second run at the U-boat.

"He's quite deep, sir," said the Asdic operator. "The signal is getting weak."

"Direction?"

"Due south, sir."

"Steer right twenty degrees!" Mulford shouted. "Prepare deep depth charge pattern!"

"I just lost him, sir," said the Asdic man.

Mulford switched to the *Corinthia*. "Where is he, Scotty?"

"It's difficult to be sure at his depth, sir, but I think he's turning north again."

"Steer to port forty degrees!"

The *Pembroke* shifted direction again as Mulford stared at the water ahead, trying to divine the position of the U-boat.

"You should be passing over her right now, sir," said Scott.

"Drop depth charges!" bellowed Mulford.

Kruger looked up as the sound of propellers drew closer. His hands were folded between his knees, and he had an expression of utter boredom on his face. Glancing at the depth gauge, he saw that they were down to maximum depth, where the Asdic would have difficulty finding him. The temperature and salinity gauges still offered no possibilities.

He didn't need to tell his men to hang on to something because they were braced already. Blohm stood only inches from Kruger in the cramped conning tower, admiring his commanding officer's aplomb.

The propellers passed overhead. Everyone on the U-boat knew that depth charges were being dropped. Kruger looked at his watch; he'd been down nearly twenty minutes already. He hoped the destroyers would return to the convoy after this pass.

The depth charges began to explode, closer this time. The U-boat jounced about in the water as men looked at each other fearfully, but the explosions weren't close enough to do real damage. Kruger didn't even ask for a damage report. The propeller sounds receded, and several more depth charges exploded, but they'd been through worse before and come out all right.

"Blind as bats," Kruger muttered. "They have no idea what they're doing, but they drop depth charges anyway, so they'll have something to write about when they make their reports at the end of their trip. I've never been able to respect the British. They're the most overrated people in the world."

Mulford watched his depth charges send tons of water bursting into the air, but could see no sign of a broken U-boat. After the explosions stopped, he ordered the *Pembroke* to make a slow run over the area he'd depth-charged so they could search for debris or an oil slick.

The *Pembroke* made another big arc and passed over the waters still boiling from the depth-charge attack. All the men rushed to their rails and looked for signs of the U-boat, but there was nothing to see.

On the bridge Mulford felt exasperated. It was dawn, but the clouds didn't let much sunlight through. Looking east, he could see the convoy far away, its burning ships sending trails of black smoke into the sky. He'd heard no more explosions for a while. Evidently the other U-boats had broken off their attack at daybreak. He ought to return to the convoy and protect it from the possibility of submerged daylight attacks, but he didn't want the U-boat he had pinned down to get away.

His officers on the bridge looked at him expectantly. They could see he was trying to reach a decision. With the back of his hand he wiped salt spray off his mustache. Looking back at the place where he'd dropped the last depth-charge pattern, he decided to make one more pass, but an extra thorough one this time.

He spoke into his phone. "Scotty?"

"Yes, sir."

"I want to do it a little differently this time. I want you to follow me, and after I drop my load I want you to drop two full patterns based on your calculation of where the bastard will be if he maintains the last course you've fixed him on. Understand that?"

"Yes, sir."

The *Pembroke* made a wide turn in the water, the *Corinthia* taking its position behind it. Asdic operators tried to get a fix on the deep-moving U-boat, discouraged because their previous fixes had not produced a U-boat kill.

The two destroyers rent the waves as they made their final pass at the U-boat far beneath the surface of the sea.

Kruger wrinkled his nose. "Sounds like there are two of them this time. Hydroplane?"

"Yes, sir."

"Are there two coming this time?"

"Yes, sir."

Kruger snorted. "So they've decided to multiply their inaccuracy by two. They're such fools, the British."

Blohm looked upward, wondering what the British were up to this time. He'd been depth-charged before by two escort ships, but one usually kept its distance to hold its target on Asdic. He heard the rippling sound of two Asdic beams against the hull of U-112 as the hum of propellers came closer. He reached for a pipe and hung on.

"Drop depth charges!" shouted Mulford.

The two depth-charge crews on the fantail of the *Pembroke* pulled the levers that released huge canisters of explosives. The charges were set to explode at depths from 250 to 300 meters. They splashed into the water, disappearing instantly in the gray-green depths.

After the last depth charge had splashed into the water, the crew returned the levers to their original positions, then loaded more depth charges on to the tracks for the next pass. Mulford trained his binoculars on the water at the rear of his ship, waiting for explosions. Seventy yards behind was the *Corinthia*, following directly in his path. Then, suddenly, the *Corinthia* veered sharply to starboard.

On the bridge of the *Corinthia*, Scott had just received a message from his Asdic man that the U-boat was making an abrupt change in course. Scott ordered that the *Corinthia* be steered in that direction, then Asdic contact broke off.

Scott looked at the waters and tried to estimate the position of the U-boat. He decided to unload his depth charges one crew at a time and thereby spread the charges over a wider range of ocean.

"Port crew — drop charges!" he shouted.

Kruger wrinkled his brow as he looked upward and tried to outthink the destroyers. He'd veered away from the first as soon as it came overhead, but now it appeared that the second was steering in his new direction.

"Hard left rudder!" she said.

"Hard left rudder," repeated the helmsman.

The U-boat turned again as depth charges exploded all around it. The first ones weren't very close, although they bounced the U-boat around.

"One can't help wondering," Kruger said, "how much time they have to waste up there?"

Then came an explosion that made the floor plates rattle. The lights dimmed for a few seconds, then came on again, revealing men looking at each other in alarm.

"That really wasn't so close," Kruger muttered. "I won't need to ask for a damage report."

An earsplitting clap of thunder flung the U-boat downward violently, knocking Kruger off his seat. The lights went out and didn't come on again. Kruger climbed to his feet in the darkness and felt the front of the U-boat dipping low. He was about to issue an order to level off when another powerful explosion rocked the U-boat and sent him crashing against a network of pipes.

"Emergency lights!" he said.

There was a pause, then somebody said: "They're not working, sir."

Kruger calmed himself. "Break out the emergency lamp." He looked at the depth gauge. The U-boat had fallen below 300 meters, its operational limit, but theoretically could dive two hundred meters beyond that with no ill effects.

"Can't we have some lights?" Kruger asked.

The lights came on as a close explosion knocked everyone in the conning tower to the floor. Water hissed from a crack in the wall as long as a man's hand, then another depth charge exploded on the bow of the U-boat, sending it into a rapid downward spin.

"Level it off!" Kruger said, trying to get to his feet. "Stop that leak!"

But the U-boat was out of control, dropping deeper into the ocean. Kruger hung on to a pipe and saw the depth gauge near 400 meters. Water poured into the conning tower. Kruger thought he'd better seal it off. His boat obviously was getting into serious trouble.

"Everybody down to the control room!"

They slid down the ladder, Kruger going last and closing the hatch above him. At the hydroplane wheels the two operators were straining to bring the U-boat under control.

"Damage report!" Kruger said.

"Forward torpedo room taking water badly, sir."

"Why haven't you plugged it up yet?"

"Can't, sir," said the desperate voice. "The water's over the floor plates."

Kruger blinked and tried to think. This was the worst situation his boat had ever been in. It was still out of control, nose-diving into the sea.

"Everybody to the aft motor room!"

Everyone except the officers and the men on duty in the control room ran backward through the U-boat to the motor room. They scraped their knuckles and bumped their knees, fearing for their lives, hoping for a miracle to save them before the pressure of the ocean collapsed their hull. Kruger looked at the depth gauge; the U-boat was at 450 meters.

The weight of the men aft leveled the boat off, but still it was sinking. Kruger smelled a bitter, acid odor and realized that saltwater had leaked into the batteries, producing chlorine gas, which could kill if it reached a sufficient concentration.

"Both motors ahead full!" Kruger shouted, hoping that the motion would stabilize the boat.

"Port motor is out of order, sir," said the voice on the loudspeaker. "Starboard motor can't go any faster."

The depth gauge reached 600 meters, which was as far as its needle would go. Kruger realized he had only two grim alternatives. He could hope to bring the U-boat under control before the water pressure crushed it, or blow the tanks and raise the U-boat to a safe depth, then flood them partially.

He turned to look at the speed gauge and saw that the boat was moving at only two knots. He needed more speed, but none was available. He became aware that his feet were wet. Looking down, he saw an inch of water on the floor plates. No batteries were under the control room to produce chlorine gas, but the added water was making the U-boat heavier. Coughing could be heard from the rear of the U-boat. Kruger glanced at Feiler, who was looking at him expectantly. Blohm's face was white as snow.

Kruger decided to take the desperate measures that were his only chance. "Blow the main ballast!" he said. "Hydroplanes on hard rise."

The hydroplane operators leaned to the side and pulled their wheels to the hard-rise position as the ballast operator pulled the appropriate levers. The U-boat shuddered and began to rise, nose first.

"Oil slick off starboard bow!"

Mulford swung his binoculars in that direction and smiled as he saw the iridescent surface of the water. But was it a trick? Sometimes U-boat captains released oil to fool British commanders into thinking that they'd made a kill. He lowered his binoculars and reached for the phone.

"No contact, sir. I think you're too close to him and you're upsetting the sound waves."

"I'll move away."

Mulford let the *Pembroke* continue in its direction away from the oil slick.

"Everybody on the bridge — keep that oil slick in view at all times!" Mulford said. "Don't let it get away from you! Asdic?"

"Asdic, sir."

"Report as soon as you make contact"

"Yes, sir."

Mulford looked back at the convoy; it was almost out of sight now.

"This is Asdic," said the voice in his earphone. "I've got him."

"Where is he?"

"Bearing two-twenty, range three hundred yards. The signal's getting louder, so I think he's coming up."

Coming up? Mulford thought. He looked in the direction given by the Asdic man and saw that the U-boat was in the vicinity of the oil slick. *Did I get him?* Mulford thought excitedly.

"Hard left rudder!" he shouted.

The *Pembroke* began to turn around. Mulford prepared to deliver a full depth-charge attack to the region of water underneath the oil slick.

In U-112 the air had become thick with chlorine gas. Blohm held his handkerchief over his nose, his eyes smarting as he looked at Kruger, who appeared calm and lost in thought. Kruger took off his hat and ran his fingers through hair that was like sauerkraut.

The U-boat was rising slowly, at the 300-meter mark already. Kruger thought he'd let it go up another fifty meters, then flood the ballast tanks.

The sound of approaching propellers could be heard. Kruger put his white hat back on and wondered what had gone wrong. He'd been depth-charged before and nothing like this had ever happened. Had his luck finally run out?

"We just have to hang on a little longer," he said softly. "They can't spend the whole day out here. They have to guard the convoy."

Propellers passed overhead. Blohm looked up, assuming depth charges were being dropped. U-112 didn't have enough speed or maneuverability to get away. He recalled how thrilled he'd been when they were sinking convoy ships, but this was the other side of the coin. Gripping the pipe more tightly, he became afraid. Something told him this was going to be his last day on earth.

A depth charge exploded beside the U-boat, then a stream of water shot across the control room. Hands groped for cranks; the stream slackened. Then three depth charges went off simultaneously. The U-boat was jolted so violently that Blohm was thrown into the air, his head crashing against the pipes on the overhead. He dropped dazed to his knees, and the lights flickered.

"Taking water in the motor room, sir!"

"Numerous leaks in the diesel room, sir!"

"Can't stop the big leak in the galley, sir!"

Reports came in from all compartments of the leaking U-boat. The smell of chlorine became stronger. A short circuit could ignite chlorine gases and blow the boat to bits. Hanging on to the ladder that rose to the conning tower, Kruger tried to think of something to do. The depth gauge showed that the boat was sinking again! A depth would soon be reached when the U-boat couldn't rise even if he blew the ballast tanks again.

Kruger's face was impassive, aware that his moment of truth had come. He could either sink and be crushed by the ocean, or surface and be blown out of the water by the British.

A depth charge exploded underneath the U-boat, and Kruger stared in horror as the floorplates buckled before his eyes. Lights on the U-boat went out. He heard a sound like a waterfall. Men started screaming. Panic was breaking out. He turned his flashlight on the depth gauge and saw that the boat was sinking below 500 meters, the needle moving quickly.

Kruger finally made the most difficult decision of his career. He decided to surface and surrender to the British before they killed everybody.

"Blow all ballast!" he shouted.

He waited, listening for the sounds of levers being thrown, but nothing happened. Flashing his light on the ballast console, he saw the operator out cold, his face resting on the levers. Coughing from the chlorine gas, Kruger dashed to the console, but Feiler got there first. Feiler pulled the levers, and the boat shook from side to side. Kruger pointed his flashlight at the depth gauge and saw that the rate of descent was slowing. Men sloshed through the water and crowded into the control room, panic on their faces.

"Who told you to leave your stations?" Kruger demanded, standing ankle deep in water.

"We're flooding, sir!" said the chief mechanic. "We've closed off the hatches!"

Kruger looked at the mechanic's face in the ghostly circle of light and saw stark terror. For the first time Kruger became afraid. He focused the flashlight on the depth gauge and saw that they were rising. A wave of claustrophobic madness overwhelmed him, but he fought it down. He closed his eyes and tried to calm himself.

"Would someone turn on the pumps, please?" he asked.

"I'll get them, sir," replied Feiler.

A switch was thrown, and the steady thump of pumps began.

"Well, at least they're working," Kruger said jovially.

"At least *something's* working," somebody said, and there was some chuckling.

They're relaxing, Kruger thought. *Even in the most difficult times, men can relax.* He hadn't turned on the pumps before because they would make too much noise and give their position away, but that game was over now and the basic struggle for survival had begun.

"All right," Kruger said, "we're going to surface. As soon as we get up there, abandon ship and swim for your lives. If you get away from the boat, the Tommies will pick you up, but if you linger on board they'll shoot you, so move quickly. Any questions?"

"Sir," said Blohm, "how can we get out of the conning tower? It's flooded."

"Officers and petty officers will go up the torpedo supply hatch, and other ranks will go up the galley hatch. Any more questions? No? Then you might as well split up now, gentlemen. Good luck to all of you."

The men moved fore or aft to the respective hatches, Kruger remaining in the control room to set the scuttling charge. It consisted of fifty pounds of explosive in the hull of the boat, activated by a little lever in a locker behind the ballast console. When Kruger pulled it, he'd have one minute to get out of the U-boat, which would be plenty of time.

He sat at the console and waited for his men to start abandoning ship. Looking up, he heard the sound of propellers coming closer. He closed his eyes and thought that the destroyer might try to ram the boat as soon as it could be seen on the surface. Swallowing hard, he thought of the ship's prow splitting the U-boat in half. His ears popped due to changing air pressure as the U-boat rose in the water. The depth gauge read 50 meters.

"Get ready, gentlemen!" he shouted. "The party is about to begin!"

The *Pembroke* was bearing down on the big oil slick, preparing to drop another pattern of depth charges, when Mulford saw the outline of the U-boat beneath the water.

"She's coming up, sir!" bellowed Peters.

Mulford thought he'd ram the U-boat but decided against it; he didn't want to ruin his Asdic as the *Alcestis* had ruined hers. "Hard right rudder!" he said. "All engines one-third ahead! Gunnery crews prepare to open fire!"

Mulford trained his binoculars on the U-boat and saw its periscope poke through the waves. It was listing to port, obviously damaged. Gritting his teeth, he remembered the *Centurion* and how it had been sunk by U-boats, with many of his crew killed.

The conning tower of the U-boat appeared, and water poured out of a hole near its base. He could read the designation of the boat painted in white letters on its side: *U-112*. His knuckles went white as he gripped his binoculars, fires of revenge burning hot in his heart.

"Open the hatch!" shouted Feiler.

Kruger, sitting before the scuttling mechanism, heard a metallic clank and then saw sunlight in the forward compartment. He saw the first man go up the hatch, then the U-boat was rocked by an explosion that threw Kruger against the console, knocking him out for a few seconds.

When he came to, he heard machine-gun fire and shell explosions. Touching his hand to his face, he felt blood. Men were screaming everywhere, and it sounded as though hell had broken loose. Turning forward, he saw men going up the hatch. One went up and fell down, half of his head blown away. Kruger took a deep breath and pulled the lever.

The scuttling charge was armed. The bottom would blow out of the U-boat in only sixty seconds, taking the secret code books and cipher machine, plus all other confidential documents, to the bottom. Kruger stood, and was struck by dizziness. Blood poured down his face from the cut on his temple. He covered it with his hand, staggering forward to the torpedo-loading hatch.

The U-boat was hit by another shell. Kruger fell to his knees, grabbed on to a pipe and pulled himself erect, then made his way to the forward hatch. When he got there, he heard machine-gun fire and screaming above. Blohm was climbing the ladder.

Blohm's head cleared the hatch and he saw men lying and writhing all over the deck. He leaped out of the hatch and bounded across the deck, and something slammed into his leg. Screaming, he tripped and fell over the side of the U-boat into the water.

Kruger climbed out of the hatch and ran across the deck, jumping over bodies as bullets whizzed around his head. He dived head first into the water and stroked as soon as he landed. Surfacing, he swam as quickly as he could away from the U-boat. Glancing quickly behind him as he swam, he saw the deck littered with bodies, and a number of heads bobbing up and down in the water. A few other men were swimming. Kruger realized that not many had got away alive.

"Hold your fire!" said Mulford on the bridge of the *Pembroke*.

The firing stopped as Mulford examined the sinking U-boat through the smoke. Its fore and after decks were covered with dead German sailors. Some had fallen in the water. Behind the U-boat were a few Germans trying to swim away. The hole at the base of the conning tower wasn't leaking anymore, and the

U-boat was sinking slowly. Mulford knew that U-boat commanders were under orders to scuttle their boats in times like this, and he expected U-112 to go at any moment.

On the bridge his officers and men were jubilant; it wasn't every day that they sank a German U-boat. The *Corinthia* was coming about on the far side of the U-boat where the Germans were swimming, evidently to pick them up.

Mulford looked at the U-boat, waiting for it to explode. The moments passed and nothing happened. He scratched his mustache, wondering if something had gone wrong with the scuttling charge. Had they failed to set it in their haste to abandon the boat?

It occurred to him that the U-boat's ciphering machine, the one Sir Percy Noble had told all the escort commanders to capture if they could, was right there before him inside the walls of the U-boat sinking slowly before him. Could he get it out? Was it worth a try?

He realized he couldn't send anyone into a U-boat that might blow up, although as the moments passed, he became more convinced that something had gone wrong with the boat's scuttling charge. He decided to go himself, with one other person.

He turned from the bridge rail. "Prepare to lower the starboard boat!"

The officers and men on the bridge looked at him in surprise, wondering what he intended to do.

"I need oarsmen and one volunteer to board that U-boat with me."

"I'll go, sir," said Peters, his executive officer.

"I need you here," Mulford told him. "Advise Commander Scott of my plans."

"How about me?" asked Stanhope, an old, gnarled boatswain's mate.

"You'll do fine. Come with me." He turned to Peters. "You take command of the *Pembroke*. Send the crew of oarsmen to the starboard boat and have someone bring two service revolvers down there right away."

"Yes, sir!"

"Let's go, Stanhope!"

Mulford descended the ladder to the main deck, followed by Stanhope. Mulford walked swiftly to the lifeboat, where the oarsmen were gathering. Another crew lowered the lifeboat to a position where it could be boarded.

An ensign came running with two navy .45s, handing them to Mulford and Stanhope, who tucked them in their belts. Mulford and Stanhope boarded the lifeboat and the crew followed, shipping their oars.

The lifeboat was swung over the side and lowered to the water, where it landed with a splash. The sailors aboard the lifeboat pushed away from *Pembroke* and began to row toward U-112. Mulford looked ahead at it, chewing his mustache. He didn't think the scuttling charges would blow at all now, he but wondered if he could get the cipher machine out of the U-boat before it sank to the bottom.

It was sitting awfully low in the water. Only the conning tower and part of its foredeck were visible now.

Kruger swam as quickly as he could from the U-boat, hoping he'd be able to escape its blast. He'd been a championship swimmer at the Naval Academy, and he cut through the water quickly.

Each second he expected the U-boat to explode, but it didn't. Seconds passed, Kruger wondering if he'd lost track of time. Stopping, he turned around and saw that he was a great distance from the U-boat. Surely it should have blown by now. Then he looked above the U-boat at the destroyer on the other side and saw a lifeboat being lowered.

"My God," muttered Kruger. He realized that the British were going to attempt the boarding of the U-boat. If they did, they might find the cipher machine and code books. Kruger realized what that would mean. Turning, he began to swim as fast as he could back to the U-boat. Somehow he had to get there before the British and sink the U-boat so that the secret machine and code books would be destroyed.

His arms like lead, his lungs bursting, he swam wildly through the water as he made his way back to the U-boat.

Blohm floated in the water, half-unconscious from loss of blood. Coughing up the seawater he'd swallowed, he was too weak to raise his arms to try to swim. The water around him was dark with his own blood, and he thought, *This is what it's like to have your ship sunk underneath you.* He remembered all the ships that U-112 had sunk and all the deaths in which he had been an accomplice. His leg ached fiercely, and he began to cry. All his life he'd been enchanted by the glory of war. Even as recently as last night he'd delighted in it, but this was where it led: a watery grave.

He tried to hold his head erect and open his eyes. U-112 shimmered before him, and he thought he saw someone swimming toward it. "I'm having hallucinations," he mumbled, then black curtains descended before him.

He closed his eyes, his head sagging to the side.

The lifeboat came alongside the U-boat. Stanhope jumped on to the deck. Someone threw him a line, and he tied it to the U-boat's deck rail. Mulford stood up and made his way toward the U-boat. Stanhope gave him a hand and pulled him aboard.

The U-boat had sunk even lower. Mulford thought it might go down at any moment. In a final decision he decided that he couldn't ask Stanhope to go below with him.

"You stay right here, Stanhope," Mulford said. "If she starts going down, cast off the line and jump clear."

"But what about you, sir?" Stanhope asked.

"Do as I say."

Mulford turned and ran toward the U-boat's torpedo supply hatch. He looked at it and saw water advancing toward it. *Once the water gets in there, it will be all over,* he thought.

Chewing his mustache, he bent down and descended the ladder into the U-boat. His feet touched water first, then the deck. He took out his flashlight and turned it on, sloshing through the knee-high water toward the radio room where the cipher machine was. He tried not to think about the U-boat sinking suddenly, but he couldn't help thinking about it. He believed he might have a chance to get out through that hatch again if it did sink. Maybe.

The boat was laid out just the way he'd seen in the diagrams, and the air was thick with chlorine gas. He passed the officers' quarters and the wardroom, and finally came to the radio shack. Shining his light inside it, he saw the cipher machine just where they'd said it would be, and nearby were stacks of papers and books.

Now he wished he'd brought Stanhope with him, but it was too late for that. He scooped up papers and books, stuffing them frantically into his pockets and the opening of his shirt. Then he grabbed the cipher machine and found that it was much heavier than an ordinary typewriter.

Lifting it, he staggered through the water, trying to step carefully so that he wouldn't trip over something and drop the machine. His breath came in short gasps as he made his way forward to the hatch, through which shone a shaft of bluish light. He thought of what would happen if he got the machine out of there — the lives it would save, the promotion he'd get, the glory and praise. Then he heard the sound of dripping water, and realized that the hatch was leaking and the U-boat was doomed.

He ran wildly toward the hatch, not caring if he fell now, willing to stake everything on getting out of there with the cipher machine. As he approached the hatch, he tripped over the body of a German and fell against the ladder, but managed to hang on to the machine. He tucked it underneath one arm and began to climb the ladder.

"Are you all right, sir?" asked Stanhope from above.

"Get ready to grab this machine!"

Mulford climbed the ladder laboriously as water poured on him and the machine. When he neared the top, Stanhope reached down and plucked it out from underneath his arm. Mulford climbed on to the deck and saw Stanhope pass the machine to one of the men in the lifeboat. "Be careful with that, now!" he shouted.

The deck was covered with water. Mulford heard a splashing sound to his right, turned and was astonished to see a German officer with blond hair climbing on to the U-boat.

Kruger was exhausted, his mind tumultuous with thoughts of defeat and disgrace. He saw the cipher machine being loaded on to the British lifeboat. "No!" he screamed. "Halt!"

He lunged toward Stanhope and Mulford, who drew his navy .45. In the excitement and close quarters Mulford only had time to take aim and pull the trigger. The pistol fired, and through the smoke Mulford saw the German drop to his knees, clutching his chest. Blood spurted out between the German's fingers, and he pitched forward into the water covering the deck.

"Hurry, sir! She's going!"

Mulford felt the deck heaving beneath his feet The bow of the U-boat was moving up into the air, the boat sinking stern first. Stanhope jumped into the lifeboat as Mulford ran across the rapidly slanting deck, but he couldn't make it. He slipped, grabbed onto the rail, and climbed over it.

"Jump, sir!"

Mulford leaped into the air, covering his face with his hands. It was only about ten feet down, and he held his legs tightly together as he fell. He hit the water, dropped beneath the surface, chilled to his bones. Kicking wildly and clutching water with his cupped hands, he swam to the surface, blinked, and saw the lifeboat heading straight for him.

"We've got you, sir," said Stanhope, leaning over the side.

Hands reached out to him and dragged him aboard. Mulford coughed and sputtered, wiping his eyes with the back of his hands as they covered him with a blanket.

"Where's the bloody machine?" Mulford yelled.

"Right here, sir!"

Mulford saw it sitting on the deck of the lifeboat It was wet but otherwise all right. He reached into his jacket and pulled out the German code books. The outside pages were soaked but could still be read, and the inside pages were dry.

"Look what I found in this locker, sir," said Stanhope, holding up the lifeboat's ration of rum.

"Give it here," Mulford replied.

Stanhope handed the flask to Mulford, who unscrewed the cork and took a sip, burning his throat and warming his heart. "Ah," he said, gazing at the cipher machine again.

"There she goes!" someone shouted.

Mulford turned around and saw the U-boat sliding stern first into the sea. The conning tower with the marking *U-112* disappeared, then the rest of the bow sank beneath the waves. A few huge bubbles erupted toward the surface, then the ocean crested into waves and rolled away as if the U-boat and its crew — with all their ambitions, patriotism, heroism, foolishness and romantic escapades — had never existed.

A NOTE TO THE READER

Dear Reader,

Thank you for reading *Tracking The Wolf Pack*. This is the second submarine novel that I wrote. It also is one of my favorite novels that I ever wrote out of 86 published.

Tracking The Wolf Pack covered the most critical period in the battle for the North Atlantic. I wanted to tell this story from both American and German points of view, with characters of all kinds from fanatical Nazis to professional patriotic German officers, from ordinary American and British sailors to highest ranking officers in the Allied navies. I also wanted interesting women because men and women tend to get crazy over each other under normal circumstances, but emotions become especially intense during wartime.

I couldn't write off the top of my head a 90,000-word novel about a specific period in history requiring detailed knowledge of complex technologies related to submarines and anti-submarine warfare. A tremendous amount of research was required. I read the below books which still are in my home library:

Memoirs: Ten Years and Twenty Days by Admiral Karl Dönitz, commander of the German U-Boat fleet

Convoy by Martin Middlebrook, about the "Greatest Convoy Battle Of All Time", said to be a turning point in the Battle of the Atlantic

Iron Coffins: A Personal Account of the German U-Boat Battles Of World War II by Herbert A. Werner, former U-boat commander

Jane's Pocket Book of Submarine Development edited by John Moore

The Bluejacket's Manual 1943

The Battle of the Atlantic: The First Complete Account of the Origins and Outcome of the Longest and Most Crucial Campaign of World War II by Terry Hughes and John Costello

Submarine Commander by Rear Admiral Ben Bryant

U-Boat Killer by Captain Donald MacIntyre

Escort Commander: The Story of Captain Frederic John Walker by Terence Robertson

Das Boot (The Boat) a novel by Lothar-Günther Buchheim who had served aboard U-boats.

U-Boat War, by Lothar-Günther Buchheim

How To Abandon Ship by Phil Richards & John J. Banigan, published in 1942 when such a book was necessary.

I also toured and took notes aboard two vintage World War II submarines at a U.S. Navy installation in Groton, Connecticut. The American submarine was the U.S.S. Croaker but I don't remember nomenclature of the German U-boat.

Research plunged my mind deeply into submarine warfare. I have a very vivid imagination and often felt panic and claustrophobia when reading about U-boats getting depth-charged, or the thrill of the hunt as British ships chased and depth-charged U-boats.

During the course of the war, 2,572 Allied merchant and war ships were sunk by U-boats, and 1,133 U-boats were sunk by Allied war ships and aircraft according to *The Battle of the Atlantic* mentioned above.

Did all my research, plans and intellectualizing actually produce something worthwhile? Only you, the reader, can be the judge. If you are able to leave a review on **Amazon** or **Goodreads**, I would be very grateful.

Len Levinson

Sapere Books is an exciting new publisher of brilliant fiction and popular history.

To find out more about our latest releases and our monthly bargain books visit our website: **saperebooks.com**

Printed in Great Britain
by Amazon

47774389R00185